Timurud - Book 1

Sferogyls

A David vs Goliath Space Battle

By Mit Sandru

Artwork by Dumitru Sandru

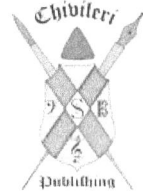

Chivileri Publishing

ISBN 13: 978-1-942612-13-1

Disclaimer:

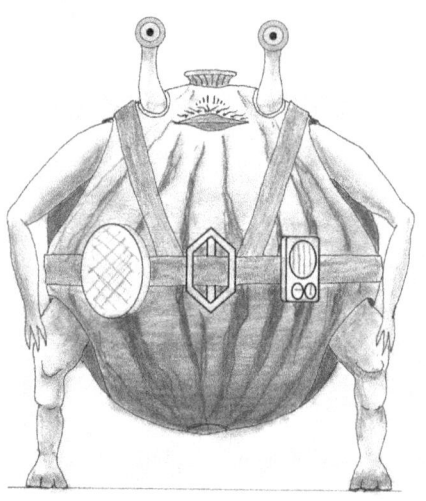

Table of Contents

Chapter 1. The Talking Head

"You're finally awake." I heard a man's deep voice talking to me.

Yes, I was awake, and I had a terrible headache—the hangover variety. I opened my eyes but couldn't see much. My vision was blurred, and I blinked repeatedly to clear the lacrimal film that made it seem as if I were underwater. Someone wiped my eyes gently with warm wet gauze, and I began to regain clear vision. Fuzzy at first, but things quickly got into focus. I was in a white room, sterile, like a hospital intensive care unit.

I cleared my throat, and it felt raw. "Where, where am I?" My voice was hoarse, and my throat was dry. Someone opened my mouth and sprayed something in it, probably a moisturizer of some kind. It tasted like alcohol and peppermint, with a metallic aftertaste. My throat felt better soon after.

"You are finally back with us," said the deep-voiced man.

I focused and saw an old man dressed in a white jumpsuit, looking at me a bit sternly. His hair was white, a bit curly, and he had a trimmed beard, but his skin was youthful. His blue eyes were piercing, as clear as blue ice.

"Welcome back," he said.

"Who are you?"

"You don't recognize me, Timurud?"

"No, I'm sorry. I don't know who you are."

"Well, at least I know who *you* are, Timurud."

"Why do you call me by that name, Timu...?"

5

"Timurud."

"That's not my name. My name is Tim Andrus."

"Ohh, that's right. Tim Andrus, the science fiction writer."

"Yes. Who are you?"

"I am Anu, your creator."

"Who? My what?" I screeched feebly.

"Anu, your creator."

"What's going on here? Where am I? Who are you, really? Am I in a hospital? I demand to know. I am an American, for Christ's sake."

"Yes, you are. And you are in a medical recovery room, of sorts."

"What happened? Was I in an accident?"

"Not exactly, although we revived you."

"I died? How did that happen?" I tried to move, but I couldn't feel the rest of my body.

"Yes, you were dead, and we brought you back to life."

"Oh, my God. What happened?"

"You are safe now and back where you belong, with us."

"Mr. Anu, I'm confused." That was putting it mildly.

"Of course you are, Timurud. And just call me Anu, your heavenly father."

I thought, *Oh, shit. I'm dead and talking to God. Well, at least he's not the devil.*

"You don't remember anything, anything at all, Timurud?"

"Remember what? And why do you call me Timurud? My name is Tim Andrus."

"Tim Andrus was your human name on Earth, and apparently you did something to your mind to gain complete amnesia. You've forgotten who you really are. But we found you. Finally."

"Am I in heaven, talking to God?"

"Many civilizations, including Earth, imagine that I am the heavenly God. However, we are not in heaven. You are among the living, about to start a new life."

I was alive. That was good. I knew who I was, Tim Andrus, and that was good, too. I knew that I was a science fiction writer. I remembered that, but not what books I'd written. But I had no idea who this man was. Maybe I was dreaming. No, it didn't feel like a dream.

"OK, are you a doctor? What's my situation? How soon will I be discharged?"

"No, I'm not a doctor. I'm Anu."

"Uh-huh, OK, I believe you. When can I get out of here?"

"As soon as you are well."

"I'm getting out of here," I tried to move. But that was all I could do—try. "Am I restrained?" I wasn't lying down. I was on a vertical bed, and I wanted to turn my head and look around, but I couldn't do that, either. "Am I paralyzed from the neck down?" My worst fear was creeping up on me.

"No, you are not paralyzed from the neck down. Maybe from the neck up, momentarily." He chuckled.

"What does that mean? What's wrong with me?"

"There is nothing wrong with you, if we ignore the fact that there is nothing below your neck."

Static noise began buzzing in my head, frightening and confusing me. Anu must have seen my desperate look, because he waved his hand and produced an oval frameless mirror so I could see myself in it.

I fainted.

Chapter 2. How They Found Me

"Wake up, Timurud," I heard a woman's voice this time.

I regained consciousness. "Let me see that mirror again, please." This time the woman, beautiful as an angel and dressed in a white jumpsuit as well, waved her hand and produced the oval mirror for me to see my head.

And that's all I could see—*my head* on top of a black fuzzy ball. I had a net over my head made of clear tubes, which changed colors at times and were presumably monitoring my brain activity.

There was nothing else underneath the black fuzzy ball—no body, no arms, and no legs. The ball was suspended above the opaque white floor. That was all I could see in the mirror. Behind the mirror, I could see this gorgeous, auburn-haired, brown-eyed woman. Maybe *she* was the doctor. She walked away, but the mirror remained in place in front of me, held by something, because I couldn't see what suspended the mirror in front of my eyes.

"What happened to me?" I asked with a trembling voice.

"Do you remember dying?" Anu asked me.

I tried to shake my head, but that was impossible. "No, I don't."

"In your Last Will and Testament you specified that, upon your death, you wanted your head severed and cryogenically frozen."

"No, I don't remember that, either."

The woman snickered. "Of course not. You were dead."

"Do you remember what happened before you died?" Anu

asked.

It was slowly coming back to me. "It's unclear. I was on a lot of pain medications. I had cancer, I think." I swallowed. "Prostate cancer. I was diagnosed too late, and I guess I died from it."

"That's right. Although the Earth's medical knowledge is not that advanced, the PSA test is good for the early detection of prostate cancer. But you did not have the test until it was too late, and you kicked the bucket." He chuckled.

I remembered that. I was just 59 years old, and I was given three months to live. Not something anyone wishes to hear. And then here I was, a talking head, defrosted and brought back to life. How the hell was I able to even talk, without lungs or a vocal box?

"You brought me back to life—my head, that is," I said.

"Yes, we did," said Anu in a fatherly tone.

"How am I able to talk without a body?"

"We reconnected all the vital supplies to your neck," said the woman doctor. "Although your neck was severed low and your vocal box was preserved, you are not really talking to us."

"But I can hear and see you talking to me, and I can hear myself." I was becoming agitated.

"Yes, we talk to you, but you imagine that you are responding to us vocally," she said, smiling. "You talk to us in your head."

I blinked to make sure that I could control some parts of my remaining physical self. I opened my mouth wide and tried to say something, but no sound came out. "How could this be?"

"It is because we are gods," she replied.

It dawned on me—the black fuzzy ball under my head was supplying me with blood and nutrients to keep me—my head—

alive. Since I didn't have a body or lungs, there was no air going through my mouth or nose. I didn't need it. My blood was oxygenated, and I was alive.

What an ironic situation! I had become a science fiction writer because of my vivid imagination, but I'd never thought of this scenario: a talking head mounted on a black fuzzy ball, levitating above the floor. Maybe I was not levitating, maybe some support held the black fuzzy ball up from behind me, where I couldn't see it.

"What is your name?" I asked the woman.

"Dalia. I'm your doctor."

And she was such a beautiful doctor. "In that case, thank you, Doctor Dalia, for reviving me."

"Thank Anu for that. He made that decision, Timurud."

There—she called me by that name again. "Why are you calling me Timurud?"

"Because that's your real name, Timurud," said Anu. "Yes, I know you are Tim Andrus, a wanna-be-famous science fiction writer back on Earth, but your real identity is Timurud, and you are a god."

Did he say I was a *god*? This was so farfetched that I couldn't stand it. But wait. *Let's play along*, I thought. "OK, Anu, please tell me what's going on. I'm listening and I'm sure I will not have a heart attack, since I don't have a heart." I couldn't resist the joke.

"You still have your sense of humor. A bit off, though," said Dalia.

"You know me?"

"Of course I do. We all do, and we thought you were a goner."

"How could a *god* like me be a goner?"

11

"Even gods die. But I'll let Anu refresh your memory."

I shifted my eyes toward Anu. I think I raised my eyebrows, too. I should have been able do that much.

"I'll tell you the short version, and maybe that will jog your memory," said Anu. "On Earth, as is the case in many other worlds in the universe, we are recognized as gods, as the ancient mythologies claim on Earth. We are ancient sapient beings, and we go back hundreds of millions of years. We are biological entities—advanced, of course—and we live for millions of years. Practically forever, if we so wish."

This sounded like the biggest bullshit I'd ever heard. Even I wouldn't have written such crap. "Gods? Tell me more," I said, faking interest.

"You may not believe me at this moment, but be that as it may," said Anu, standing in front of me with his hands behind his back. "We did not evolve the way human beings evolved. We were engineered by another advanced species."

"Who are they?"

"We don't know, and we've never found them."

"Maybe they were the real gods."

"No, they were not the *real* gods, either. They were sapient beings, very technologically advanced. We found their base here in the Milky Way but not a trace of them anywhere else. We don't even know what they looked like. Besides engineering us, our creators seeded the galaxies with carbon-based genetic life. And it flourished on many planets. The asteroids and comets spread the life spores farther, to many other solar systems' planets that were suitable to support this form of self-replicating matter, the living organisms."

"Panspermia," I said. "That's how life started on Earth, by asteroids?"

"Yes, along with Mars. But unlike Earth, Mars didn't do as well. Millions of years ago, after we mastered the technology of our creators, we explored the galaxies, looking for other life forms, and we found plenty. Not surprisingly, here and there we found sapient beings, some rather advanced. We contacted some, observed others, experimented with a few—"

"Experimented?"

"Sure, we wanted to know who they were, what they were, if they were on track to become highly intelligent. And the ones we found promising, in some cases, we tweaked to make them more intelligent."

"Did you do something to us humans?"

"Indeed we did. We came to Earth during the dinosaurs' reign. The Suarichian-Theropod species, as it is classified by Earth scientists, showed some promise." He must have noticed my questioning look. "The T-Rex type, from the same line from which the birds evolved. The problem with the dinosaurs was that they had all the food they needed—they grew large for defensive purposes, but their brains stayed small. And then a comet wiped them out, as you know. We revisited Earth several times, observing the birds, but there was not much improvement from their dinosaur ancestors. The mammals showed more promise. And then, millions of years later, we discovered the Ape Cladogram."

"So we did evolve from apes."

"Of course. Somehow. Invariably, throughout the Milky Way Galaxy, the sapient biped, like the hominid form, evolved more frequently. And Earth was no different. That's why we look hominid, too."

"Why are hominids better suited to becoming sapient?"

"More precisely, I should say hominidal, meaning in the shape of a human—a biped, with two free upper limbs and at least three opposable fingers. It is the most efficient packaging for a being to tinker and explore the environment."

"So, if those other bipeds are not human, what are they?" I asked.

"Carbon-based sapient bipeds evolved from other type of mammals, dinosaurs, reptiles, and mollusks, among many other species."

I gaped. "Then you're saying that two legs, two arms, and two hands are essential."

"Not at all. There are species with tentacles instead of articulated fingers, or with four legs and more than two arms. But it seems four limbs—two legs for support and two independent arms—is the more efficient package."

"You also said carbon-based. Are there other types of life?"

"Sure, but that's a vaster subject."

I was more curious about me and asked, "And what's my story?"

"Your story, which you seem to have forgotten, is that you are a god, like us." He paused. "Or you used to be."

"What happened?"

"Only you know that, but you don't remember. We know that about sixty Earth years ago, you disappeared. It is not uncommon for gods to die; after all, we're made of flesh and blood, from the same gene pool. But we can always find a god's body or a DNA sample, and in many cases we can resurrect that god, if he or she died accidentally."

"Wait a second—if you are made of flesh and blood and can die, you are not a god."

"Technically correct, but humans did not know that when we taught them about gods. As humans envisioned it, gods were not of this world. They lived forever in heaven. Even advanced civilizations believe in us as gods. Well, we've been around for hundreds of millions of years, all over the universe and this galaxy, and we are technologically and scientifically the most advanced species. Now, the spiritual God that humans envision in the heavens is a different matter."

"But most everyone on Earth believes in a spiritual god."

"We gave that concept of the spiritual god to Earth people and others, when we first lived among them. A spiritual god is easier to obey, and we introduced religion to prevent humans from forgetting about God and degenerating back into animals."

"And yet, God and religions can cause death and destruction."

"Not God, only religions. Unfortunately, we live in a relative universe. There are no absolutes. Religion can do good, and it can do bad. For there to be good, bad must exist. For there to be life, death must exist. For there to be day, night must exist—the two sides of a coin.

"Anyway, back to you, Timurud. You disappeared. We stopped actively searching for you after a few years but kept an open case on you. It was not until a year ago when Dalia stumbled on a piece of information from one of your science fiction books, which indicated your advanced knowledge of the laws of the universe."

That made me feel proud. But wait, that wasn't from my imagination—it must have been my recollection from when I supposedly was a god.

"You remembered something from your past and wrote about it," Anu confirmed. "We tracked you down, just to find your frozen head. And here we've brought you back to life."

"To experiment with me."

Chapter 3. Stupidly Intelligent

"Experiment with you? Not at all."

"Well, you experimented with our ancestors—"

"Not our ancestors," corrected Anu. "We're of a different kind."

"Uh-huh. How much genesplicing did you do on the prehistoric apes?"

"None. We prefer to let nature take its course. Then, when the primitive ape-man appeared, we intervened, and eventually, about five million years ago, we spread a virus among the Australopithecus and created the Hominin genus."

"A virus? Why not use gene manipulation?"

"Intervening externally and modifying the genes is the quickest method to get results. In the short term it works, but the genes of living things have a mind of their own, so to speak. Many variables, including the environment, affect gene coding and eventually, generations later, the species evolve in their own way, according to the embedded gene intelligence. The outcome over time may not be what the original tinkering intended to do.

"Now, a virus is an effective method of mutating species. It seems to be an external intervention, but most everything is an external intervention affecting the gene codes anyway. Therefore, the viruses mutate the gene coding in a natural way. It takes longer than direct gene modification, but it produces better and more stable results over time, as in the case of humankind evolving eventually to become Homo sapiens."

"How many times did you intervene?" I asked.

"Several times. And many more different species evolved than the Earth paleoanthropologists discovered. Some species died out, others were outright killed by newer and more intelligent humans.

"We let the modern humans settle in, as it were, and about fifty thousand years ago, we began teaching them about agriculture, animal domestication, even sciences. They had mastered toolmaking long before that time. And of course, we taught them about religion to keep them civilized. We became their ancient gods."

"If humanity could only know the truth," I mused, as my interest rose.

"They have to discover all these things on their own. And even if they do, we are still gods."

That god-thing, about being a god, that didn't make sense to me yet. "Why are you telling me all this?"

"Because you're a god, Timurud."

"Yes, you mentioned that, although it is hard to believe. You look human to me, and I haven't seen much of you on Earth. What's the god's role today?"

"To keep an eye on the sapient civilizations, including Earth. For many reasons, the sapient worlds either self-destroy, are destroyed by others, or collapse into stupidity of their own making. Very simply put, our task is to stabilize the civilizations at risk."

"I see. You're like the guardians of the stupidly intelligent."

"Yeah, something like that." He chuckled and added, "When sapient beings appear on a planet, they may not be the most intelligent beings. But being the first intelligent beings prevents other more-intelligent beings from sprouting up."

"But on Earth, Neanderthals were first, before modern humans," I argued.

"Yes, but the Neanderthals were not smart enough and were replaced with the current intelligent population of modern humans, and no other more-intelligent species could have evolved as another branch of humans."

"But humans could become more intelligent as well and stop being hostile and combative, and recognize the good of peace and cooperation."

"Of course. Many intelligent civilizations have advanced to super intelligence through natural selection, gene alterations, and computer implants, just to name a few ways. And many—most of them extinct—super-intelligent civilizations had set up utopian societies, with equal resources for all and peaceful intentions. When sapient societies have all they need without struggle, they degenerate. But most important, even if a civilization is peaceful, the next-door ET may not be, and the ET with the bigger gun wins."

"Scary," I said.

"Perhaps."

"But I'm just a head. Why did you revive me?"

Chapter 4. Gods and Duty

"Because you're one of us."

"That's heartwarming, but I don't buy it." I wanted to shake my head but couldn't.

Anu sighed. "There are not many of us left. We must take care of each other."

"Don't you have children?"

"It's complicated. That's all I can say for now."

"Why don't you clone yourselves?"

"Now that's an idea. Then we don't need you. Dalia, what do you say—should we place Tim Andrus back in the cryogenics?"

I shifted my eyes from Anu to Dalia, waiting for them to sentence me to more frozen sleep or death. Maybe I had overplayed my hand.

"I don't know," said Dalia. "He's a god, after all. He could be useful."

They had an ulterior motive. I was going to push my luck. "How can a head on a fuzzy black ball be useful to you? You must have computers more powerful than my brain."

Dalia smiled conspiratorially. "We can grow you a body. Would you like a new body?"

A new body? That would be nice, but... "Yeah, sure, an old man's head on a young body."

"Who said anything about a young body?" Dalia said.

Contradicting thoughts raced through my mind. Get my 59-year-old body back? A young body would be better. "How would you get me my old body back?"

"We'll grow you a new one."

"Bodies grow?"

"You mentioned cloning," Dalia said.

"I see—clone my body, then chop its head off and sew mine onto that body. That's barbaric!"

"It would be if we did that," said Anu.

"Then how?"

"We have the technology to grow your body from where your neck was severed. It will be your own body."

"But my body will be old."

"It starts young. But if you insist, we'll age it for you. Would you prefer that?" said Delia with a mischievous smile.

"No. I changed my mind—I want a young body."

"Good choice."

"Now, to have my body, arms, and feet back, what's the catch?"

"You'll have to redeem yourself," said Anu.

"Heh, heh, heh. Even gods have motives."

"Sure. But considering the state you're in, you must prove yourself."

"Let me see if I understand this. You revived my head. You'll grow me a new, young body. I'll be a complete healthy man again, and then I have to redeem myself. How?"

"Do what gods do—defend threatened civilizations."

"How would I do that? Superman, I'm not. I didn't even serve in the military or the clergy, and I'm not good at politics."

"The human you conspired to be in your past is what you're referring to. The god in you will arise, and you'll figure out what to do and how to do your godly works."

"That's how I'll redeem myself? By fighting for justice?" I closed my eyes, puzzling through this information. "OK. Maybe. What's the plan?"

"As it happens, we have a problem on the planet Nisip. It is a matter of slavery and eventually the extinction of that civilization. The Sferogyls—that's what the people there are called—will need our help, and currently we're spread thin. We found your head just in time to reconstitute you and send you to help them."

"Slavery and extinction?" I wondered aloud.

"Another civilization, the Maggotrolls, had almost decimated the Sferogyls thousands of years ago. A small part of the Sferogyl population escaped from their home planet, Vestrallum, and settled on a new planet, Nisip, where they've lived peacefully ever since. They reduced their use of technology to camouflage their existence. But they were nevertheless found by the Maggotrolls, who want to enslave them again."

"Slavery exists in the galaxy?"

"Yes, it does, just as it exists today on Earth."

"I need more details. Who are these people, and who are their enemies?"

"The Sferogyls measure about one meter high when they stand up. They vaguely resemble hominids, although they are snails—"

"Snails?"

"Yes, known on Earth as the *Gastropoda* class of the *Mollusca* phylum."

"Intelligent snails?"

"Yes, but they don't look like snails. They have a round body enclosed in a hard shell, with two legs, two arms, ears and eyes, a mouth, nose, anus, and sex organs, although they're hermaphrodites."

"Say what?"

"Hermaphrodites. Each individual has a set of both sex organs, and they don't need to pair to procreate, if they choose to do so."

"Uh-huh," I commented dumbly. I wanted to shake my head so badly. Luckily, nothing on my head or face itched.

"And they take on the shape of a ball when they retract their limbs," Anu continued.

"Like a turtle?" I asked.

"Similar, although their genes are gastropoda. They are smart, they talk, they sing—actually, they do all that by whistling—and they are peaceful. Too peaceful."

"Hmm, what do you expect if they don't have to fight for sex," I quipped.

"You may have a point."

"Did you create them?"

"A little bit. The Sferogyls' original snail body evolved to have

24

legs and arms, but it kept the exoskeleton, the shell, as a defensive trait."

"They use their shells to protect themselves from predators?"

"Predators, gravity, and temperature shaped them. Their ancestral planet, Sferogyl, was 50% larger than Earth, and it rotated around its axis once a year for six months of summer, six months of winter. They adapted very well to survive the cold, so they don't go into hibernation, as snails do. Gravity and the cold aided their round form. They eventually migrated to another planet, Vestrallum, which was warmer, and they lived there for a million years or so, until the Maggotroll Empire invaded and enslaved them."

"Ma-ggo-tro-ll?"

"Yes, the Maggotrolls, from their home planet Maggotrollia. The Maggotrolls are a species similar to mammals and humanoids, similar to us, although they're slightly taller and their blood is blue, because it is copper-based and has hemocyanin instead of hemoglobin. They are a warring species, and after they mastered interstellar travel, they conquered other planets and became an empire. They enslaved many civilizations, as they did to the Sferogyls."

"You'd think that ET would be more civilized than that."

"ET is us."

"So you're saying the universe is full of ETs. Prove it."

Anu chuckled. "I wondered when were you going to ask for proof. Very well. I'll show you a real bad-ass ET." He snapped his fingers.

The wall behind him disappeared to reveal a room, where I could see a metallic half dome in the middle of it. The dome became transparent, and there was something squirming inside it. I'm sure my eyes bulged out when I saw it.

And then I fainted.

Chapter 5. ET

"Wake up, scaredy-cat." Dalia called me.

I awoke and stared again at the hideous creature under the clear dome.

It was a she, judging by her breasts. Her eyes were burning red, like ambers, and she had a protruding mouth with two rows of teeth, like those of a constrictor snake. Her head—oh my god!— her head had stubby spikes instead of hair. This species was definitely reptilian, judging by the scales on her body and her snake-like tail. She stood on two hind legs, similar to a raptor, with sharp claws and spurs. As she turned, observing her environment, I saw wings, insect wings, folded neatly on her back.

I was staring at the Devil.

The creature screeched, a sound like that of a metal table being dragged over a concrete pavement, and she came close to my side of the dome, plunging her clawed fingers into the transparent wall. I swear I could see those sharp claws almost piercing the dome's thin membrane. She opened her mouth and hissed, extending a bifurcated blue tongue.

It was worse than a nightmare.

"What in hell is that, Anu?"

"This is a Coshmar."

"God help me, but that is the most hideous creature I've ever seen."

"It is not the most hideous creature in the universe, but it is one of the most deadly. Venomous, too. It is the result of a failed experiment by the Maggotrolls. They wanted to create an army of them. Instead, they escaped from their labs and multiplied. They are semi-intelligent and able to learn even how to pilot a spaceship. Now that scares me."

"My god, it looks like the cross-breed of a snake and a devil."

"And that is what this creature is."

"What? The devil exists?"

"Creatures similar to the devil do exist on some planets."

"And you want me to do battle with those creatures? I cannot do that." The Coshmar screeched at me again, to scare me some more. It sensed my fear.

Anu snapped his fingers and the dome turned to metal, obscuring the hideous creature. The dome became soundproof, too, which was good. Then the wall in front of it rematerialized, obscuring the dome.

"This is not real, this is not real, this is not real." I wanted to shake my head to dispel this reality as a nightmare. But I couldn't.

"But it is real," said Anu. "How about seeing something more pleasant?"

I was afraid to ask what he had in mind when a small man, a gnome, but without a red hat, with his arms folded on his chest and dressed in a blue jumpsuit, floated near me.

"Hello, Timurud," the small man said in a high-pitched voice. "I am Freggor."

Small was the wrong word. *Miniature* was more like it. He was no taller than a forearm. He did not frighten me, but I was baffled at the size of this man. I managed to untangle my "mental" tongue. "You're so small. And how do you float in midair? Are you held up by strings from the ceiling?" I managed to glance upward, but there was no ceiling that I could see, except for white fluff.

"Tsk, tsk. You've forgotten how levitation works," he said. He stamped his foot on something solid that he was standing on. "My pad levitates, solid and invisible."

"Are you a holographic image?" I looked at Anu. "Is he a holo-image?"

"Let's find out." The little man jumped from his pad onto my black fuzzy ball and pinched my left cheek. "Does this feel real?"

I looked cross-eyed at him and yelled, "Get off me!" I was considering blowing on him, like some bug, but I couldn't even if I tried.

"As you wish." He jumped back, away on whatever that thing was, supporting him. "I am a god, too," he said.

"Jesus," I whispered. "I've ended up on Dr. Moreau's island."

"Not at all," said Anu. "You've ended up on—"

"Olympus," I said, exasperated, "judging by the fluffy, resembling clouds above."

"That would be funny," said an amused Anu. "We are in a low orbit around Jupiter."

My jaw dropped. I shifted my eyes from Anu to Dalia to the little man, who was snickering, with his bearded chin resting on his knuckles. "Are we in a spaceship?" I managed to ask after a while.

"A spaceship of sorts," said Anu. "It looks something like this, when it is visible." Anu moved his hand, and an object resembling a crystalline cube appeared in my view. It was rotating slowly on its apex, and I realized it was a hexahedron, not a cube.

"What is that?"

"The spaceship of sorts, in the shape of a triangular dipyramid." He saw me thinking about the name he gave to the shape of the spaceship. "It is made of two tetrahedrons, a triangular dipyramid."

"Why do you call it a spaceship of sorts?"

"Because this is an energy blip in time, an EBT. And we occupy it now, until we can settle the matter with you."

"What is an energy blip in time?" The object was mesmerizing, as it rotated on its pinnacle in front of my eyes.

"You should know, but you don't remember." Anu sighed. "The physics to describe it is advanced. But simply explained, we are in a bubble of energy and time warp."

"That's why everything seems to be transparent or in white clouds?"

"Yes, but we can give it any properties we like, just as we made the dome metallic."

"And that's how you made the mirror appear, and the Coshmar?"

"Yes, we manipulate energy and time to resemble anything we want. But the monster is real. We caught it on Earth, of all paces. But that's another problem we want to solve, to find out how the Coshmar arrived on Earth in the first place."

That was a lot of information to take in all at once, but I decided to stay on the topic of the spaceship. "This is how you traveled from Earth to Jupiter?"

"'Travel' is not the correct term. More like 'teleportation'."

I'm sure there was a scientific explanation for why he used the word "teleportation" instead of "travel," but I had other questions on my mind. "Why are we around Jupiter?"

"We are on a very low orbit around Jupiter to cloak our presence," said Anu.

"Whom are you hiding from?"

"Not hiding, more like cloaking our presence from the Maggotrolls, among many others. We don't want them to know that we've rescued you. Yet."

Thoughts and questions were bouncing around in my head. Could all this be an illusion? And why am I imagining all this? Am I dreaming while sleeping in the cryogenic container? But I was dead; there shouldn't be any sleeping or dreaming.

I tried to inhale, more from habit than anything else, and I mentally said, "Can I see Jupiter?"

"But of course." Anu snapped his fingers, and Jupiter's cloudy atmosphere appeared all around us, as far as my eyes could see. We were inside Jupiter's atmosphere, in between layers of clouds. I could see orange, white, and yellow clouds to the left, right, above, and below us, although there was a distinctly clear layer between the immediate clouds above and below.

This time, I did not faint.

Jupiter! I couldn't believe my eyes. The immensity of this planet, with its many layers of clouds of different colors, swirling at different speeds, was mesmerizing.

"Wow! What a view!" I couldn't take my eyes from the panorama I was seeing. The planet was massive, and I couldn't even see its curvature. Fortunately, I couldn't sense how cold or hot it was outside, the speed of the winds, or the poisons they contained. Not to mention the deadly radiation bombarding us. I hoped this triangular dipyramid craft could protect us well.

"Are you ready, then?" Dalia asked after a minute or so.

"For getting a body under my head? Certainly." I pulled my eyes away from the colorful clouds and looked at Dalia. "How long will it take? Will it hurt?"

"It will not hurt a bit. You're going to be asleep and time won't matter," she said, while her fingers ran over the fuzzy ball under my chin, probably programming something.

"Well, Timurud, we'll see you when you are back on your feet," said Anu.

And with that, I sank into oblivion.

Chapter 6. My New Body

When I opened my eyes I saw the deep blue sky above. I was outdoors, and was alive and awake, lying on my back, levitating in midair among lush green foliage and beautiful red and orange flowers. An iridescent rainbow-colored butterfly fluttered over me. I could hear the water from a brook splashing softly, and the birds sang joyfully. *This must be heaven*, I thought.

I raised my arms and I saw my strong hands, healthy, with young skin. Thanks to a neck and torso, I could rotate and lift my head, noticing my feet, my bare legs, and my naked body. What a splendid sight!

Was I dreaming? I jumped up from whatever was supporting me on the horizontal and landed on my feet. It didn't feel strange to stand up on my two own feet, as I had never experienced life without them, except for a brief period of time when my head floated on a fuzzy, black ball. It felt natural, standing on the mossy ground with my toes wiggling in it. I felt a little unsteady and my legs were aching slightly. As self-therapy on my new, but unused muscles, I did a few knee bends to warm them up.

I was whole again. These people *were* gods. And to think I doubted them!

The crystal-clear brook captured my attention. It was so inviting, I wanted to touch the water, and so I kneeled next to it to see myself in better detail. My hair was thick, no longer white but dark brown, with some salt and pepper. My moustache and goatee were gone. My skin was smoother, and I looked as I used to in my forties. Early forties. Yes, these people *were* gods.

With my cupped hands, I scooped up the crystal water. I

splashed my face with it, and it cooled and invigorated me.

I was about to scoop up some water to drink when I heard, "Don't drink that water just yet."

There was no one around, but I recognized Dalia's voice. "Where are you?" I asked, standing up.

"Right behind you," she said. I turned abruptly and saw her behind a red flowering bush. "How do you feel?" she asked me.

I inhaled deeply, feeling the fresh air in my lungs. Everything was so crisp, so flavorful, so new, and so vibrant. "I feel great. Where are we?"

"Home. We are on Gardenia."

"Gardenia? Why, because of the lush vegetation? Or because this is the Garden of Eden?"

"All of the above." She stepped out from behind the bush in all her naked splendor. Her white Carrara-marble body was perfect in every respect. Her auburn hair cascaded onto her shoulders, and her breasts, ohhh, her breasts. I couldn't take my eyes off them, feeling like a teenager seeing a naked woman for the first time.

I blinked to dispel a hallucination, but she was real. "We must be in paradise, like Adam and Eve."

"You mean our nakedness? You're not a prude, are you?"

"Prude? No, not me. I've been to Hollywood." I was so self-assured and then I noticed the woody between my legs, and it was not of the vintage variety as I remembered it, but rather a young, vigorous log. "Maybe horny." I'm sure I blushed.

"It's a natural reaction." As she came closer, I—both of us—*rose* to attention. "Remember, I'm your doctor until I discharge you.

And no, we don't run naked on Gardenia, but I wanted to see your reaction. You passed. Your body and head are completely integrated."

I wasn't sure which head she was referring to, so I couldn't help but look down at my manhood. "An arousal is a sign of well-being?"

"Yes." When I looked up, she stood fully dressed in front of me, in the same white jumpsuit as before.

"How did you get dressed so fast?" I was sure I hadn't seen any clothes around anywhere.

"That's what you'll have to learn while here," she said, as she pulled me by the hand toward a clearing. "Here is a good place to learn how to dress."

We stood on a rose stone slab. "Is this place special?"

"Not really, but it will help you focus. How would you like to be dressed?"

I looked at my slim and trim body, several sizes smaller and dozens of pounds lighter than I used to be, wondering what my sizes were now. "How about shorts and T-shirt? I think I'm size 30 and large."

She chuckled. "What do you think, I'm going to run to Wal-Mart to get you a pair of short pants and a T-shirt?"

"You know about Wal-Mart?"

"Like, yeah! Anu and I've been on Earth for six months, searching for you. I've experienced Earthly things."

"Huh," I mumbled dumbly.

"On Gardenia, or any other energy-controlled environment, you can create any object. All you have to do is imagine the clothes you want to wear, and you'll be dressed."

"Really? Like magic?"

"There is no magic in it, just technology. Now concentrate on how you'd like to be dressed."

"OK, OK," I said, trying to relax. I closed my eyes and imagined being dressed in khaki cargo shorts and a black T-shirt—I wanted to start simple. I opened my eyes and I was dressed. "Holy shit! It worked."

"Very good, but the holy shit had nothing to do with it. I may mention that you don't have any underwear or shoes."

"I feel comfortable." I jumped slightly up and down. Then I imagined a pair of sandals, and they appeared on my feet. "But I'm thirsty."

"You cannot drink or eat anything yet. Let's go and see Anu."

"Oh, yeah, where is the old man?"

"He can hear you," she said with a smirk, as she pulled me by the hand down a path. "Besides, he can change his appearance to any age he wants to be." I nodded stupidly, following her.

We arrived near a waterfall from where a creek began flowing away. A curious-looking gazebo in the shape of a pagoda straddled the creek like a bridge, and we walked to it and then up on wide stairs to the deck. The roof, beams, and floor were made of transparent material, making it luminous and airy inside. Anu was sitting on a blue metallic chair, looking at quickly flickering holograms appearing out of thin air. Freggor sat on his shoulder, watching as well.

"Well, well, if it's not the complete Timurud. What a good-looking lad you are!" Anu smiled widely at me.

"He's taller than I thought," said Freggor.

My original good disposition turned into a sneer when I heard that. In my young days, I was six feet tall, give or take an inch at the end of the day. Of course, to Freggor, everyone looked tall, so I calmed down.

"Thank you, Anu and Dalia. It's good to be alive and back with a body, standing on my own two feet. Still an old head, but the body is great." I touched my clean-shaven chin. I wasn't missing my goatee and moustache.

"Don't worry," said Anu. "Your twenty-something body will continue to rejuvenate your head's appearance—maybe not all the way to twenty-something, but to about thirty years old. Isn't that right, Dalia?"

"Oh, yes. In a short time, I won't be able to keep my hands off him."

I blushed. Was she serious or toying with me to get me aroused again?

"How are your legs feeling?" Anu asked.

"I don't feel the ache I felt when I first stood up. I feel great now."

"That's good. Then we can begin with the initiation. Ready, Freggor?"

"At your command." Freggor levitated toward me, holding a transparent bucket with a clear liquid in it. The bucket was as tall as he was, but he had no problem holding it over his head. Or maybe he was hanging from the bucket.

"What initiation? Is this some kind of baptism?" I felt downright frightened, especially seeing that I was naked again.

"Well, you see, it's this way," Anu said. "You forfeited your status as a god when you became human sixty years ago. You still have a human body now, and we must convert you into a god."

"And what's Freggor going to do with that bucket?" I pointed to it.

"Pour it on you."

Without any warning, Freggor dumped the liquid over my head. It was not water, more like syrup. It was sticky and it stuck to my head like glue. It flowed slowly down over my face, into my ears, my nose, and my mouth, which I couldn't keep closed. I felt suffocated, and I dropped to all fours, grasping for air, but the darn goo kept my head enclosed in a sticky bubble.

I passed out.

Chapter 7. A God Am I

I woke up in the creek and jumped to my feet, gulping for air. There was no trace of the goo on my head. The darn stuff must have infiltrated my body through every opening on my head. I was still naked, and now I was wet.

And I was pissed.

High above me, Anu, Dalia, and Freggor were watching me with satisfied grins from the edge of a round hole in the gazebo's transparent deck, through which I must had fallen into the creek. I looked at them all with malicious intent. Without giving it any thought, I jumped from the gravel bottom of the creek all the way up onto the floor above and landed on my feet.

"What in hell is the meaning of what you've just done to me? I've never passed out this many times in my entire life."

"You're a *god* now," said Anu. "Look how high you jumped!"

The creek was three meters below the floor.

"What did you dump on my head?"

"God's biological nanorobots," said Dalia. "Bionanobots, for short."

Whatever she said didn't sink in, and I looked from her to Anu and even Freggor, the bastard, who was levitating at my eye level, smirking. "Bionanobots?" I finally managed to ask. "Why?"

"To make you a god," said Anu.

"Was that necessary?"

"Yes, if you want to be a god," Anu replied.

"I thought I was already a god. And if I needed more godliness, why didn't you give me more god-DNA when you grew my godly body?"

"You didn't need any more god-DNA. You had enough."

"Why didn't you put the nano-things in my body, then, when you grew it?"

"Your body had to be fully developed, and the bionanobots had to enter your body the natural way," said Anu. "It seems primitive, but it's procedurally correct."

"Yes, it is primitive. Freggor dumps a bucket of stuff over my head, right here in nature, with no clean room, no machines with a zillion blinking lights monitoring my vitals and the progress, no team of experts, no shiny stuff..." I looked around me, and I was in the clean room environment I had just described.

"Futuristic enough for you?" asked Anu, appearing next to me. "You want to hang around here or go back to nature?"

I motioned with my head to go back, and we were back on the deck of the gazebo, in full nature. I sighed and accepted the new reality. "So, my body is full of little creatures, crawling inside me?" I squirmed and felt like scratching myself.

Anu just nodded.

"Jesus!" I shivered, realizing that I was still naked and wet. I put my hand out and imagined a white fluffy towel, which appeared instantly in my opened hand. It was a large soft white towel and I wrapped it around me. "Are those things making me a superman of some kind?" I asked, combing my fingers through my thick hair.

"In a way, yes," said Anu. "They are biological entities and are integrating with your body as we speak. They are undetectable, unlike the artificial nanobots, and they will serve you well."

"How do you feel?" I heard Dalia asking. Her lips did not move. She only looked at me with a smile.

I squinted and thought, *What the hell?*

"That's right. You've forgotten how we communicated with you when you were just a head," said Dalia in my head.

"Telepathically?" I wondered. "Two-way communication?"

"You're a god," I heard Anu in my head. "The bionanobots went to work. From now on, we can communicate telepathically among us gods."

Wow, I thought. *What else did those bugs do to me?*

"You've acquired extra strength. Remember how high you jumped?" Anu communicated.

He was right; I had jumped three meters and landed on the floor on my feet, like a cat. By now the floor had resealed itself, and I could see the creek flowing gently below.

"Your senses are superior to those of mere mortals, and you will be able to move extremely quickly, if needed," piped up Freggor. "It comes in handy if you're attacked."

I raised my arms halfway and admired them. I was a fit biological machine. Then it dawned on me. "Attacked? By whom?"

"Whatever or whomever you'll encounter in your missions."

I had no idea what he was talking about.

"And of course, your mind will be sharper," added Dalia.

A sharper mind and a stronger and younger body were good. I toweled off the rest of my body and noticed that Dalia was wearing a black evening gown with gold accessories. Freggor and Anu wore black tuxedos with bow ties. "Are we going to a ball?"

41

"Just dinner," Anu replied.

"Then I'd better change into something more appropriate." I imagined being in a tuxedo with a black bow tie—including underwear—and in an instant I was dressed, with shiny black shoes, too. I mentally requested a comb and then combed my hair. "How do I look?" I asked loudly.

"Fabulous, darling." Dalia put her arm through mine. "Let's have dinner."

We exited the pagoda-shaped gazebo and ascended to a white and blue-streaked marble terrace nearby, where a round table was set for four, if you counted Freggor's tiny chair and table, which were on the round table. The terrace had a great view over the valley below. It was getting late, and I looked up to gauge how low the sun was. But there was no sun in the cloudless sky.

"Where is the sun?" I asked, unsettled.

"Gardenia doesn't have a sun," Freggor said as we sat down. He sat in his small chair at his little table on our table.

"What? Where do you get light from?" I looked around and saw no discernable shadows.

"Gardenia is a rogue planet," said Freggor. "It escaped its sun many millions of years ago. We discovered it, a frozen rock, and terra-formed it, making it our home. The planet is enclosed in an energy shell, which focuses the light of the galaxy's stars to provide the illusion of sunlight. The luminescence revolves around the shell every 24 hours, giving us day and night. The shell also keeps the heat from escaping the planet and protects us from cosmic radiation."

"Mindboggling," I whispered, looking up. "But why 24 hours?"

"As it happens, on average, a 24-hour spin for a planet this size that were exposed to a sun is optimal to spread the heat evenly on the surface," said Freggor. "A faster spin, and the planet stays constantly hot, but too slow, and one side freezes every night."

"Huh," I mumbled at this information.

We were all seated, and out of nowhere, four waiters—one for each of us—appeared. The servers were automatons, perfect machines with impeccable manners, but they spoke like machines. They even wore aprons over their metallic bodies. Their eyes were two camera lenses and their mouths a perforated grill, just like on the robots you'd see in a 1950s movie. I gawked at them and heard Dalia giggle at seeing my gaping mouth. My waiter asked me what I would like to have as an appetizer, followed by soup, salad, a main course, and my beverage preference, after which he scurried away. For sure he would return later with a choice of desserts.

"So, gods eat, too," I said, as my server returned with my cocktail, a double Black Russian. I so needed it.

"And we eat well," Anu said, sipping his martini. "We need nutrients to survive, just like any biological creature."

"And the waiters, the automatons, I've never seen anything like them before." My waiter placed a shallow bowl with jumbo shrimp and cocktail sauce in front of me.

"Yes, you have seen automatons, but you've forgotten," said Anu. "And you may be wondering why we don't use androids that resemble us."

Mmm, the shrimp and cocktail sauce were delicious, and I was hungry. I nodded, wanting to hear the answer.

"All our helpers are artificial entities here on Gardenia. We can give them any shape we want, and for tonight we chose automatons. Would you like instead an android? Or an English butler, perhaps?"

"Are you finished with your appetizer, sir?" my server asked in a British accent. He was now a middle-aged English butler, and he had on a white shirt, black tie, gray vest, black morning coat, striped gray trousers, and white gloves.

"I'll be," I said, marveling at the android standing beside me. "Yes, yes, I'm finished. My compliments to the chef."

"I will relate your compliments to our chef, sir. It will be pleased." The server took my dish, bowed, and departed to the kitchen, I presumed. Then something occurred to me: Did they have a kitchen here? "Where is all this food for our dinner coming from?" I asked watching a herd of deer grazing in the valley.

"We could raise animals and plants for food, but it is more humane to synthesize it." Anu observed me looking at the deer and said, "Although Gardenia has an abundant wild life we don't eat the animals.

"But the food tastes so good, even if it's not real," I said.

"It is real, and it is made out of organic molecules, proteins, and hydrocarbons, and all the minerals to impart the specific taste that the meal should have," Anu said. "Tonight we decided on an Earth cuisine that you were accustomed to. Our chef, who is a machine, can synthesize over a million dishes from a thousand worlds. All edible by humans, I may add."

I took another sip of my drink. I needed it. This was too much information to absorb all at once.

The dusk was upon us. "How do you have a sunset without a sun?"

"We can make anything we want," said Freggor from across his little table. "Sunsets and sunrises are always nice. So we made them as well."

"This is paradise," I said, sipping from my wine now, which my waiter had just served. It was an excellent cabernet. "Freggor, if I may, what do you do?"

"Other than being a god? Or you may wonder what can I do, being so little?" I felt embarrassed, but that's exactly what I wanted to know. "I am the keeper of Gardenia." He opened his arms wide.

"You manage Gardenia? Just you?"

"How many people does it take when you have an army of automatons, androids, and other specialized intelligent robots?"

"That's true. I'm just trying to wrap my head around all this."

"Well, enjoy it," said Anu. "I would have liked to give you more time to spend on Gardenia, but trouble on Nisip is approaching fast. You'll depart tomorrow on your first mission to save the Sferogyls."

I felt a knot form in my stomach, just as I was about to attack my real-looking and real-smelling synthesized steak and lobster tail.

"Don't worry, you'll do well," Anu assured me. "As a matter of fact, after tomorrow, Freggor will be the only occupant of Gardenia."

"You and Dalia will be departing, too?" I asked.

"Yes, but on different missions," said Anu. "Also, when you're on Nisip, use your Earth name, Tim Andrus. Use your god name, Timurud, only when it is necessary or appropriate."

I rubbed my cheek, puzzling over what he said.

"If the Maggotrolls find out that a god has arrived on Nisip to help the Sferogyls, they'll come after you first," Anu warned. "They may even send Coshmars after you. Remember, you'll be there to help the Sferogyls defend themselves, not to fight for your life."

"I don't think I even know how to fight."

"Use your head." Anu pointed with his fork at my head. "Glave o'Sfero, the Sferogyls' leader, is expecting you. You can tell him who you really are, and you'll be welcomed as the Messiah."

My eyes bulged at such a notion. "Isn't a Messiah supposed to arrive brandishing a laser saber?"

"A what?" Anu chuckled. "Ahh, that must be Earth's latest fantasy, I guess. No, no weapons."

"How am I going to defend myself? I should have at least a laser gun."

"You won't need one," Anu assured me, while taking a bite of his lamb chop.

"I don't know how to fight."

"Oh, you know how to fight," said Anu. "You were our best bare-handed combat fighter. You'll remember when the situation arises."

"Throw me in the deep end and see if I can swim." I ran my fingers inside my collar, suddenly feeling flushed.

"Something like that." Anu smiled.

I snapped my fingers and my waiter came right away. "Give me a triple Black Russian." He bowed and returned quickly with my drink. I downed the glass in a couple of big gulps. "This will cool my nerves." I wiped my mouth with the back of my hand.

"Unfortunately, as a god, you'll not get drunk," said Dalia with a wink. "Besides, you need to preserve your strength for tonight."

I was totally confused—not about not getting drunk, which I intended to do, but about *tonight*.

Freggor slapped his knee and burst out laughing at my confusion.

"You'd better finish your dinner," said Dalia. "And then I'll be your dessert."

I finished my meal and, as promised, but to my disbelief, Dalia took me by the hand to her love nest. I almost fainted with anticipation.

Mit Sandru

Chapter 8. Bionanobots

I woke up in the middle of the night. A full moon lit the landscape around us. But it was not the light of a full moon—it was much brighter. Sweeping aside the canopy that hung over the bed for a better view, I gawked at the brilliant sky. Billions of stars, sparkling in different colors, filled the sky. They provided so much light that I could have read a book by it. The nearby lake, its colors of turquoise near the shore, was alit, reflecting the sky like a mirror. It didn't look Earthly; it looked magical.

For a minute, I forgot that Dalia was sleeping next to me. The starlight made her face and naked body even more beautiful. I was in heaven, where the weather was perfect, the stars were brilliant, the flowers smelled sweetly, the food and drinks were sublime, and you didn't have to jump through hoops to make love to a goddess. This was paradise. I fell asleep again with a satisfied smile on my face, cuddling up to Dalia.

The "sunrise," reflecting over the lake, woke me up early in the morning. Or maybe the chirping birds interrupted my restful sleep. I propped myself up on an elbow and analyzed my immediate surroundings in the morning light. We were on the sandy beach of a tranquil lake. Occasionally, a jumping fish broke the mirror-like surface. We were surrounded by manicured, luscious flowering gardens, filling the air with an aromatic fragrance. Dalia was sleeping next to me, wrapped in a silk sheet, and we were outdoors in a four-poster canopy bed. Dalia was so beautiful, and I was the lucky guy to have slept with her. Boy, she had a way with everything, including the words she whispered in my mind while we were making love during the night.

Dalia stirred and moved closer to me. Part of the silk sheet slipped off, revealing her angelic breasts. And they were natural. I couldn't restrain myself, so I cupped my hand over one of them. It felt warm, firm, and tender.

Then I remembered that I was going to have to leave soon on a dangerous mission. That chilled me. I was going to be taken to an alien planet, to live among creatures that looked like balls, and make them get off their round butts to defend themselves against evil aliens. What was Anu thinking? A stupid mission for a stupid guy like me.

Suddenly a thought crossed my mind. I remembered the "got milk?" commercial—at first you think you're in heaven, then the next, without milk, you're in hell. Dalia was my heaven. Nisip and Sferogyls were going to be my hell. Small drops of sweat cooled my forehead, and I wiped them off. I was scared. What was I going to do? There was no escape from this mission, other than looking like a coward in front of Dalia.

She caressed my face. "Good morning, Timurud. Why are you so worried?"

Seeing her awake, my fear somehow disappeared. "Good morning, beautiful." But I was not completely relaxed.

"Are you concerned about your mission?"

There was no reason to lie. I nodded with a sigh.

"Don't worry at all. You'll be safe."

"Safe? I'll meet creatures I never conceived could exist. And how will I communicate with them?"

"The bionanobots will help."

"How?"

"You'll be able to understand and communicate with the

Sferogyls or Maggotrolls in their languages," she answered.

"How is that possible?"

"Simulated telepathy. You'll speak in English and they'll understand you in their own language, and vice versa."

"Hmm. I guess that would work. And how about my senses or their senses? Are we going to correlate with each other?"

"Bionanobots."

"How about nourishment, the air I'll breathe, alien viruses, my physiological needs?"

"Bionanobots."

"Is there anything these bio-nano-bots-can-not-do?" I grinned sarcastically.

"They cannot do everything, but that's when you take over and use your god-like ingenuity and acumen to help the societies in need. In this case the Sferogyls," she said sweetly, propped up on one elbow.

I collapsed onto my back, and Dalia reached over and began kissing me.

Oh, God, have mercy!

Mit Sandru

Chapter 9. The Suit

"Well, stud, it's time to get up and get ready," Dalia said after five minutes of cooling down after our morning lovemaking.

"Sure. Where is the shower?"

"The lake." She got up, ran toward the lake, inviting me to follow her, and plunged in, revealing her curvaceous derrière.

I ran and jumped in, expecting to find the water cold, but it was pleasantly cool. It must have been my metabolism or those bionanobots.

We frolicked, splashed, and even washed, and eventually we came out.

"Well, it's time you put on your expeditionary uniform," said Dalia.

"What's that?"

"Don't worry, I'll do it for you, since you don't remember yet." She snapped her fingers and I found myself dressed in a brown leather-like one-piece suit. On my feet I had combat boots. Even my hands had gloves on them. There were some appurtenances on the suit, but there weren't any zippers, fasteners, or even pockets.

I looked at Dalia, and she was dressed in a similar suit, except it was in blue. "Interesting suit," I said, checking some more of what I was wearing, which felt like a second skin. "How do I remove my gloves?"

"You don't need to. But if you want to, just imagine them off," she explained. "This suit will protect you like no other suit out there. First, even if you don't see anything around your head, you have an invisible force field helmet. That helmet will protect you from any poisonous atmosphere, and it will keep you from drowning, too."

"How much air do I have? How do I open it to drink or eat?"

"You'll never run out of air. Your suit will scrub the carbon dioxide or convert any gases in the atmosphere into the air you use to breathe. You don't need to open your helmet. It will do that on its own when needed. The helmet is invisible, but you can make it opaque, if you don't want to show your face. Your suit is waterproof, temperature-shielding, impact-resistant to rocks, knives, or bullets."

"Bullets? Aliens are using guns?"

"Chemically propelled projectiles are the cheapest weapons out there. They are still in use. Also, the suit is radiation-resistant. It is even resistant, for short durations, to laser and plasma blasts. Any questions?"

"Better than the Ironman." I felt bewildered. "Can I fly in it?"

"No, it's strictly terrestrial. And with this suit, you have close-contact combat weapons."

"I thought I wasn't going to have any guns."

"Not guns, blades."

"Come again?"

She raised my chin with a one-meter-long blade coming out of her hand. It was two centimeters wide and barely visible.

"I guess you don't have light sabers." I looked crossed eyed at the blade.

"Ha, ha, you and your science fiction movies. I amused myself watching *Star Wars* when I was on Earth. I even watched *Star Trek*. Yeah, light sabers." She made a dismissive gesture.

"What's so funny? Those movies are good."

"Yeah, right. Earthly science fiction is so far off from reality."

"It is?"

"Let me put it to you from this perspective. Imagine the ancient Greeks on Earth, trying to make a play about the 21st century. What would they think of spaceships or airplanes? Chariots of fire rolling in the sky. How about your communication systems, like phones? Two soup cans with a string between them. How about your TV? Mirrors. Get my point?"

"But those were the ancient Greeks. They didn't know as much about science as we know today."

"Well, George Lucas should have known better than to make spaceships look like naval battleships."

"I think George Lucas is a genius. And in his defense, a spaceship resembling a naval battleship is more appealing for Earthlings, more believable."

"That I understand, and I gave you the example of how the Greeks would have thought of the future versus today's reality on Earth. You use what you know today for what will be tomorrow."

"Yeah, I see your point," I said meekly, remembering that the EBT, the energy blip in time, did not look anything remotely like a spaceship. "So there is no resemblance between our sci-fi and what is out there?" I gestured up to the sky.

"Some is. You'll find out."

"Why the blade?" I pointed to the saber she was holding.

"Remember, I said close-combat fights. You don't shoot a plasma gun at someone who's on top of you. But if you have a blade like this…" She swished it in the air and it whistled. "You'll kill your enemy swiftly."

"I guess," I was unimpressed and gave her a half-smirk.

"The edge of this blade is one atom sharp, and it oscillates at high frequency. The thickest part of the blade is at most only two millimeters thick. It cuts through anything—flesh, bone, armor, granite, steel, titanium, or even the highest alloys ever devised, like carbodurium. The blade can change its length or shape, as you desire, and you're not limited to one blade—you can have two or three, but they'll be shorter. The maximum length is based on the mass your suit will generate to create the blade, as you see coming out of my hand now.

"You can have blades or spikes coming out of your hands, or out of the tip or heel of your boot. Good for kicking." She generated those features as she was explaining them. "From your shoulders, elbows, or a spine of spikes on your back—practically from any part of your body, to defend yourself or kill your enemy. As I said, you can cut through titanium or carbodurium, and it will never go dull, because the edge regenerates to stay one atom sharp." She produced blades from all parts of her suit, even from her boobs. Fascinating and deadly.

"As long as I'm not required to duel with anyone," I said.

"Why duel? Grab their weapon with your gloved hand and kill the sucker with your blade in the other hand."

"That's not gentlemanly."

"Gentlemanly is overrated when it comes to life and death."

What a woman! An Amazon, for sure. "You've convinced me. I hope I don't cut myself." I experimented and extended some blades from various parts of my suit. "These heel spurs are dangerous. I could kick myself and puncture the suit."

"No, your own blades will not work against your suit, although these blades are the only object that can slice through such a suit."

"Well, some of my worries have dissipated. It seems that I will be well protected. But let me ask you this: Why is your suit blue and mine, brown?"

"The suits can be any color, including skin color, if you want to pass as naked. It is also capable of camouflage and invisibility."

"Invisible? Now you're talking."

"Yes, but invisibility can be revealed with the proper sensors, and it has some limitations. Camouflage is best when you stand still near a wall or an object. Mine is blue, because that will be the nature of my mission. You'll be on a brown, maroon, and beige planet, and your suit will blend better with the brown environment. Remember, you can change your suit to any color or pattern, if it serves you better."

I nodded and looked at my suit. "I guess this is all I have to protect myself."

"For now, until you rediscover your telekinetic powers."

"Like bending spoons?"

"Like moving objects with the power of your mind. You were one of the best among gods when it came to psychokinetic ability."

"I wish I'd remember how to do it."

"Don't worry it will come back. Any questions?"

"Not at this time."

"Good, because your ride is here." She wrapped her arms around my neck and gave me a long kiss. "Good luck, and we will spend more time together soon. I'm glad you're back from being missing-in-action."

"Ready, lover boy?" Freggor said from a clear bubble he was levitating in.

I looked at him, annoyed, and then I turned back to Dalia.

She was gone.

Chapter 10. Facts of the Universe

"Where did she go?"

"She left for her mission," said Freggor.

"How did she do that?"

"On Gardenia, you can teleport anywhere you want. With proper training."

I scratched my chin. Everything here was as if in a magic world, minus the wands.

"Time to go," said Freggor. "Hop in." He motioned with his head to get in the bubble, which now was large enough to accommodate me as well.

"Where are we going?"

"To the spaceport. Anu is waiting for you there."

"What does this thing do, fly?" I pointed to the bubble.

"Yes, and it does it very well."

I climbed in and sat down in what I imagined was a seat. "How does this thing levitate?"

"Antigravity."

"Would you explain that for someone like me who's forgotten?"

"It's simple. Matter causes gravity. Antimatter causes antigravity."

"There is antimatter in this thing?"

"Simulated antimatter to obtain the antigravity. I told you, it's simple." The bubble shot up into the sky like a bullet.

I didn't feel any acceleration. What a marvelous thing this antigravity is! "Do you use this for space travel?"

"Yes, we can, but the antigravity is useful mostly around planets. You need gravity—well, a planet—for repulsion or attraction, as the need may be. The farther from a planet, the weaker the gravity gets, and the less repulsion or attraction power you'd have. Let me give you a quick spin around the planet."

"Uh-huh," I said dumbly. I looked outside. We were out of the atmosphere, and the continents, seas, and cloud formations down below were fascinating. It was just like Earth, but with different landmasses and seas. "How much water do you have on Gardenia?"

"Half-water, half-land," Freggor replied. "And we balanced evenly the area of the continents and the oceans to keep a stable climate."

"Are there deserts?"

"Yes, the spaceport is in a desert."

The craft entered the dark side of Gardenia, created by a reduction in the energy shell's luminescence. The Milky Way, in its entire splendor, was more brilliant than I remembered it from last night. The center of the galaxy was blinding and enormous.

"How far are we from the center of the galaxy?"

"About 16.3 Kly," said Freggor, looking up. "Beautiful, isn't it?"

"Fantastic! Why is the light even more brilliant than what I saw last night?"

"The energy shell dims the galaxy's brightness. Otherwise, we wouldn't have night, especially when we face the center of the galaxy. Now we are above the shell, and you see the true brightness of the Milky Way."

I cleared my throat. "What's Kly?"

"Kilo light years. Or 16,300 light years."

"Where are we exactly in the Galaxy?" I asked.

"Spherical coordinates are 16.3, 45.24, 3.01. Down to the minute accuracy." Freggor noticed my raised eyebrows. "16.3 Kly from the center of Milky Way, 45 degrees 24 minutes azimuthal angle, and 3 degrees 1 minute polar angle."

"What does that mean?"

"We're in the Sector 1, Ring 3 of the galaxy."

"What does that mean?" I sounded like a kid.

Freggor sighed. "Since you forgot even the galactic coordinates, I'll explain it. Once. Because the galaxy is rather flat, it is divided in 12 sectors, like an analog clock, from zero to 11. Zero is aligned with the galactic bar at the center of the galaxy. Then the galaxy is divided in 12 rings. Zero ring starts at the center of the galaxy. For simplicity the polar angle from the center of the galaxy is omitted, and it is good enough for determining our location in the galaxy."

"Uh-huh. What arm would that be?"

"Norma Arm for earthlings like you."

"That's clearer. The Earth is on the Orion Arm," I said remembering the Earth's mapping of the galaxy. "You mapped the galaxy in 12 sectors not four quadrants as it is on Earth."

Freggor snorted. I got the message. I was not on Earth.

The bubble-craft descended on the morning side of the planet, in the southern hemisphere, approaching what seemed to be a crater, and we landed on a platform outside a large dome. Its roof resembled the desert terrain surrounding us.

"Let's go," said Freggor, jumping out of the craft onto a levitating disc.

I jumped down onto the platform's deck and followed him into the enormous dome. Inside there were several triangular dipyramids, or spaceships. One of them was the craft I'd seen when we were around Jupiter. It was the largest of them all, dwarfing the next two parked near it.

"Good morning, Timurud. I trust you had a restful night," said Anu, who was seated at a table in an alcove nearby, having breakfast.

I didn't know how to interpret the "restful night" comment, so I said, "Yes, I did. Nature always makes me sleep restfully."

"Good, good. Did you have breakfast? Would you care to join me?"

I hadn't had breakfast, and it was a good idea to eat something, considering that I would end up God-knows-where on my first day on the job as a god. Freggor floated toward one of the smaller craft, where several automatons were busy with exotic apparatuses. I sat at the table and eyed the goodies on it.

An android-waiter approached and asked, "Would you like coffee, espresso, cappuccino, or tea?"

"I'll have a cappuccino, please. And a glass of orange juice." I reached into a basket for a croissant and a boiled egg.

"That's your EBT, the one on the right," said Anu, pointing to it. That was the craft the automatons were busying themselves with, preparing it for my trip.

"I get my own spaceship?" The android waiter brought me a large cappuccino and the orange juice.

"But of course. How else would you get to Nisip?"

"How far away is this planet?"

"It is in Sector 10, Ring 4. About 25 thousand light years away, in the Sagittarius Arm."

I almost choked on my cappuccino. "How long will it take to get there?"

"Instantly," Anu said with a serious expression on his face.

I placed my cup on the table and eyed him in disbelief. "How could that be? Nothing can travel faster than the speed of light. Even I, a science fiction writer who bends the truth all the time, know what science says, and I believe it."

"And you should, based on how advanced the Earth's science is," said Anu. "Therefore, a quick lesson about space travel speeds: The sapient civilizations are classified as non-space and space-capable. The space-capable civilizations are classified as standard-speed, near-light-speed, and hyper-light-speed. Only the gods can travel instantaneously."

"How much energy would that require? How is it done?" My curiosity was at its maximum.

"Considering what you know from Earth, that's a valid question. First, standard-speed, or SS, is speed up to 30,000 kilometers/second. Different types of propulsion engines are used on these craft. They are very inefficient and dangerous.

"Now, near-light-speed, or NLS, for speeds as high as 99% of the speed of light, would require a great amount of energy if propulsion engines would be used, which would make them impractical. Civilizations that achieve NLS don't use propulsion. They use space warping."

I raised my eyebrows.

"This technology deals with the fabric of space. Space is flat, but it is bent by gravity. Imagine a spaceship that deforms the space in front of it by creating a gravity-well in the membrane of space. The craft will fall into the GW, and if the curvature of the GW is maintained constant, the spaceship will continue to accelerate and achieve NLS."

I vaguely remembered reading about such a theory, but how it was done in practice was a mystery to me. Apparently, advanced civilizations in this galaxy had developed that technology.

"Let's say that is so," I said agreeably. "But the higher the speeds, the higher the chances of the spacecraft disintegrating when colliding with even a grain of sand."

"Sure. Not to mention mini black holes. That's why the spaceship has an additional gravity field around it, like a protecting cone, to deflect any object, large or small, from its path. The near-light-speed spaceships are mostly long and slim, like a cigar. The conical gravitational shield requires energy, and the larger the cross section of the craft, the greater the energy needed. I mention this so in the future you'll be able to recognize the types of craft used by different civilizations."

"Has anyone achieved the speed of light?" I asked.

"The short answer is no. It is an impossibility," said Anu.

"Why?"

"To achieve true speed of light, the spaceship must distort the space fabric continuously. But the incremental distortion becomes less and less as the speed increases, until it becomes zero at infinity, where the speed of light can be reached."

"So the speed of light can never be achieved because it will take infinity."

"Yes. However, there is something else you must know," said Anu, raising an eyebrow.

I got a feeling that he was about to tell me a great secret. A godly secret.

"Timurud, everything you see around you, including you and me, is an illusion."

I straightened up. "What do you mean, an illusion?"

"To use a word that you'd understand at this time, the entire universe is a giant hologram."

What the fuck—pardon my French—was he talking about? What hologram? "But, based on my senses, I know everything around me is real, not smoke and mirrors."

"How do you know? You, yourself, are a hologram."

I shook my head, confused about what he was saying. "You mean here and the vast universe out there are all an illusion?"

"And you and I are illusions as well," said Anu. "What's more important to understand is that this grand illusion is generated at the speed of light."

"So we cannot go faster than we are generated." I was dumbfounded.

"You got it. That's why in the visible universe, VU, the speed of light is the maximum speed."

"Who is generating this hologram?"

"Us. We do."

"We as gods?"

He shook his head. "All of us."

"Please explain."

"Life, all life forms, generates the grand illusion of the universe. That's what it does."

"Like a byproduct?"

Anu acknowledged with his eyes.

I stood up and rubbed the back of my neck, then sat down again, but I got it, strange as it sounded. Life generated the grand illusion, and the illusion generated us. It was a continuous loop, and that was the big mystery of the universe.

"For you, with only scientific knowledge from Earth, it may sound unreal, but it is the only real thing. And I gather you understand now."

I inhaled and nodded.

Chapter 11. Space Travel

"How close to the speed of light can they get?" I asked after I had recovered from my bewilderment.

"Some can get near 99% of the speed of light."

"But they will be affected by the passage of time between their home planets and the spaceship as they approach the speed of light," I said.

"Of course. Say, at 98% of the speed of light, for every year on the spaceship, the home planet will have aged five years. They'll have to plan for the time disparity. That's why there are very few civilizations that venture more than ten light years from their home planets to trade or establish empires."

"It still baffles me that such advanced civilizations conquer each other," I said.

"Unfortunately, at our core, there is no difference between a hungry bacteria and a hungry sapient entity." He contemplated for a moment. "Not all civilizations are empires, and there are some empires that resemble federations of planets. There are many unions of planets as well. There are many reasons why they formed."

The universe was stranger than I could imagine.

"What kind of energy do they use to achieve these speeds?" I asked.

"It varies, but the most efficient and abundant is dark energy."

"Dark energy exists?"

"And dark matter, for that matter. The VU, the visible universe, the hologram illusion, is embedded within the Dark Universe, the DU."

"How big is the DU, if the visible universe is infinite?"

"It's infinite as well. Size is irrelevant within the scope of everything there is. It is relevant to us but not to the big picture." He paused for a moment and took a sip of his coffee. "Shall I continue about travel speeds?"

"By all means."

"The hyper-light-speed civilizations, HLS, had figured out what this entire universe is made of and discovered the Dark Universe. The way they travel faster than the speed of light is by taking their spaceship from the VU and transferring it to the DU. A visible universe spaceship is invisible in the DU, and the laws of our VU physics are not applicable there. Nevertheless, once in the DU, they use dark energy and can travel thousands of times the speed of light."

"Amazing—travel faster than the speed of light!"

Anu nodded. "Yes, but remember, the spacecraft is not traveling in the VU. The characteristics of the DU spacecraft are, again, unique for that type of travel. The DU must engulf the visible matter and energy of the spacecraft, and for that reason the craft will have an internal tunnel going through it. At its most basic, the DU craft resembles a tube.

"In the DU everything seems distorted and it makes a very boring passage. Most crews go into hibernation to preserve their supplies and eliminate boredom. The most advanced civilizations travel at ten thousand times the speed of light."

"They could cross the Milky Way in ten years." I was astounded.

"Yes."

"Is that the fastest they can go?"

"So far. Fortunately, there are not that many such civilizations. But each one that mastered the faster speeds became an empire."

"It's not much different than what George Lucas envisioned in *Star Wars*." I smirked. "Maybe he's a god."

"No. We would know if that's the case," said Anu. "And finally there is us, who can travel instantaneously anywhere."

"Have you ever reached the edge of the universe?"

"The universe is infinite, and there isn't an edge, or an end, or a loop to take us back where we started from."

I understood, but at the same time I was having difficulty with the concept of infinity. "How can you travel at instant speed?"

"Not instant speed, mind you. We appear where we want to be instantly."

"Quantum mechanics," I said.

"Yes. On Earth, you learned that an electron could be in many places at the same time. Earth has a long way to advance to discover how objects bigger than an electron can exist in all locations at the same time. And time is what makes it all possible."

"What does time have to do with all this?"

"Time is the only thing that's real, and time makes the universe real."

I swallowed, trying to comprehend what he had just said. "What do you mean, time is the only thing that makes the universe real? How about matter and energy and forces and space?"

Anu smiled. "Matter, energy, space, and forces cannot exist without time. When time stops, 'the everything' ceases to exist. When this universe was created before the so-called Big Bang, there was nothing. The Big Bang was the beginning of time, when the Pandora's box opened to create the forces, energy, and matter, as we know them. As this stuff came to be, because of time, space was created."

"But if the Big Bang happened and there was an origin of the universe, how come now it is infinite?"

"That's why time is so fascinating. Zero time and infinite time are the same. Try to wrap your head around that concept."

I didn't even try to comprehend what he had just said. "Is there more than one universe? Have you traveled to any other?"

"There are infinite numbers of universes. We cannot travel to other universes, but we know they exist, each one with a different time continuum. Universes are created all the time and die all the time."

"Where are they?"

"Here, around us." He opened his arms.

"What do you mean, here? Where, exactly?"

"Here," he repeated. "They are not far, far away, but they occupy the same space as we do, and yet we cannot cross into the other universes. We only can exist in our own universe, dependent on our time continuum."

I scratched my ear. "So how do you travel instantly?"

"Remember when I said that zero time and infinite time are the same?"

I nodded.

"Now, between zero and infinity there are an infinite number of seconds. We just select the 'when' we will be in an instant and that gives us the option to select the 'where' in the universe."

"And that's why you cannot get to the edge of the universe. It exists at infinity, and you cannot select infinity," I said, feeling proud of myself.

"Nor zero, for that matter of fact. We cannot freeze time."

"Can you travel back in time?"

"We cannot travel back in time. Negative time does not exist, although mathematically it can. Time is a continuous one-way entity, at least in this universe."

"How about communication over large distances?"

"As you know in the visible universe, the maximum speed of electromagnetic waves is the speed of light," said Anu. "So far, Earth has managed to communicate using electromagnetic, or E-M, waves. Spacefaring civilizations have learned how to use quantum mechanics, and they communicate instantly using the all-over-the-place electron.

"However, the time must be taken into account when communicating this way. Time is not constant through out the universe and it varies depending of the speed of the sender and receiver, and gravity."

"This is amazing. Now I see why Earth cannot 'hear' transmissions by other civilizations. We don't have the technology. That's why the universe seems lifeless."

"Exactly. E-M communication is like using sound waves, compared to quantum communication."

"Can the other civilizations hear Earth?"

"Sure, if they want to listen to such primitive forms of communication. But some may listen to discover new, primitive worlds to conquer."

"Do they know about Earth?"

"It depends how hard they listen, however, the E-M waves from Earth have traveled only 100-plus light years away so far. And that is not far enough."

I sighed with relief.

"But it is a matter of time before Earth will be spotted, anyway. It's a small galaxy," added Anu.

"So many people on Earth want to know about ET, new sapient civilizations. It will be scary when that happens." I shuddered.

"It will be scary and wonderful. Don't worry. We keep an eye on Earth and other emerging civilizations. That's our job as gods."

That assurance made me feel a little better. No matter what Anu said about being a god, I still felt human and cared about Earth. I reached for my cappuccino, contemplating what I had been told, but my drink was cold. I turned to call for the waiter, but it was already at my side with a new, hot cup of cappuccino. That's what I call service.

"Let's get back to your mission," Anu said.

"Do I have a say in this matter?"

"What would you like to say?"

"What if I don't want to go?"

Chapter 12. Doubts

"You don't want to go. Why?" Anu raised his eyebrows.

"I don't feel qualified for such a job. Before you thawed my head, the extraterrestrials were a fantasy, even if the UFO buffs claimed otherwise. I'm shocked to find out that ETs are real and they travel all over the universe. This mission requires someone with an adventurous spirit, a Special Forces-type of guy. I told you that I never served in the military and can hardly fire a gun. Not to mention my slim diplomatic skills or ability to persuade people."

"Special Forces?" He guffawed. "You are a god. You can do anything."

"Thank you for the vote of confidence. But let's say that you wanted me to go back to Earth and fix Earth's problems. I would say, no way. I couldn't."

"No? Why?"

"OK, so I go back to Earth and I tell everyone that I am a god and have come back to solve Earth's problems. You know what people will say? That I'm cuckoo. Others will ask me to prove myself by walking on water, turning water into wine, or curing all the diseases known to mankind. Some others will believe and prostrate themselves in front of me, while others will call me an imposter or the devil. I wouldn't be surprised if an Ayatollah would put a fatwa on me." I ran a finger across my throat.

"You think that a god like you should deliver godly results? Not at all," said Anu. "We, or in this case, you, will help with a specific problem on a mission. You think Earth needs help. Earth needs to solve its own problems, and humanity is not in danger of extinction. Yet. However, the Sferogyls are in danger and have asked for god's help."

"If you are god, Anu, why don't you impose a god's peace? I'm sure you have the technology to annihilate any military force. Or give them an ultimatum: If you cross this line, you'll lose your technologies."

"I, we, could do that," said Anu. "Long ago, we destroyed an empire's military force, and that empire ceased to exist. But just decades later, one of the former colonies conquered the old empire's home planet and slowly all the other colonies, and a new empire emerged. Who was right and who was wrong? Why should we side with one or the other? We protect civilizations against extermination. That's when we grant god's help."

"But you, as a god, could give technologies to other civilizations to satisfy all their needs, and there would be no need for them to conquer each other. There would be eternal peace and prosperity."

Anu laughed. "We don't have to do that. Many of these civilizations have discovered and put to use those technologies."

"Then what's the problem?"

"When a civilization achieves that level of technology, like here on Gardenia, where everything is done by machines, that civilization either collapses or becomes an empire."

"Why would it collapse?"

"Once the people of that civilization receive everything they need and they don't have to struggle and work for their daily bread, they grow fat and dumb. In just a few generations, they forget how the machines they've created work. They rely on the machines until the machines stop working. In the meanwhile, that population is so unused to learning and working that collapse is inevitable."

"I see what you're saying." I thought for a moment. "Was there ever a case when the machines took over?"

"Yes, but it didn't last. No matter how smart the machines are, they don't have a soul and a reason to be."

This was fascinating stuff he was telling me.

"But we have a reason to be. That's why we help and send one of us, a god, to help, which happens to be you in this case." Anu narrowed his eyes. "If you don't want to take the mission, what would you do?"

"I don't know." I rubbed the back of my neck, unsure. "Stay here?" I asked, knowing full well that I had no chance of remaining on Gardenia.

Anu chuckled. "How would you earn your keep?"

"Write, paint—I can compose music, too."

"What do you know? A man of many talents—a Renaissance man. And who will be your customers, your audience? How long can you do that before you're bored to death? Trust me, I knew people like that."

He had a point. There were not many people on Gardenia to appreciate my "genius." Even gods must earn their keep. And since I would live for millions of years, what would I do after 100 or even 1,000 years of creative work? There would be only so much in my creative well before it would run dry.

"Besides," said Anu, scratching his beard. "Why did you ask in your will to save your head after you died?"

"To live another day."

"Very well, I'll send you back to Earth. Not as Timurud, the god, but as you, Tim Andrus. You can write, paint, and make music until the last day of your new life."

I began blinking rapidly. I wasn't expecting that. Return to Earth? I could continue doing what I did before, but after seeing what I'd seen since I had been resurrected, I wasn't sure I wanted to go back. Negative emotions ran through me.

"Let me ask you again—why did you ask to preserve your head after you died?"

That was a good question.

Did I do it because I wanted another chance to live? Maybe.

Or what if I am a god, and my god subconsciousness instructed me to preserve my head, so it could be found and resurrected by Anu?

I had two choices: Go back to Earth and be a human, or stay here and be a god. Oh hell, what was I? A man or a mouse? Besides, Anu said that all this is an illusion. Why not live the illusion to its full potential?

And then a question popped into my head. "You say this is all an illusion, a hologram."

"The greatest there is."

"Then you didn't grow my body, you holo-created it."

"Possibly," replied Anu.

The paradigm was changing. Only gods could alter the illusion. "But I have one more question."

"Yes?"

"How can I go out there and pretend to be a god, when I eat, drink, screw, and poop like all the other mortals?"

Anu threw me a disappointed look.

I answered my own question: *The same way that Jesus walked among mortals.*

"I want to be a god," I whispered.

"Hmm?" Anu cupped one of his ears as if to hear me better.

"I want to be a god," I said decisively.

"You want to be a god? You are a god."

I stood up with renewed determination. "I am a god. What is my mission, Anu?"

Anu stood up and embraced me. "Welcome back, Timurud."

Mit Sandru

Chapter 13. The Mission Ahead

Above our breakfast table, Anu generated a hologram of a reddish-brown planet surrounded by a blue atmosphere, with a few white clouds scattered in the atmosphere. Both poles were white, indicating ice. The planet's surface resembled a cracked eggshell, and the cracks were dark blue with liquid water. There were hardly any seas to speak of, just long lakes and river canyons. Tectonic plates, the lowest points on Nisip, must have caused those cracks and the water accumulated in them. It was a dry planet, a desert planet.

"That's Nisip," confirmed Anu. "It is the second planet of its solar system, after the gas giant next to the sun, and it was unlucky to lose most of its water. But it was good enough for one million Sferogyl refugees to start a new life a thousand years ago, after they traveled for two thousand years in hibernation to reach Nisip. Their ancestors are extinct from slavery and attrition. At 1,500 light years away, they thought Nisip was far enough to escape from the Maggotroll Empire. Back then, the Maggotrolls and Sferogyls were NLS civilizations. But since then, the Maggotrolls stole the HLS technology from another civilization, and they can travel faster and farther. Their maximum speed is 1,000 times the speed of light.

"A week ago, four personnel-cargo transporters and one battle-carrier warship departed from the planet Vestrallum toward Nisip. Vestrallum was the Sferogyls' planet, and Orbyzykhan, the Overlord of Vestrallum—" Anu stopped and looked intently at me, but seeing my blank face he continued, "Orbyzykhan is on a conquering mission in the name of the Maggotroll Empire. Give me your hand." I gave it to him and he touched my palm with his. "I just gave you the information we have about their invasion.

When you are in touch with the Sferogyl leadership, you'll be able to give them the information.

"It will take the Maggotrolls a year and a half to reach Nisip. The four personnel-cargo transporters contain four million Maggotrolls and materiel. Those four million are military, mercenaries, and colonists. I believe that all four million are battle trained. They intend to expand their population to Nisip and make it their future colony. The battle-carrier is the largest class military warship allowed to imperial overlords by the Maggotroll Emperor, and Orbyzykhan is coming to conquer."

Anu generated a hologram showing a humanoid. "This is a Maggotroll. It resembles a human, except it's slightly bigger. They are ferocious fighters."

I stared at the hulk rotating in the hologram. He had a bluish-hued skin, with alien features and orange hair, which grew on both sides of its baldhead, as if he had two manes. The eyebrows were orange as well. The nose resembled two tubes coming down from between the eyes. The ear lobes had three studs in each. They were probably electronic devices not jewelry. The eyes were spaced farther apart, orange, and different than that of a human.

Anu changed the hologram to a comparison chart representing maggotroll, human, and sferogyl physiques.

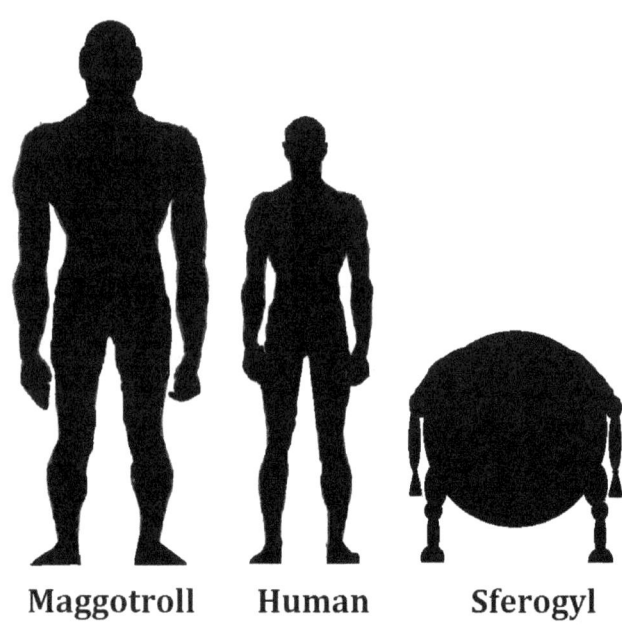

Maggotroll   **Human**   **Sferogyl**

Holly mackerel, the maggotroll was big. The fingertips of his hands reached to his knees. That meant they had a longer reach, an advantage over a human, and definitely over the ball-shaped Sferogyls, which was less than half the maggotroll's height.

Maybe I volunteered to be a god too fast. Too late now.

"The Maggotroll ground soldiers will be the four million colonizers," I reflected. "How many soldiers and battleships do the Sferogyls have?"

"Battleships, none. I'm not sure if they have any class of spaceships. Their population is one hundred million, and anything resembling a military is their peacekeeping force. They're one nation, very peaceful, and they've never had a war since they colonized Nisip."

"Lambs ready for the slaughter." I shook my head in sadness.

"Not if you can help them," said Anu.

"Why are the Maggotrolls doing this?" I asked. "Why are they going after the Sferogyls again?"

"Wealth and power. They discovered an outer rocky planet in the Gatoony solar system, twenty light years from Nisip, which contains diamonds."

"Diamonds? Can't they make diamonds artificially?"

"These are high-quality blue diamonds used in the dark energy engines."

"I see. But don't they have mining machineries to extract the diamonds?"

"Sure they do, but why build them when they can get Sferogyls to mine the diamonds for a lot less cost? Most of the diamonds are located in long and narrow veins in the planet's rocky crust. A one-and-a-half-meter-round tunnel will be plenty wide to send Sferogyls with drills to mine the diamonds. As they depopulate Nisip, they gain new land for their people, doubling the return on their venture."

"Poor Sferogyls. Do they know what's about to happen?"

"They had a premonition and then they asked us for help. We discovered the Maggotrolls' intention, and now we know they just launched their expedition. I promised the Sferogyls that the gods would help when the need arose. In a year and a half, they will need a god's help. We're the only ones standing between them and their invaders."

"Do they know they'll get only one god? Me?"

"Even one god can manage the impossible. One god is enough."

"I could only offer moral support." I ran my fingers through my hair. "And they don't have any weapons whatsoever?"

"They might have the original spaceships that brought them to Nisip and whatever other weapons they may contain. Their technology is what they used to have 3,000 years ago on Vestrallum."

"Do they expect new weapon technology from us?" I asked.

"Even if they do, we will not give them any. New weapon technology is more of a curse than a gift. And since you don't know, or don't remember, of any such technologies, they will have to use what they have."

One god, me, to help them fight an invasion force of four million Maggotrolls armed to the teeth. "Just a year and a half away," I commented, feeling sorry for the Sferogyls and myself.

"Yes. While in transit through the DU, communication is impossible. The invasion force won't be able to communicate with Vestrallum until they arrive at Nisip."

"In that case, whatever the Sferogyls build to defend themselves, the invasion force would not know about it until they arrive," I said.

"Vestrallum has a spy satellite around Nisip, informing them of any Sferogyl military buildup," Anu said.

"Everything will have to be accomplished under stealth. Now, if we are victorious, it will take the Maggotrolls at least a year and a half to renew their military campaign," I said.

"Are you ready?"

"I'm ready."

"In case you're in danger, we can communicate telepathically.

But only if you're in danger, and gods do not ask for help."

"Good to know that." I'm sure there was a reason I could contact him only in case of emergency, and if I did, I would be a lesser god perhaps. I didn't press for details. "Anything else I should know before I 'boldly go where no man has gone before'?" I smirked, smug in my use of the old *Star Trek* lingo.

"When you arrive on Nisip, go west."

"Anyone in particular I should ask for?"

"Ask for Glave o'Sfero, in case he doesn't find you first," said Anu.

"Glave o'Sfero," I repeated. It sounded Irish. I shrugged.

"Your EBT craft is ready to take you to Nisip," said Anu.

"I don't know how to fly it," I was getting nervous again.

"Neither do I, but the craft knows. All you have to do is think Nisip. Have faith and have a successful mission."

We shook hands and I walked to my EBT. At the moment, the so-called craft resembled two tetrahedrons spaced two meters apart on the vertical. I expected the two tetrahedrons to join together and form a triangular dipyramid after I boarded it. For such an incredible journey, the craft was rather small, about six meters across.

I stepped inside between the two tetrahedrons, and I was levitated to the center of the craft. The two tetrahedrons joined and formed the dipyramid, encapsulating me. My capsule was a translucent pod, not a futuristic and fantastic cabin. There weren't any monitor screens or buttons or lights or joysticks to navigate with. There wasn't even a comfortable captain's chair to sit in. Nothing. In a way, it was a letdown. The most advanced spaceship in the universe, and I was completely surrounded by a semitransparent crystalline substance. Although when I boarded the ship I was standing up, now I wasn't sure if I was standing on any recognizable surface or if I was standing at all. Maybe I was just suspended, levitating in some energy field.

What a crazy contraption! Just me, surrounded by blurry stuff I had never seen before. Through the transparency of the crystalline mass I could see Anu outside. I felt that I should salute him, and I did so. He responded in kind and smiled at me.

As instructed, I thought: Nisip.

And then it happened.

Chapter 14. Nisip

I sensed a slight distortion in my surroundings, followed by a slight but fast diminution in the ambient light, and the spaceport vanished. Outside my EBT, I saw a desert vista. I turned in place, staring at the undulating sand dunes. It didn't seem much different from the Sahara. Frankly, I wasn't too sure that I had traveled anywhere. The two tetrahedrons slipped apart, and I was lowered to the sandy ground.

The EBT glowed softly, levitating above me at the top of a small hill. Both confused and curious, I walked around the craft, which made no sound, as you would expect a machine to, or give any indication that it was made of pure energy by emitting some kind of buzzing noise. There were no scratches or smudges on the outside skin of the crystalline dipyramid to indicate the 25,000 light years of travel, which according to Anu, it didn't travel but teleported.

Nothing but sand dunes surrounded my location, as far as I could see, resembling smooth waves made of sand. I walked down the slope to more level ground, and once there I realized that the surface was not soft like sand. It was coarse like sand, but packed. The ground was reddish-brown and beige in color, and its rubber-like surface had particles of sand imbedded in it.

This was Nisip, and it was early in the morning. The temperature was pleasant, and the air was dry but breathable. I located the sun and began walking west to find someone. It would have been so much easier to arrive in a flying saucer and ask the Sferogyls to take me to their leader. Instead I was walking like a nomad, a pedestrian, on this undulating sandy-rubbery surface, with not a living thing in sight. My boots left no tracks on the ground, which could be a problem if I needed to return to my EBT craft. I looked back and located it on top of that small hill. And then slowly the EBT faded, becoming invisible. No one would find it unless they bumped into it.

A cowbell sounded from somewhere ahead of me. Who would have cows in this desert? I picked up my pace and after I climbed over a gentle ridge, I saw what seemed to be a giant snail. Every so often, as it waddled, the bell attached to the top of its shell clanged. It was a veritable snail, except it was gigantic. Its milky-white body must have been around seven meters long, and the reddish-brown shell, striated in brown and beige, gave the impression of a round millstone. Was this a Sferogyl? They were snails and here was a snail. But it was not round like a ball.

Not wanting to disturb or annoy the creature, —snails have teeth, thousands of them— I approached it cautiously from behind. The top of its shell was higher than my head. Its body was over a meter wide, and it left a slimy trail behind it as far as the eye could see. It was sticky too, I discovered when I stepped in it by accident. Obviously, the slime had caused the rubbery layer of the sand. After another look, I realized that there were more, older trails like this one, crisscrossing all over the land. There must have been more of them. The creature seemed to be foraging, and it was sucking on the surface, collecting microorganisms I could not see but presumed were there.

Approaching carefully, I came around on the side the snail. It moved its head up and one of the eye tentacles turned toward me. It spotted me, and it turned its head rather fast, extending the other eye tentacle and the olfactory tentacles to get a good sniff of me. The movement caused the bell on top to bang loudly. Not knowing what this creature would do if provoked, I walked quickly due west, looking over my shoulder from time to time, just in case it followed me.

From up on top of one dune, a ball-like creature on two small bowed legs came running toward me, or perhaps toward the snail.

That was a Sferogyl! When it was close enough, we both stopped and eyed each other. Its reddish-brown body, like that of a hazel nut, was about half a meter in diameter, and his black eyes were staring at me. The encounter didn't last long. The creature retracted its arms into its round body and began rolling uphill with the help of its feet, cranking round and round. At the top of the mound, the legs retreated, and the ball rolled down the other side of the slope. It didn't go west, but I followed it anyway.

The ball moved fast and I had to run after him to catch it. The chase went on for a few minutes, when suddenly it vanished. Where the heck did it go? It must have fallen into a crack or a hole, but I could not see any openings in the ground. I circled around from the spot I'd seen it last, but I couldn't see any signs of it or the hole it dropped into. To get a better chance of finding it, I climbed up and sideways on the shallow hill nearby for a better vantage point. Near the top I almost fell into a hollow contained by the hill.

The hollow was in the shape of a bowl with concave walls, and only the opposite side was visible. The inner curving walls were dotted with holes, and at the bottom there were several Sferogyls going about their chores. They didn't see me gawking from the edge of the bowl, but soon the little one that I had been following shot out of a hole near the bottom and began squeaking and whistling and waving its arms. Then it spotted me and pointed. The other Sferogyls stopped, shaded their eyes, and looked up at me. I had made contact with the first Sferogyl settlement! I waved to them, smiling broadly, like any respectable and honorable ambassador from afar.

However, getting down there to talk to them didn't seem possible from where I was standing. The bottom was at least fifteen meters down, and I didn't think I would land softly if I jumped. I paced around the rim, observing the Sferogyls talking among themselves and having a cow about what they were seeing or perhaps about what to do. Several more came out through the holes, and soon the whole bowl was full of bobbing and thin-arm-pointing balls.

There had to be an entrance somewhere at the bottom of the hill, so I spiraled down to its base. At the bottom of the hill, four Sferogyls, each nearly a meter across, were coming toward me. They were rocking side to side on their skinny legs, as they advanced. I stopped and crossed my arms, waiting for them. Each of their bodies was a different shade of reddish-brown, with lighter, random, vertical stripes. The shells were not smooth and shiny like that of a snail shell, but rather dull.

They didn't have any clothes or shoes on, but they had shiny leather belts and suspenders attached to the belts, on which several devices were hanging. Each one held a two-meter-tall spear-like pole with a hook or spear head. Midway down the shafts of these poles there were other metallic accessories, resembling a trigger. I wasn't sure if those were weapons of some kind or maybe long muskets. The good news was, they weren't holding the spears as if they were intending to spear or shoot me. Dalia had told me that my suit was bulletproof, but I didn't want to find out just yet how protected I was.

To my surprise, I discovered that the Sferogyls had only three fingers on each hand, one thumb and two opposable fingers. Their fingers were not thin like a human's, but thicker and slightly longer. It seems that the three fingers were all they needed to grab or work with. My eyes went down to their feet. There were no digits on their feet; rather, they were flat oval pads, which were covered with thick gray skin. Their arms and legs were creamy-white like snail skin, although there were traces of brown spots here and there.

They stopped a few paces in front of me and stared with their beady black eyes at this creature—me—that they had never seen before. The little Sferogyl I had encountered earlier came running, but it stopped behind them and watched me curiously.

And then I saw their eyes.

Mit Sandru

Chapter 15. The Sferogyls

Strangely, Anu hadn't shown me a hologram of their appearance. I couldn't take my eyes off their eyes. Each eyeball was at the end of a tentacle. It made sense, since they were snails and, just like snails, their eyes were at the end of tentacles. They were able to move their eyes in any direction to see without turning their "heads" or better said bodies. Below the eyes there were several vertical slits that looked to serve as nostrils, and below the nostrils they had filament tentacles for additional olfactory detection. Since the filaments were dark brown or even black, they looked like a moustache. Their mouths were horizontal, which resembled the partition between the two halves of a walnut shell.

I gawked back at them. It was stranger than science fiction to see in 3-D these living things in the shape of balls, standing on two bowed legs and having two arms. They didn't resemble anything even remotely similar to any creature on Earth, except maybe some sort of beetle. The four of them didn't stand still; occasionally one would twitch or whistle, move its arms slightly, or shift its weight on its skinny bowed legs.

I was towering over them, so I raised my hands to project even more importance. "I come in peace and seek Glave o'Sfero," I said in my most godly, English-speaking voice. They did not even blink, which they probably could not. I wondered if they understood me. "Do you understand me?"

"Yes, we do," I heard one of them say in my head. Actually, its speech was whistle patterns. The one who was second from my right was the one who spoke, according to the way his mouth puckered. "Who are you?"

"My name is Tim Andrus, and I come in peace to see Glave o'Sfero."

They looked at each other. Since they didn't have necks, the ones on the ends turned their bodies partway, and one of their tentacle eyes moved as well, although I swear that each one kept one eye on me at all times. The same Sferogyl asked me, "Why?"

Good question—why had I come here? "I'm an envoy from far away, and I bring important tidings to Glave o'Sfero." I hoped that was satisfactory.

The one who spoke turned slightly to the Sferogyl on its right and I heard it conferring in many whistles. "He doesn't seem to be dangerous or armed." I heard it say in my head.

"But how did he get here?" the other asked.

A third one said, "He looks very similar to the Maggotrolls."

"He sure does," said the fourth one, who curled even tighter its three fingers around the shaft of the spear-hook-gun.

"I am not a Maggotroll," I said, and all four turned all their eyes toward me, surprised that I had overheard them. "But I need to talk to Glave o'Sfero about the Maggotrolls. Would you lead me to Glave o'Sfero?"

That got their attention. Two of them waved me to follow them. I did, while the other two came behind me and the little one lagged behind. At a round opening in the hill they went in, and I followed them, bent over, through a corridor until we exited into the bowl's courtyard. Sferogyls of all sizes and stripes parted to let us get to the center of the court.

"We will inquire," one of them said. I didn't know who that was, because frankly, they all looked alike to me. "Would you like to sit down?" It pointed to a bowl.

My puzzlement dissipated when I saw some of them farther away sitting in bowls. Of course those were their chairs—bowls to accommodate their rotund posteriors. I turned one of the bowls upside down and sat on it. That precipitated whistling comments among them and even laughter. Yes, they were capable of whistle-laughing.

Their settlement, located below the top of a small hill in a hollow about forty meters in diameter, was unusual. The concave walls had many round openings that were presumably doors and windows. In some spots, there were violet climbing plants with round leaves clinging to the rust-colored walls. Ramps that served as stairs descended to the courtyard's bottom from some of the round openings above in the wall. The rim at the top from where I had spied on them cantilevered over the bowl itself but the opening still allowed plenty of light to come in. The floor was gray stone, paved with irregular slabs.

Around me stood many Sferogyls, talking among themselves in low whistling voices. In front of me, the four Sferogyls who had come to meet me outside each sat in a bowl. Others behind them held their spear-guns.

"My name is Tim Andrus. What is your name?" I asked the one sitting in the nearest bowl.

"Turnd l'Sfero, Tim Andrus. Where do you come from?"

"A faraway place." I smiled at it and wondered how could I identify it in the future. They were so similar. "Were you the one who spoke to me first?" Not a particularly delicate question, but I had to be sure who was who.

"Kland l'Sfero spoke to you first, Tim Andrus." It pointed to his right, my left.

They remembered my name, but I couldn't tell them apart. "Kland l'Sfero, has there been a messenger sent to contact Glave o'Sfero?"

"Yes, we are waiting to hear from him, Tim Andrus."

Interesting, they were referring to each other as him. Being hermaphrodites they preferred the male pronoun.

I concentrated really hard to find a distinguishing feature on Kland l'Sfero, and I realized that their stripes were different in pattern and in colors. Simple. Kland's pattern was different than Turnd's on his left. And so was the one at his right.

"I'm Logrn e'Sfero, Tim Andrus. What species are you?" asked the Sferogyl at Kland's right.

"I'm a hominid from a faraway planet, Logrn e'Sfero. Although I have the hominidal body shape, I am not related to the Maggotrolls."

Some of their tentacle eyes moved sideways to make eye contact with each other.

"I'm Varna e'Sfero, Tim Andrus," said the Sferogyl on the left side. "Where did you learn our language? You speak it very well."

"It is an ability that I acquired recently, Varna e'Sfero." I took their custom of repeating their names. It seemed that was a sign of respect for them. I smiled, not sure if it meant anything to them. They didn't react one way or another.

"Where is the little one who found me?" I asked.

Someone pushed to the front the smaller Sferogyl. He looked shyly at me.

"Hello, what's your name?"

"Bovern k'Sfero."

"You're a young Sferogyl, aren't you?"

"I am twelve years old."

"Good for you. Do you shepherd the snails?"

"Yes. I'm a watcher."

I nodded and smiled. "And what do you do?" I asked the elders to pass the time.

We spent the time inquiring about each other while waiting for Glave o'Sfero. As we warmed up toward one another, I was offered cold beer, amber in color. It came in a glass stein, but the rim had two outward, opposite protrusions, like a water pitcher, and with two side handles, obviously made for their anatomy. I tasted it, not sure what I was about to drink, but to my surprise it was beer, real beer—cold, delicious, and refreshing.

So far, so good.

I found out, while having a few more beers, that the giant snails were their equivalent of cows, providing them with milk, meat, and leather. The bowls they were sitting in were from the snail shells. Agriculture was carried out around the water bodies far away from this area. The four Sferogyls who had come to meet me, Turnd, Kland, Varna and Logrn, had a rather important status in their society, but they were here to tend the snails and unwind from their routine life.

The gadgets hanging on their belts and suspenders were communication devices and other personal containers. The belts and suspenders made sense, since they didn't wear clothes and therefore had no pockets. Because they didn't have shoulders, I couldn't see how they could carry a bag over a shoulder. Their single ears were near the top of their bodies, or heads, and resembled a small beret. All their limbs, eyes, beret-ears, and moustaches had the ability to retract inside their bodies, a snail's defensive feature that had never diminished over their evolution.

It was almost noon when a sudden commotion happened among the Sferogyls. To my surprise, they knelt on one knee, as if waiting for someone important.

Chapter 16. Glave o'Sfero

I stood up, curious; somehow I felt that Glave o'Sfero was about to enter the courtyard. And indeed he made his appearance, escorted by many other dignitaries, judging by the golden buckles on their white belts. Glave seemed to be the oldest, full of marks on his round gray body.

Glave o'Sfero came forward and observed me for a moment. He said, "Our prayers have been answered. Welcome, Tim Andrus." He extended his three-fingered right hand, its narrow palm opened, toward me.

I figured I should do the same with my right hand, when I noticed from the corner of my eye Kland showing me what to do. Instead of the right palm, I extended my left and touched Glave o'Sfero's palm. This was the first time I had touched a Sferogyl, an actual alien being, and his hand was colder than mine, but the skin was soft. I felt a surge of electricity coursing through me, and I realized that our minds somehow had connected. Or maybe it was just static electricity.

Glave o'Sfero went down on one knee in front of me. A hush settled over the audience when they realized that their leader was bowing, in a way, to me. He then stood up and addressed the crowd: "Tim Andrus is the most illustrious visitor from the stars we have had in millennia."

The crowd raised their three-fingered hands and gave a long whistling sound. And then everyone went down on one knee toward me.

"Thank you for your warm welcome, Glave o'Sfero," I said. "We have much to discuss and prepare."

Glave o'Sfero motioned with his hands to get everyone to stand up. "Let's go to Tandalo, our capital. It is more private there."

"Certainly," I agreed, figuring that there might be prying eyes up in the sky. I followed him through one of the round openings and we entered into a modest-sized cave, lit by artificial light.

"Who found Tim Andrus?" Glave o'Sfero asked.

They ushered Bovern k'Sfero to the front. "I did, oh great Glave o'Sfero," he said. The kid went down on one knee. "But Kland, Turnd, Logrn, and Varna x'Sferos brought him amongst us."

"Tim Andrus, would you like to be hosted and escorted by the Sferogyls who first encountered you?" Glave o'Sfero asked.

"Sure, Glave o'Sfero," I said, seeing Bovern's excitement.

"Good choice, Tim Andrus. They'll serve you well," said Glave o'Sfero. "We shall go to Tandalo, our capital."

Glave o'Sfero, his entourage, my newly assigned escort, and I exited the cave into an underground tunnel, which housed a moving sidewalk that whisked us to a central station. There we boarded individual levitating spherical vehicles. I sat cross-legged on the bottom of the bowl-shaped vehicle and prepared to witness this alien place. The bubble vehicle was self-driven and I almost expected to hear the voice of a narrator while being taken through a theme park.

The vehicle, like the others, seemed to function like cars and speeded up on a multilane highway. On the walls of the freeway's tunnel, animated hologram billboards advertised the products and services of this world, from beer, which I had tasted, to black spaghetti, to plates with some kind of balls on them, and even massages administered with perforated paddles. I was sure those were massages because the Sferogyl slapped with those paddles stood up, seemingly reinvigorated and cheery.

As far as I could see, all the cars were in the shape of spheres and held only one occupant. The taillights were purple, and the headlights were orange. At times, these sphere cars drove one after another, as if they were linked. It amused me, because it reminded me of an egg-packing house, with eggs rolling down conveyor belts. We traveled through many tunnels, crossed many mini-city caves, and finally arrived in an enormous cave. Perhaps "cave" was not the right word, because I couldn't see the end of it, but it had a ceiling supported by columns and many oculi to let the sunlight in. This must be Tandalo, their capital.

The enormity of the cave was beyond words. The columns that held up the roof reminded me of the ancient Egyptian temples in Luxor, surrounded by a forest of columns. We were traveling on a wide thoroughfare, with thick columns on either side supporting the ceiling high above. The ceiling in that area had a longitudinal opening to allow the sunlight in.

Occasionally the columns supported dwellings, which were stacking up attached to the columns. As we progressed into Tandalo the columns became laden with dwelling modules with round or semi-round windows. In many cases the columns resembled high-rise towers, serving as support for the cave ceiling as well. Among the column-buildings there were openings in the ceiling serving as oculi, allowing the sunlight to stream down to a park of sorts at the ground level, where bushes and other vegetation grew. Most of the trees resembled palm trees, and the foliage colors were not green, but dark blue to violet, even black.

The cave's ceiling must have been hundreds of meters above, and the sferogyls built a multi level city inside it. There were at least two more levels of highways and rapid transit lines at higher levels. Bridges, facilitating access from building to building without descending to the ground, connected some of the round tower-buildings. Besides the enormous tower-buildings there were other round buildings that didn't go all the way to the cave's ceiling. By far, most of the cladding of the tower building was glass, or a similar transparent material.

Our final destination was a large, shiny sphere. It seems that, when you're a ball, as the Sferogyls were, the best shape is a round one, like a sphere or a circle or a cylinder. Four massive stone columns supporting the cave's ceiling penetrated through the outer perimeter of the giant sphere. Our cars stopped at the entrance at the bottom of an incline. Considering the Sferogyls' physique there might not be any steps anywhere here in their world, only ramps.

After disembarking at the entrance, Glave o'Sfero pointed up at the sphere above us. "This is our Assembly House, Tim Andrus. In here we as a civilization debate and approve our laws for all of us to follow."

I imagined it must have contained a great hall inside, where the elected Sferogyl politicians gathered and passed laws.

"But first, Tim Andrus, let's meet in my office." He and I were taken through the building's foyer through another tunnel, and we entered through a round door into a vaulted round chamber, with its walls painted violet. In the middle of it stood a half-donut desk surrounded by half-bowl chairs. Behind the half-donut desk there was another bowl-chair for Glave o'Sfero. The violet walls were adorned with many holograms of important Sferogyls, I suspected.

In this world, most structures would probably be underground. Everything seemed to be round, spherical and stairless. And there were no green colors. But then I looked, amazed, at a lamp hanging from the ceiling, glowing softly with orange light— it was in the shape of a cube. I guess there's always an exception.

Glave o'Sfero motioned for me to sit in the customary bowl made of snail shell in front of his desk, which I turned over and sat on top of. He watched me with amusement, judging by the raised corners of his mouth, and then he sat in his bowl-chair.

"Thank God, you've come, Tim Andrus," Glave o'Sfero said with obvious relief. "I fear dark times are ahead of us."

"Unfortunately, your fears are correct, Glave o'Sfero," I responded.

"I figured we need to talk in private first and divulge to our people only what is appropriate for them to know," Glave o'Sfero said.

I nodded, but then I realized that nodding might be unknown to the Sferogyls, so I said, "As you think is best for your people."

"What tidings do you bring us, Tim Andrus?"

I waved my hand and a hologram appeared above the desk. Above it a blue planet engulfed in a rusty haze, five large, dark-gray spacecraft were orbiting in formation. One was slimmer and more menacing-looking, undoubtedly the battle-carrier warship. Its overall shape was that of three cylinders strapped together, with three arrowheads and tails. The other four ships resembled fat cargo or personnel transport spaceships, having two sets of arrowheads at each end.

Anu's voice began: "Greetings, Glave o'Sfero. I'm Anu, and I'm sending the god Timurud to bring you important news, but unfortunately, not good news. The Maggotrolls have started on a new expedition to subjugate the Sferogyls, as you envisioned. You are the last of your civilization, and we cannot allow the Maggotrolls to succeed. This flotilla of four cargo-personnel transporters and one battle-carrier has just departed toward Nisip. Each cargo-personnel transporter contains one million colonizers and the armament and materiel needed for a successful invasion. In total, four million Maggotrolls will be invading Nisip.

"The battle-carrier, *Mangle*, is the Maggotroll Empire's second-highest-class capital warship, and it carries 750 fighter-crafts, twelve frigates, and other spacecrafts. It is an interstellar-class warship armed with missiles and heavy proton cannons to penetrate underground settlements.

"The Maggotrolls have known about you for the past nine years, and they've kept a satellite in orbit to spy on you. Unfortunately for you, they discovered a rich source of blue diamonds in the Gatoony solar system, and Sferogyls would make good miners. The planet Nisip would be icing on the cake for their imperial expansion.

"They will arrive in eighteen months. Their strategy is to invade and land the first four million colonizers. They'll capture four million Sferogyls and take them to Gatoony. The battle-carrier is to assist in case of opposition. They will not kill many of you, unless you resist and fight them. The enslavement will continue until there are no more Sferogyls on Nisip.

"I know you are a peaceful people and may not have any weapons, short of what was left over from your ancestors. You renounced space travel and kept a low profile so as not to be discovered. But if you don't arm yourself and fight, your species will become extinct.

"I have sent the god Timurud to help you plan, organize, develop weapons, mobilize, and even assist you in fighting, if it is necessary. The responsibility to survive is with you and your people. Good luck!"

I sat silently, observing Glave o'Sfero. His eyes were retracted, thinking about what he had just seen and heard. I wondered what was going through his mind. There were dark times ahead, and he had only one god to defend against four million invaders and an enormous carrier-battleship?

"We are thankful you have come to our aid, Timurud," Glave said finally.

I felt rather unsure if he was serious. "You realize that it's just me, Glave o'Sfero. No other gods, no other help, and no weapons will be offered."

"One god is all we need."

Mit Sandru

Chapter 17. Dinner

Unless Glave o'Sfero was bluffing, he and his people's faith in me, a god, might be enough to inspire them to defend themselves. But what would I deliver? Was I a magnificent enough god, who could help them in this moment of dire need? Even I was curious to see what I could do for them.

"What can I tell my people about upcoming events, Timurud?"

"Everything you want, except my real name, Timurud. I am Tim Andrus, an emissary from the gods, and I was sent by them to help you."

"May I ask why not tell them your true name, Tim Andrus?"

"There is concern that this knowledge may change the Maggotrolls' plans. If they find out, they may increase their invading force. Right now, we have a year and a half to build up your defenses and destroy their armada to convince them not to come back."

"Understood," Glave said. "That is wise."

"The holograms we saw, plus additional military information about the Maggotrolls, were downloaded to your network."

"Very well, Tim Andrus. I'll have our experts analyze it. In the meanwhile, we'll offer you accommodations, and you will let me know whatever else we need to do for you."

I was taken to a nearby round tower near the Assembly House, where I was given a suite. It occupied the entire tenth floor in a toroid shape, encircling the stone pillar, which supported the cave's ceiling. The accommodations were excellent, although the doors were round and only 1.5 meters high, so I had to bend down to get through them. The external wall was a continuous glass wall offering an outstanding view over the immediate neighborhood. The bed in my room was a large bowl, and two Sferogyl workers were hurrying to replace the bowl bed with something more suitable for my anatomy.

The Sferogyl Ministries requested the presence of Kland l'Sfero and Logrn e'Sfero for special duties because of their expertise. Turnd l'Sfero and Varna e'Sfero, along with Bovern k'Sfero, became my companions while on their planet.

From the time I arrived in the city, I began smelling vanilla and cinnamon. At first I thought it came from their local bakeries, but I soon realized that the Sferogyls' natural odor gave off the vanilla and cinnamon fragrance. It gave me the impression of being in a donut shop all the time.

I stepped onto the balcony to admire the new and strange environment around my building. Most of the buildings had balconies as well. The large sphere of the Assembly House was nearby, along with many other tower-column buildings surrounding it. Elevated highways and rapid transit lines snaked among the tower-buildings, which also served as the supports for the aerial ways. Occasionally the highways helically encircled a tower-building descending to the ground.

We were in a giant cave, and I wasn't sure if it was naturally formed or Sferogyl-made. I suspected the Sferogyls had constructed most of it to hide their cities from the Maggotrolls or other galactic enemies.

It was rather quiet in the city of Tandalo, although there was plenty of traffic down below on their boulevards and more traffic above. Then again, all their vehicles levitated and there was hardly any noise coming from them. An occasional purple beetle or orange butterfly flew by the potted plants on my balcony. None of the plants had any green in them, and most had dark-violet leaves, some even completely black with curly fronds.

Down in the streets, the stores were open for business, and Sferogyls went about their daily affairs. In the plaza below, surrounded by my building and others like it, the sun shone through the oculus on part of it, and I saw some Sferogyls basking in the light while seated in their bowl park chairs. In the shaft of light coming from the ceiling, bugs and even birds flew around. They liked the sunlight, too.

Although there seemed to be plenty of light in the city, the daylight pouring through the round oculi in the cave's ceiling would not have been enough to illuminate the giant cave. Soft light was emitted by many of the buildings, including the one I was in. Additional light came from the mall and store signs and advertising billboards located at different levels on the buildings. In the purple, violet, and orange hues of light, Tandalo, the capital of the Sferogyls, was strange, but at the same time a city like any other.

Varna e'Sfero approached me on the balcony. "Tim Andrus, we will offer an early dinner soon. But since we don't know your taste preferences, I ordered a sampler of many dishes. I hope that's alright with you."

"That would be great, Varna e'Sfero."

"Would you like a cocktail before dinner, Tim Andrus?"

"Why, certainly. A Scotch would be good." Fanciful wish, I thought.

"Scotch." Varna raised a metallic box with a display to one of his eyes and read, "A 40% alcohol content drink made from grains and aged in wood barrels. We can do that. We'll order one right away, Tim Andrus." He punched a few buttons with two of his fingers, ordering my drink. To my surprise, he snapped his fingers, concluding his task, and returned inside, seemingly happy that he could please me.

A minute later, a drone approached our terrace. It landed and deposited a container on a low, round table. The drone was what I had earlier mistaken for birds flying around. Bovern k'Sfero came onto the balcony holding a stem glass, and he poured out of the container the drone had deposited an amber liquid into the glass. He then offered it to me. That was my cocktail, delivered by drone. If that really were Scotch, it would be an incredible feat. I took the glass and smelled it. It smelled like Scotch. I took a small taste and it tasted like Scotch, and not bad Scotch, either.

"How did you manage to get this?" I asked Bovern.

"Varna e'Sfero ordered it from the bar down below," said Bovern, raising his hands as if he was amazed as well.

I went inside. "Varna e'Sfero, how do you know about Scotch?"

"From our records, we learned that this drink is rather popular with other civilizations, Tim Andrus. But your drink was made by a synthesizer."

It's a small universe. I didn't know from what ingredients they synthesized the Scotch, but it occurred to me that my bionanobots had something to do with my olfactory and taste glands as well. Without them, this liquid may have tasted like wood alcohol. Everything is perception, created by a grand illusion. But as long as it smelled and tasted good, and I was told that nothing would poison me, why not enjoy the experience? This mission was not as bad as I thought it would be. I went out onto the round balcony, gawking at the alien city while sipping my Scotch and walking around to see more if this city.

From the other buildings surrounding us I could see many Sferogyls on their balconies below and above, gawking back at me. I raised my glass and waved to them with the other hand, and some waved back. I was the curiosity of the town. Heck, I was E.T.

"Bovern, would you ask Varna e'Sfero and Turnd l'Sfero if they would join me for a cocktail?" I asked as I completed my walk on the circular balcony.

"Certainly, Tim Andrus." Bovern went inside to deliver my request.

Soon both Varna and Turnd joined me on the balcony, each with his own purple drink in stem glasses, probably better for gripping with three-fingered hands.

"Had you ever met an alien before?" I asked them.

"Not in person, Tim Andrus," replied Turnd.

"But we've seen them in holograms," said Varna. "Many different species."

"Are all your cities underground?" I asked.

"Yes, either in natural caves or made by us," said Turnd. "Most of the ground on Nisip is limestone, and in previous epochs, the planet was much wetter and the caves formed abundantly."

"Why do you dwell underground?"

"Security," said Varna. "Billions of our people perished at the hands of the Maggotrolls. We are the last remaining Sferogyls, and for protection, we keep a very low profile and a low electromagnetic signature."

"Are you saying you don't use wireless communication?"

"For short distances or underground, we use wireless communication," said Varna. "But most of our communications are by underground cables."

"But your caves can be seen from space," I said, pointing to the oculus above.

"We enjoy the sunlight," Turnd said. "That's why our cities have openings to the sky. However, those opening are camouflaged, and the city and its lights are not visible from space."

I took another sip of my Scotch. "What do you do? What kind of profession do you have?"

"I am a city planner," said Turnd. "Mostly dealing with traffic."

"I am a professor," said Varna. "Liberal arts."

"And you spend time in the country tending snails?"

"We were on our sabbaticals," Varna said. "Kland l'Sfero and Logrn e'Sfero as well." Without my asking him to elaborate, he continued, "Every year or so, we take a month off and join the simple life of shepherding our domestic animals, tending the crops, or fishing."

"Is that your vacation?" I wondered.

"What's a vacation?" Turnd asked.

"Time off from work to relax."

"Then that's our vacation," said Turnd, and his mouth depicted a smile.

"What do Kland l'Sfero and Logrn e'Sfero do?"

"Kland l'Sfero is a police chief," said Varna. "And an enthusiastic battle-simulations hobbyist. His rank is that of a general in those games." Varna saw my inquiring expression. "We are peaceful people. We don't have much crime. And we don't war among ourselves. However, some of our people have a more warlike inclination and we play war games to release our aggressiveness. His skills will be needed now." It seemed Varna and Logrn had already heard the news I had brought to Glave o'Sfero. "Both Turnd l'Sfero and I participate in clubs where we entertain ourselves in simulated battles."

"Huh. And Logrn e'Sfero?"

"He is an engineer, a technical guru," said Varna. "He has learned and rebuilt, as a hobby, many of the old technologies. Even weapons. Yes."

"Peaceful as we may be, having experts to rebuild our armed forces is good insurance for survival," said Turnd. "And now he will be very much needed."

A larger drone came to the terrace and deposited a container.

Bovern approached us. "That's your dinner, Tim Andrus." He picked up the container, holding it over his head, and walked inside.

We stepped inside and Bovern set the table for me. "Aren't you going to join me?" I asked the Sferogyls.

"Gladly," said Varna, and they brought bowl chairs to the table.

Turnd ordered more dishes from the local restaurant via one of his belt devices, and we sat around the table to have dinner.

I suppose what was on the round platters was food—or food in the shape of bite-sized balls of different colors, textures, and opacity. Varna, Turnd, and Bovern watched me curiously.

"What type of food is this?" I asked to make sure I wasn't going to break a tooth, crunching on a rock-hard morsel.

"Our food is made of carbohydrates, proteins, and minerals,"

113

Turnd said. "Some are from fruits and cereals, others from meats, milk, and eggs. Some are cooked, some are synthesized. The shiny balls are sweet."

"What is this clear one?" I pointed to a transparent ball that contained a small creature resembling a tadpole swimming inside it.

"That is a newly hatched egg," said Varna. "A delicacy for us."

I picked up a white ball with my fingers and put it in my mouth. It tasted like rice. I tried a brown ball and it tasted like meat, similar to chicken. But I didn't try the newly hatched egg, not wanting any living creature to swim in my stomach.

Bovern snickered, watching me pick up the balls with my fingers. "Am I doing this right, Bovern k'Sfero?" I asked.

"Yes, Tim Andrus. But you have so many fingers. How do you decide which one to use?"

"I am used to all my fingers, and it comes automatically to me which ones to use."

Another drone delivered more food, and we ate and talked. The food was good, and we finished our dinner with a few sweet balls.

One question begged to be answered. "Everything around here is round, either a circle or a sphere," I said. "Why don't you use other geometrical shapes?"

"Like squares or triangles?" Varna asked.

I nodded. "Yes."

"Well, when you're a sphere, round is the most natural shape." Varna began to laugh. Turnd and Bovern joined in.

"We use other shapes when necessary, but we prefer round," said Turnd. "What kind of shapes are you most comfortable with,

Tim Andrus?"

"All geometric shapes, but mostly rectangular," I said. "However, we consider the rectangular shapes to be hard and the round shapes, soft."

They seemed eager to know about my experiences in other worlds, and so I told them about Earth, the only other world I remembered.

"So Bovern k'Sfero, do you go to school?" I asked him.

"I sure do, Tim Andrus. But I'm not sure about what I'll do in the near future."

"What would you like to do?"

"When I grow up, I want to be chief of police, like Kland l'Sfero."

"Is that so?" I thought about my first dream job when I was a kid: being a dogcatcher, working for the Humane Society. "How about your parents? Where are they?"

"Parents?" Bovern seemed to be confused.

"Well, Tim Andrus, we are different from most species in the galaxy," said Varna. "As you may know, we are hermaphrodites, or intersex. Although we don't have to pair to procreate, we do pair to expand our gene pool. We lay eggs that are hatched, and we don't have parental affinity toward our own eggs. Most Sferogyls don't know their biological parents."

"Then who is raising and rearing the young ones?" I asked.

"Once we lay the eggs, we bring them to a hatchery. The eggs are not marked for identification, and after the young ones are hatched they are taken to nurseries. We don't know who is the biological parent of a young Sferogyl. At the age of seven years, the young Sferogyls are adopted into a pod and raised as one of the pod members."

"What is a pod?"

"It is small community of Sferogyls who live together for social needs," said Varna. "It is every pod's responsibility to raise the young ones, like Bovern k'Sfero here." He patted Bovern on his "head."

"Then you are all in the same pod." I motioned with my fingers to indicate the three of them.

"Yes, we are in a pod along with Logrn e'Sfero, Kland l'Sfero and a many others you saw, Tim Andrus, but didn't meet," said Varna. "As a matter of fact, the Sferogyls you saw on the balconies of the other buildings belong to different pods."

"Usually a pod occupies an entire floor of a building," added Turnd. "Do you find our social arrangement strange, Tim Andrus?"

"Not at all. You are like an extended family in other civilizations."

Night fell, and we decided to get some sleep. Turnd, Varna, and Bovern retired to their nest beds in the adjacent rooms in the suite. I retired, after ducking through the round door of my bedroom, which now contained an oval, flat-bottom box with a soft mattress inside it. My bed.

Chapter 18. The War Council

The Sferogyls instituted a War Council, which was tasked with defending Nisip against the Maggotroll aggressors. The members of the council were the best Sferogyl society had to offer in terms of technical, military, and industrial brains. What they didn't have was a military force of any kind—and one was badly needed.

I was made an honorary member of the council and invited to attend their meetings, which were held in a compound deep underground near Tandalo. Two dozen Sferogyls sat around a large round black table, which had circular indentations in front of every seat to accommodate a Sferogyl's round physique. I was offered a seat at the table, and my seat was not a bowl but a chair ergonomically constructed for my posterior. Surprisingly, there was a leaf underneath the table that, when opened, re-established the curvature of the table at my station, which was better for me. Several rows of seats encircled our conference table, where many more Sferogyls sat to observe and participate if needed. Turnd and Varna sat nearby, behind me. Logrn and Kland, on the other hand, sat at the table. A hologram depicting the Maggotroll armada rotated slowly above the table.

Glave o'Sfero rang a silver bell to bring the audience to order. "In light of what we have learned recently, I call to order the newly instituted War Council. Tim Andrus, the gods' emissary, has brought us important news essential to our survival, but disturbing at the same time. The Maggotrolls are on their way to annihilate us. It is time to fight and defend ourselves, or die a painful death as slaves. The Great Assembly will be gathering this afternoon in the Assembly House to hear our recommendation. They will make the final decision regarding our fate.

"Before we start, I'd like to inform you of the following appointments. Kland l'Sfero was appointed the Military General for our armed forces. Reporting to General Kland l'Sfero, Alvuteran l'Sfero was appointed as the general of the Tandalo region; Razvij l'Sfero, the general for the Dengholan region; Jongen l'Sfero, the general for the Marjon region; and Pantongev l'Sfero, the general for the Sferogug region. Also, Lantolan l'Sfero was named the general for our future spaceforce. Logrn e'Sfero will be our science and technology chief; Xirxyg e'Sfero, the armament and weapons leader; and Nurvig e'Sfero, the industrial leader. They in turn will be responsible to recruit and appoint the other leaders needed for the war looming ahead of us.

"Logrn e'Sfero and other scientists have studied the information sent to us by the gods, and he'll tell us the potential danger we're facing." Glave extended his hand to Logrn.

The Sferogyls had acted quickly in making appointments to the War Council. Although, truth be told, the time was short to build up a military force strong enough to resist the Maggotrolls.

When speaking, the Sferogyls did not stand up, but an orange spotlight from the ceiling illuminated the speaker. Logrn pointed a purple laser beam at one of the transport ships in the hologram. A bulky, boxy craft filled the entire hologram.

"This is a Maggotroll high-capacity cargo-transport ship, about four kilometers in length, 800 meters in diameter, and with a volume of two billion cubic meters. It can travel at hyper light speed, HLS, in the dark universe and near light speed, NLS, in our visible universe. Each transport carries one million armed colonists and mercenaries, four million of them, all together. During travel through the dark universe, they are kept in hibernation. After the invasion, the hibernation pods will be used to carry four million of us to the Gatoony solar system. The transporters are lightly armed, but on board they have materiel, armament, and vehicles for a quick ground and air invasion. We expect the transporters to land on Nisip and begin the abduction of our first four million people immediately after they arrive."

"If they land on Nisip, do you know where?" a Sferogyl asked.

"We don't know their strategy, General Alvuteran l'Sfero," answered General Kland l'Sfero. "But we expect each transport ship to land near one of our largest cities. Therefore, the first cities to be assaulted would be Tandalo, Marjon, Dengholan, and Sferogug."

Logrn e'Sfero changed the hologram to depict the carrier-battleship the Maggotrolls would be using as their assault warship. It was a mean-looking craft, with its three cylindrical hulls strapped together. Each hull had an arrowhead appendage at the bow and a sharp, longer arrowhead, which served as the arrowtail in the aft, adding up to three pairs of arrowheads.

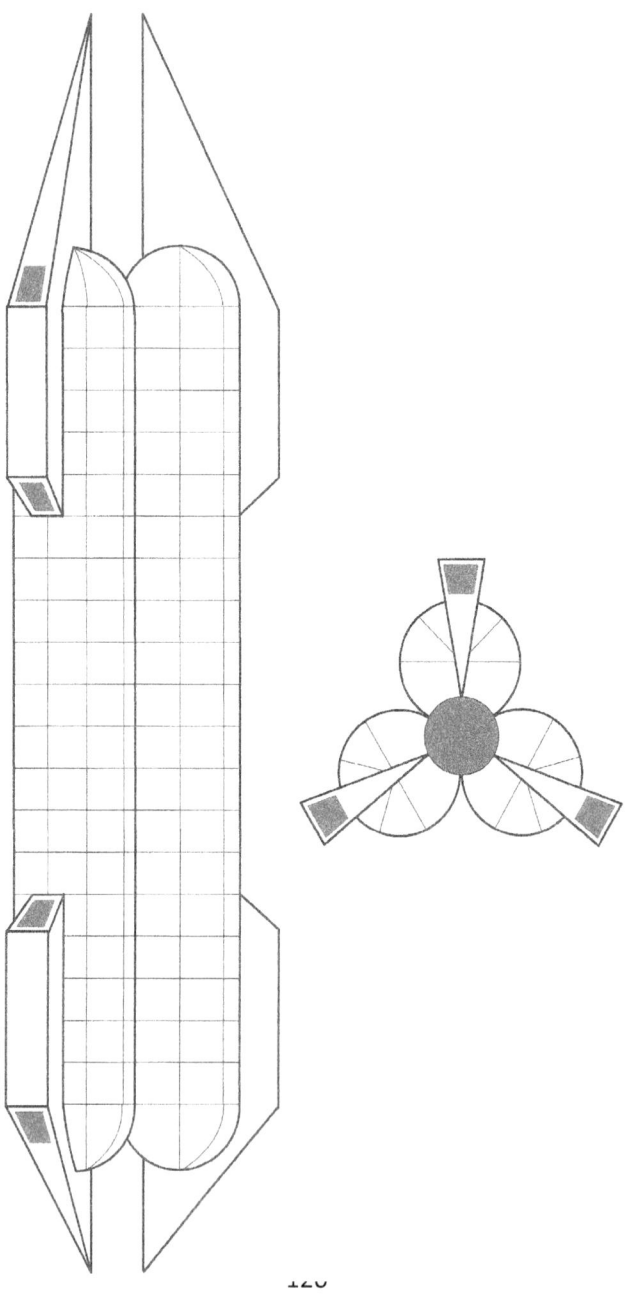

<u>Mangle Specs</u>

Tip to tip length: 3,000 m

Hull length: 2,205 m

Nominal Diameter: 803 m

Hull Diameter: 303 m

Volume: 152 million cubic meters

Dark Universe Engines. DU Speed: 1,000 Light Years

Near Light Speed Engines. NLS Speed: 98% Light Year

Anti-Gravity Engines

Fleet:

12-Frigates

750-Fighters

300-Shuttles

Crew: 10,000

Arsenal:

3-Proton Cannons

150-Proton Guns

150-Laser Guns

150-Projectile Rail-Guns

10,000 Missiles

"This is the warship *Mangle*," said Logrn. "Tip to tip, it is 3,000 meters long. Each hull is 2,205 meters long and 303 meters in diameter. The volume of this craft is 152 million cubic meters. The weight is anyone's guess, depending on the amount of neutrons and protons in their batteries. As you see from the three arrowhead appendages, it has a three-plane NLS engine, and it achieves 98% of the speed of light. In the dark universe, DU, it travels at 1,000 times the speed of light. And of course, it has antigravity engines for maneuvering around planets."

"What is that tunnel in the center of the craft?" Varna asked.

"Just as the transporters have one, the tunnel is necessary for DU travel, Varna e'Sfero. The craft needs to be surrounded by dark matter. Therefore, it has an inner passage to counter the outer hull exposure to dark matter. The dark energy engines are mounted in each of the arrowheads housing. Next, I'll let Kland l'Sfero—my apologies, General Kland l'Sfero—elaborate on the weapons carried by this capital warship."

General Kland cleared his throat and the orange spot light shined on him. "*Mangle* is in the second largest class of warships the Maggotroll Empire possesses in its arsenal. As a carrier, *Mangle* has a fleet of 12 frigates, 750 fighter-crafts, and 300 shuttles, and it has a crew of 10,000. Its armament is made of three super-heavy proton cannons, 150 laser guns, 150 plasma guns, and 150 projectile-rail guns. It carries at least 10,000 missiles with a variety of warheads."

"Do we have any information about the three super-heavy proton cannons on *Mangle*?" asked a Sferogyl at the table.

"We have some preliminary information, Sarmal l'Sfero," replied General Kland. "They have a maximum capacity of 1,000 kg-proton-mass blasts, be they focused or scattered."

There were several gasps of horror from the audience. I tried to make sense of what he had said, and I was about to gasp, too. Each heavy proton cannon on *Mangle* was capable of shooting a slug of 1,000 kg of mass, a ton, at essentially the speed of light. The amount of kinetic energy upon impact would be . . . I made a quick mental calculation, which was easy now that I was a god . . . 44.4 TJ. That's 11 KT of TNT or 71% of a Hiroshima nuke. And that was just one blast—powerful and deadly, if the slug was concentrated, with the protons tightly packed.

"Each blast will heat the atmosphere in its wake to many thousands of degrees," said Sarmal. "Not to mention the depth of penetration and residual radiation."

"Our cities will not be safe," said Glave o'Sfero. "We must evacuate them and go deep underground." Several Sferogyls voiced their approval.

Another Sferogyl raised his hand. "What are those tracks running on the exterior of the hull?" He was referring to what I thought of as bands that may have held the hulls together.

"That's exactly what they are, tracks, General Pantongev l'Sfero. The turrets holding the variety of guns travel on those tracks to protect the warship from attacks. *Mangle* has flexible firepower, being able to dispatch its combination of 450 guns to the spot where the attack is more threatening. Besides the firepower, the hulls are five-meters-thick carbodurium, the strongest material we know of, with a backup of hull-resealing armor to resist projectiles or missile blasts. Also, the hull is dotted with energy shield emitters, providing additional protection against laser, plasma, and proton blasts." Kland magnified a section of the hull's skin, where what seemed to be rivets were actually emitters-receivers for the energy shields. "If all this protection is not enough, the warship can deploy its NLS engines, gaining an additional space-warping force field around its hull and deflecting any energy or even projectile blasts."

My mouth was open in awe. This sucker would be able to destroy the Earth's entire military arsenal—before breakfast. I could not fathom how anyone could fight such a behemoth.

Kland changed the hologram to another warship, which resembled a marine animal, something like a trilobite, with two pinchers in the front.

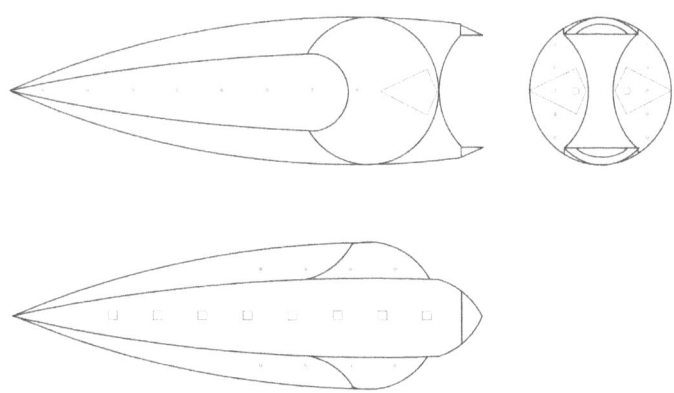

Frigate Spec

Light-speed Engine

HL speed: 95% light-year

Anti-gravity Engine

Tip to tip length: 106m

Hull diameter: 32m

Volume: 11,000 cubic meters

Crew: 200

Arsenal:

5-Proton Gun

30-Laser and Plasma Guns

10-Plasma-Guns

10-Projectile Rail-Guns

600-Missiles

"This is one of the twelve frigates on board *Mangle*," said General Kland. "It is only 106 meters long, 32 meters in hull diameter at its widest, with a volume of 11,000 cubic meters and a crew of 200. The frigates are not equipped with DU engines, they are too small, but they're capable of 95% of the speed of light. The two pinchers at the bow are its two-plane NLS engine. Its arsenal consists of five medium proton guns—three at the bow and two aft—30 laser, 10 plasma, and 10 projectile-rail guns. And it carries at least 600 missiles. It has similar energy shielding as the mother ship, *Mangle*." General Kland paused. "Any questions?"

No one had any.

Kland changed the hologram, depicting the fighters.

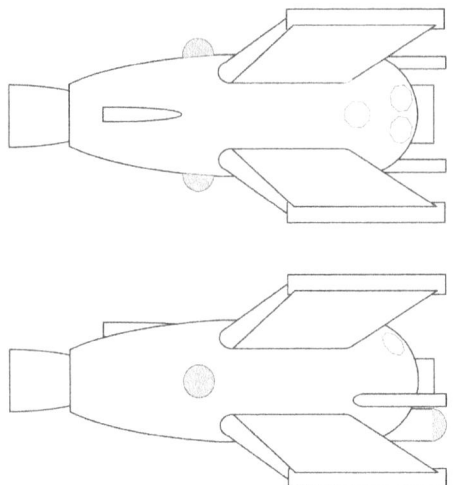
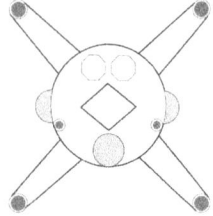

Fighter Spec

Length: 11m

Nominal diameter: 7m

Hull diameter: 3m

Weight: 120 tons

Crew: 2

2-Atomic Propulsion Engine

Sub-light speed: 1,000 km/s

Anti-gravity Engine

Arsenal:

3-Laser Guns

3-Projectile Rail-Guns

20-Missiles or 4 Proton Guns

"The fighters, 750 of them, are a two-crew craft, pilot and gunner. It is eleven meters long, and the hull is three meters in diameter. Besides the antigrav engine, it has one atomic propulsion engine capable of $100m/sec^2$ acceleration. It can achieve at least 1,000 km/s, standard speed. Its arsenal consists of three laser and three projectile-rail guns. It carries twenty missiles. The four appendages radiating out of the hull contain the missile launch tubes. Each appendage is the magazine, containing five missiles each. The fighter is an offensive craft, loaded with missiles to destroy warships. However, if needed, the four missile launchers can be replaced with proton guns.

"Now, just in case the Maggotrolls make it to the surface, this is what we should expect." General Kland changed the hologram to show military carriers and soldiers. "They'll have military armored vehicles armed with projectile and laser guns. Additionally, they have proton, laser, and rapid-fire projectile guns to protect their ground bases after landing. Some of these may be positioned as needed around the periphery of their bases on the ground.

"The transporters have hundreds of space shuttles, but their intent is to land the transporters on the surface and not to use the shuttles for space-to-surface landing. The shuttles double as air defense and are equipped with laser and rapid-fire projectile guns. And they have the capability of missile launchers, if needed.

"The information we have shows a few large ground personnel transport vehicles and trucks. These vehicles would be needed to transport us to their ships as slaves, but they don't seem to have enough of them for a speedy extraction. I guess they'd planned to use our transport vehicles for that purpose."

General Kland changed the hologram to depict a Maggotroll soldier. "The Maggotrolls are hominidal: two and a half meters tall, strong, and agile. A Maggotroll soldier suited for combat has armor to resist small projectiles, and as you can see, the suit is reflective to deflect laser fire. The suit is not vented to our atmosphere; therefore, it is chemical and biological warfare-proof. Standard issue for each soldier is a laser gun. Some soldiers may carry larger weapons and even mini-missile launchers. Also, their helmets have nighttime, infrared, and ultraviolet vision. The helmet is equipped with mini-radar and motion sensors. Basically, a soldier can see the enemy in the middle of a sandstorm at night. We don't recommend hand-to-hand combat with the Maggotrolls. Their arms are long and powerful."

General Kland paused for a moment and looked at the Sferogyls around him. "And that concludes this brief presentation of our enemy's military capabilities. Any questions?"

There were no questions. Everyone was either numb by the dump of information or didn't know what questions to ask.

I had one, but it was imprudent to ask here. My question would have been: *Which weapon would inflict the quickest and least painful death?* But then I slapped myself, mentally. I was a god, for crying out loud. I should not be worried about dying.

"If you want to analyze in more detail the Maggotrolls' weapons, you can access the specs on the info-network. I want to thank Tim Andrus for bringing us the information about the enemy's military capabilities."

"What weapons do we have to counter the Maggotrolls?" a Sferogyl on my right finally asked.

"General Jongen l'Sfero, at this time, we don't have any military weapons."

Chapter 19. Victory Will Be Ours

There was dead silence in the conference room. Judging by the grim expressions, a better name for the room would have been the "quiet panic room."

General Kland looked around the room, undisturbed by his frank answer on what a dire situation they were in. "Since there are no other questions, let's continue and discuss the weaknesses of the Maggotroll military."

"If there are any," quipped a Sferogyl. That elicited a few nervous chuckles.

"There are always weaknesses, General Razvij l'Sfero," said General Kland. "Logrn e'Sfero, would you give us some details about their armor, energy shields, and force fields protecting *Mangle*?"

"Certainly, General Kland l'Sfero. There is no defensive weapon that will protect or destroy incoming energy blasts from laser or proton guns. The blasts travel at the speed of light, and you'd know when you were hit after you were hit, if you survived. Energy shields are the only protection for a craft against energy discharge weapons like lasers and protons, and *Mangle* has such shields.

"The armor on *Mangle*'s hull provides good protection against projectile blasts, be they explosions or direct impacts. A lot of kinetic energy is required to penetrate five meters of carbodurium armor. And they'll use their missiles, laser, and rail guns to destroy any incoming projectiles or missiles before they impact the hull. For plasma blasts, they might use sacrificial missiles to explode and dissipate the energy, or use their energy shields.

"The force fields, such as the space warp created by the NLS engines, work fairly well against both energy and projectiles. The force fields act as deflectors. But if either the energy or projectiles have superior energy or mass, and are directed perpendicularly against the force fields, they'll penetrate them.

"How, then, can we breach their defenses?" asked Logrn rhetorically. "Projectiles and missiles will penetrate the energy shields and have a chance to rupture the hull, provided they're not destroyed by *Mangle's* guns before impact. Of course, to rupture the hull, the more mass or explosive energy, the better. But that would make the projectiles and missiles larger and therefore easier to be targeted by *Mangle's* guns and fighters. We would gain an advantage by using missiles and projectiles, but only if we posses and launch large numbers of them against *Mangle* at close range, thereby overwhelming their defenses."

"We'll need to manufacture thousands of them," said a Sferogyl.

"Precisely, Xirxyg e'Sfero," said General Kland. "I'm counting on you and Nurvig e'Sfero to provide them for us."

"The energy shields can be destroyed by high power energy blasts, such as proton and laser fire," continued Logrn. "The energy shields work by absorbing the incoming energy blasts. The more energy hits them, the more they'll overload the receivers, causing them to fry and leave gaps in the shields. Since we don't yet have warships to attack *Mangle*, the proton blasts have to be generated from the ground. That's a positive—practically speaking, we have unlimited energy compared to *Mangle*, and we can build heavy cannons to blast their ships out of the sky."

"Would such cannons be used to destroy the transporters?" asked a Sferogyl.

"*Especially* the transporters, Nurvig e'Sfero," General Kland answered. "Each transporter destroyed before it touches our ground prevents one million Maggotrolls from killing us."

"The most effective weapons for us, at this time, will be the ground proton cannons. Yet to be built," said Logrn. "Ground laser and plasma blasts to attack the enemy in space are not a good choice, since some of their energy would be dissipated by the atmosphere before impact."

"It seems our best weapons will be defensive and ground-based," said General Lantolan l'Sfero. "But they will also be subject to the enemy's frigate and fighter attacks. Even *Mangle*'s massive proton cannons could be used against our ground cannons."

"Not to mention that our cannons would be stationary," said General Pantongev.

"I agree with your assessments, Generals Lantolan and Pantongev," said Logrn. "We have to be smart about how we build the proton cannons. For one, the proton accelerators would have to be deep underground, and each cannon should have many discharge muzzles, camouflaged and spread radially from the proton generators and accelerators."

Agreeing murmurs sounded in the room.

"Do not forget that, unlike *Mangle*, which is in space and has limited banks of neutrons and protons, we have enormous reserves on the ground. It is just a matter of generating the volume of protons we'd need and the frequency of firing. We should definitely build larger proton cannons than *Mangle*'s."

"Now you're talking!" said Nurvig e'Sfero. "And we have the technology to build the cannons."

"That is the good news," said General Lantolan. "The bad news is that we don't have any warships or fighters."

"But we possess our ancestors' technology," said Xirxyg e'Sfero. "And some—"

"Relics?" quipped General Razvij.

"True, but that's better than nothing," said Xirxyg e'Sfero. "We'll need to build a new fleet of spaceships, and the 'relics' are a good start."

"Well, that means we need to shift all our manufacturing ability into producing weapons," said Nurvig e'Sfero. "And we've got less than eighteen months."

Glave o'Sfero rang the bell. "Although there are many other issues that we need to discuss, we are short of time before the Great Assembly needs to hear our recommendations. My first motion is: Who is in favor of surrendering to the Maggotrolls?"

No one voiced support for the motion.

"My second motion is: Arm ourselves and fight to the death?"

All hands went up.

"Our recommendation to the Great Assembly is to go to war." Glave rang the bell to end the meeting.

After lunch, we entered the giant sphere of the Assembly House, where the Great Assembly was gathered. The bleachers in this hall circled the round deliberation floor below. It was curious that, after a certain point, the bleachers went up on the vertical and then curved inward over the floor below. It pays to have flexible eyes and be round. The rotund Sferogyls sitting in their seats resembled a giant ball-bearing machine, producing a white noise of squeaks and whistles. And it smelled like vanilla and cinnamon, yet stronger than before. A large hologram hovered above the deliberation floor, depicting the Maggotroll invasion force.

The War Council members, including me, were seated in the lowest front row. The special session soon began, chaired by Glave o'Sfero, who spoke from the middle of the deliberation floor. First, he introduced me as Tim Andrus, the envoy from the gods. Some of the Sferogyls stood up to see me better, and it seemed that they were in awe and humbled by my presence.

Glave o'Sfero related the situation to the assembly, pointed at some of the warships in the hologram as he spoke, and concluded that the War Council recommended unanimously arming and fighting the invading enemy. He asked for the assembly's approval, which was given unanimously as well.

"In conclusion," said Glave o'Sfero. "The time ahead of us will be trying. There will be hardships, inevitable deaths, and injuries after the fighting begins. I count on all of you to let our population know our immense appreciation to them for standing together. Our survival is at stake. And one more thing, and this is very important: Life on Nisip should continue as it was before. We need to act normally to deceive the spy satellite orbiting our planet. Our military buildup will be carried out underground and exercises performed at night. Our enemy expects a rural and peaceful Sferogyl population. Surprise will be one of our weapons. Go in peace, and prepare for war. We will be victorious."

All the assembly stood up, raised their arms, and whistled, "We will be victorious!"

Chapter 20. The Busting Balls

As the assembly hall was emptying, Logrn e'Sfero and General Kland came by to talk to me.

"Congratulations on your appointments, General Kland l'Sfero and Chief Logrn e'Sfero."

"Many thanks, Tim Andrus," they both replied.

"We wondered if you would impart some of your thoughts about our situation, Tim Andrus," said Logrn e'Sfero.

I inhaled and exhaled thoughtfully. "Your entire population will have to work very, very hard to make this happen, to build up your weapons and join the armed forces."

"What are our chances, Tim Andrus? Have other civilizations ever won against similar odds?" General Kland asked.

"At times, a smaller or technologically inferior military has won over larger and more advanced enemies. You have nothing to fear. All Sferogyls will have to understand this and act for the same result—victory."

"Have we overlooked any aspects of their weaknesses?" asked General Kland, referring to the Maggotrolls.

"Both of you did a good job, considering the short time you've had to analyze the data," I answered. "As for defensive weapons, powerful ground proton guns will keep *Mangle* away. Just remember, the big weapons, once destroyed, are difficult to replace. So make your guns mobile, or give the impression that they are mobile, and camouflage them. If you can imitate the proton blast signature, I'd suggest you have many sites as decoys to give the impression of overwhelming firing power.

"You'll have to build an army, General Kland. I suggest you start recruiting your officers first. They should be the first soldiers, fighting war games and simulations. As they gain experience, bring in the next wave of officers, and so on, until you have a trained military force."

"Thank you, Tim Andrus. That is very helpful," said General Kland.

"I know you already know this, but your spaceforce is the biggest weakness you have," I said. "Without an equivalent spaceforce, your ground troops will be haunted by the enemy fighters."

"We kept our technological knowledge from the past, although it is 3,000 years old," said Logrn. "Our next step will be to visit the depository where our ancestors' spaceships are mothballed."

"Then you have a starting point," I said. "I believe strongly in the motto 'don't reinvent the wheel' if what you have works. Use the old technology as much as possible, because you barely have time to build up your old weapons."

The cargo and transporter ships, which had brought their ancestors to Nisip, were stored underground in a large cave. Six old spaceships would be their first fleet, if they were even capable of flying. The caves had been sealed and filled with argon gas to maintain the craft in as good a condition as possible. But now the internal atmosphere was replaced with Nisip's air to allow the Sferogyls to work inside the cave without breathing apparatuses.

The largest vessel, the *Swan*, was the most damaged, as it had hard landed on the surface because of malfunctioning antigrav engines. It was 900 meters long and only 150 meters in diameter.

This was a NLS spaceship, long and slim, with two prongs at the bow for space warping. Unfortunately, the bow and the bottom of this vessel were shorn off. One of the space-warping prongs was obliterated, but the other one was intact. Some of the antigravity engines survived. The *Swan* had no weapons on board, only a lot of spherical shells, which served as the hibernation chambers for the old Sferogyls. With their half shells opened, the interior looked like a giant empty egg crate.

The next two craft, *Goose* and *Duck*, were slightly smaller, only 800 meters long and 80 meters in diameter, and 700 meters long and 85 meters in diameter, respectively, but they were intact and their engines were functional, according to the instruments. Although these vessels were cargo ships that served as personnel carriers, they were equipped with laser and plasma guns, and a few space mines.

The last three craft were military escorts. The *Eagle*, *Hawk*, and *Vulture* were each 300 meters long and 25 meters in diameter. The slimness indicated that they were built for speed. Their arsenals contained missiles, laser and proton guns, and something very peculiar: grey balls over a meter in diameter. At first I thought they were hibernators, rather than space mines, but soon I found out they were neither.

"Those are busting balls," said General Kland, seeing my puzzlement. He was in the *Eagle* with several officers, downloading military information.

"Busting balls?" I asked "Are you sure they're not ball-busters?"

"No, they are busting balls," said General Kland. "This is an amazing weapon. They roll on the ground and bust through anything: buildings, rock walls, or armored vehicles."

"This weapon doesn't seem to have made any difference. Your ancestors lost," I said.

General Kland put a hand on one of the dark-gray busting balls. "This weapon was invented too late. From the records we examined, our ancestors devised this weapon just before the great escape. These balls here are all they produced, and they took them on the escort warships to prevent them from falling into the enemy's hands."

"Hmm. How good are they?" I was skeptical.

"Each ball can bust through anything and can reach 200 km/h, even on rough terrain," said Logrn e'Sfero. "They cannot be cracked, even if they're blasted with a missile or average laser fire, even for a whole minute."

"I can see how a projectile would have a hard time with the ball, it can easily be deflected," I said, rubbing my chin. "How are they guided? Remotely? By AI?"

"No, they are driven," said Logrn.

"What? A Sferogyl would be inside the ball?"

"Indeed," said General Kland. He pushed a button on a handheld device. The ball in front of us opened in half, as if it were an orange, pried apart. He pointed inside. "This is the driver's cabin."

I looked inside the spherical cavity. It had some controls and buttons and many displays for visual monitoring. The walls were about fifteen centimeters thick. "If this thing goes at 200 km/h and hits something, the driver would become scrambled eggs." I shouldn't have said that.

"Not in this thing," said Logrn, unbothered by my comment.

"OK, Logrn e'Sfero, explain how you neutralize all that kinetic energy during the impact."

"There is no impact felt inside." Logrn saw my dumbstruck face and smiled. "The ball travels on a special antigrav engine that contains its own gravity field around the driver for protection. The driver does not feel the impacts. Then the ball's outside skin is made of a specialized layer of atoms that vibrate and oscillate at millions of cycles per second. We call it VAL, Vibrating Atomic Layer, which will help penetrate anything through abrasion. Therefore, the faster the ball travels, the easier the busting, although the ball will slow down as it continues to punch through matter. But in most cases, it goes through solid matter as if going through water."

"It's a wrecking ball," I commented. "Does it have any other weapons?"

"No. What for? It punches and crashes through everything in its way."

"And it cannot be destroyed?" I asked.

"It has its limits, but only when it's standing still or when the VAL is turned off."

"So it must move all the time," I said.

"It has to," said General Kland.

"The drawback is if it stands in place and the VAL is active, the ball will sink into the ground," added Logrn.

"That's a good hideout. It can hide and wait in ambush." Then a thought crossed my mind. "Can it travel underground?"

"I don't know, but I'll make a note to try it," said General Kland. "That may be useful."

"How many are here?"

"Two hundred and seventeen, divided between the three warships," said Logrn "What do you think?"

"Sounds good for ground defense," I said. "Can they fly?"

"Not these. The antigrav engine is too weak. But this is the terrific news." Logrn's tentacle eyes shone with excitement. "We found advanced plans for making the balls spaceworthy by using more powerful antigrav engines."

"Good deal," I said. "They could become your space fighters."

"That's what my team thinks as well," said Logrn, smiling.

"We sure need fighters," said General Kland. "General Lantolan will be delighted."

"How maneuverable would they be?" I asked. "What is the escape speed on Nisip?"

"Ten km/s," said Logrn. "That would be its maximum speed, but we can also latch onto the enemy craft and pull the ball toward it."

"You said the ball has a shell of protective antigravity inside," I said.

"Yes," agreed Logrn.

"In that case, you have instant acceleration and can maneuver on a pinhead," I said.

"Exactly," said Logrn.

"Although the enemy fighters use antigrav and propulsion engines," said General Kland, "they will not be as quick to accelerate and change direction as our balls will be. On the other hand, the fighters have atomic propulsion engines and can travel faster than our balls. We need to consider that in our strategy."

"For deep space fighting, antigrav engines won't work," Logrn said. "Propulsion engines are necessary. But the balls won't need to venture far from Nisip. That's good."

"For immediate planet protection, it will have to do," General Kland agreed.

"How many can you build, Logrn e'Sfero?" I asked.

"We're working on that with Xirxyg e'Sfero and Nurvig e'Sfero. Each ball needs twelve tons of depleted uranium. I think the flying balls will be larger and heavier."

"What kind of energy source are these balls using?" I pointed to the balls in front of us.

"Neutron decay."

I'd have to learn about what neutron decay was. "Not dark energy?" I asked, and then I realized I should not have asked that question, since I didn't know what that was, either.

"We don't have the dark energy technology," said Logrn, thinking for a moment. "That's why the flying balls would have to be larger and heavier."

"As long as they move fast, the heavier the better," I said.

"After all, they are busting balls, not bouncing balls." General Kland chuckled.

"Very true," and I joined him in the humorous moment. "Now, if you fabricate new balls, you should make only the flying types. In this way, you'll be able to defend Nisip in space, in the air, on the ground, and perhaps, underground."

"Yes. We have a lot of work ahead of us," Logrn said thoughtfully.

"And we have less than eighteen months left," I reminded.

Chapter 21. Alien Technology

As a former science fiction writer with an engineering background, I found my interest aroused by alien civilizations' technologies. But I had to be careful how I asked questions to satisfy my curiosity; after all, what kind of god would I be if I didn't know about these technologies? But how could I learn about these advanced technologies? Bovern could help me out.

The following morning, with some idle time on my hands, I asked him, "Bovern k'Sfero, considering that one day you want to be a chief of police, or even a general, you must learn about the technology used by the Maggotroll warship."

"Yes, Tim Andrus, but I know a lot already."

"Is that so? Show me."

Bovern took me to into a room of my suite and turned on a hologram display over the desk. "I've been studying on the info-network about spacefaring technologies. I don't know many of the technical details, but so far I've learned enough to understand what's going on."

He brought up the *Mangle* hologram. "This warship travels through DU at 1,000 light years per second."

"How do you know that, besides being told about its capability?"

"It has the characteristics of a DU ship. First, the internal tunnel is necessary to allow dark matter inside the craft." He then pointed to the rectangular openings on the arrowheads. "This is for the intake of dark energy. They are paired with intakes at the back of the arrowtails. Then the dark energy is fused between the front and back intakes, right above the hull at the back of the arrowheads, causing the motion through the DU."

"What do you know about dark energy fusion?"

"That is beyond my understanding at this time. But it seems that the fusion doesn't act like propulsion but more like a displacement force. A big displacement force, I'd say."

"How about the light speed?" I asked.

Bovern rotated the hologram. "NLS is achieved by distorting the space in front of the craft, and it falls down into the depression it creates in space. *Mangle* is three-plane NLS. You can see that by the three arrowheads at the front. The more planes a craft has, the faster and closer to the speed of light it can travel, and the wider across the ship can be. This one can achieve 98% of light speed. Of course, all NLS crafts must close the space warping with the arrowtail appendages, also three of them." He pointed to the three arrowtails.

These types of spaceships did not have to obey the laws of aerodynamics, but nevertheless they had to obey the laws of space dynamics, be that in the visible universe or the dark universe. And one way or another, they ended up streamlined, like the old futuristic rocket depictions on Earth.

"The enemy frigates are two-plane NLS," he continued. "Not as fast as the three-plane, but they can get to 95% of the speed of light. The two-plane NLS craft are squatter in shape, like these frigates. The frigates don't have DU capability, but they have antigrav engines for lifting off or landing on planets."

"What do you know about their weapons and how they function?" I asked, with my fingers steepled under my chin.

Bovern opened the weaponry information on the net. "The

proton gun is the main offensive weapon. Basically, it shoots a slug of an enormous amount of protons. The protons must be accelerated to 99.9% of the speed of light; otherwise, the protons diverge and lose the destructive power of the original narrow beam. Eventually, over vast distances, it dissipates in a cloud of protons. That's because the protons are positive and repulse each other," he said knowingly.

"The protons are accelerated in an acceletron to achieve the speed of light. The longer the straight portion of the gun, the more efficient the gun is. Being over two km long, *Mangle* has powerful proton cannons. However, all proton guns have a circular accelerator to get the protons up to over 250,000 km/s before they are discharged in the straight raceway of the acceletron. On *Mangle*, the circular acceletron is a coil wrapped radially around the straight barrel of the cannon. When length is not available, a flat helical coil is used before going in the linear chamber for discharge. A target cannot detect a proton shot, because it travels at the speed of light. Usually a proton blast will go right through the hull of a spacecraft, resulting in the explosion of the craft, or it will exit through the other side of the hull, making a bigger hole. The distance to a target is the greatest disadvantage for proton guns, though. The effectiveness will decrease over 100,000 km."

It occurred to me that the mighty proton gun was a glorified shotgun. Instead of pellets, it shot protons, gazillions of them at the near speed of light. In a way, a proton gun was not much different from the cyclotrons on Earth, except incredibly more powerful. It must have used inconceivable amounts of energy to propel hundreds of kilograms of mass at nearly the speed of light. No doubt, it was a weapon of choice.

"How about the supply of energy and protons for the gun?" I asked.

"The protons and neutrons are stored in special containment

batteries. After they're allowed to decay for around fourteen minutes, the neutrons are used to supply protons, electrons, and neutrinos. And neutrons, being chargeless, can be stored at a higher density per unit of volume, many more times than the densest element."

I would have thought that the neutrons packed in container chambers, in batteries, would make a spaceship extremely heavy. But when using gravity to accelerate the craft, the heavier the mass, the faster the acceleration. How simple. Probably the electrons were used as the E-M force to accelerate the proton slugs in the gun barrel.

This was good preliminary information for me to know. "Well, I see you know a lot. Very well done, Bovern k'Sfero."

"Thank you, Tim Andrus."

"If I want to learn more about your planet, I'll just have to access your net. How do I do that?" I planned to learn more from their net later, on my own.

"Just place your hand on this pad and search the library on the info-network."

Chapter 22. War Meetings

In the following days, it occurred to me that my role as a god was that of a cheerleader, advisor, and what-if devil's advocate. I stuck my nose in all the meetings they were having, giving my two cents when needed, or not.

Logrn e'Sfero and his team prepared a test busting ball for field trials, and no one other than General Kland took it for a ride. The ball was heavy, and anywhere it stood it created a sizable dimple in the ground. If its VAL was active, it sank as if in quicksand. When it moved, it cracked the rubbery surface of the desert, and all that was left were grooves of sand and crushed rocks.

The busting ball rode without any problems up 60-degree inclines at 100 km/h, and even steeper inclines at reduced speeds. When traveling above 120 km/h on uneven terrain like the sand dunes, it became airborne between the peaks of the dunes. Any abrupt landing was marked by deep grooves and tons of dirt spewed on its impact. The ultimate test was when it rode at a maximum speed of 200 km/h and made a perfectly round tunnel into a small hill. It came out at the other end at a reduced speed of 155 km/h. The ball went through like a red-hot cannonball through ice.

To make an additional point, Kland drove the ball at maximum speed against the granite cliff of a nearby mountain. It left a round hole in the stone face, as if a machine had bored a tunnel; hot, disintegrated rock and sand kept spewing from its mouth, and a mound of debris formed rapidly outside the entrance. A minute later, with a final blowout of sand, the ball came back out of the hole like a projectile, crushing through the sand mound ejected from the tunnel.

The only drawback was that General Kland, inside the ball, was not able to communicate with the outside world by any means. The vibrating layers of atoms on the outer skin blocked the world outside for any communication other than visual. That fact had to be taken into account when attacking as a pack of wrecking balls, and procedures had to be established for communication codes by the military team.

After the test ended, General Kland's ball came to a stop and we gathered around it.

"Well, how was it inside?" I asked him as he came out of the opened shell.

"Fantastic!" he said with excitement. "When I hit the hill, I didn't feel the slightest deceleration."

"How about the stone mountain?" I asked.

"Smooth as if I went through smoke. The inner antigravity shell did its job well, in conjunction with the VAL. I was more afraid of losing track of where I was in the mountain, so I reversed. At the time I stopped, before reversing, my speed settled to a constant 20 km/h. I bored a more than three-hundred-meter-deep tunnel."

"It seems to me that, on the surface against any armored vehicle or ground force, the busting ball will have a superior advantage," I said. "Although there will be four million armed Maggotrolls on the ground. Logrn e'Sfero, have you figured out how to make this thing fly, and how many balls could be manufactured?"

"We modified one of the old balls with a larger antigrav engine, and it levitated well," said Logrn proudly. "We went up to 100 kilometers and achieved a decaying orbit. We'll need to make the ball larger because of a larger neutron decay generator and a larger antigrav engine, not to mention more work is needed on the controls. I'm confident that within two weeks we will produce the first prototype."

I smiled. It was going well, and the Maggotrolls would have the surprise of their lives in encountering the busting balls.

Shortly after that, I became a de facto project manager and overseer, sticking my nose deeper into all the initiatives undertaken to defend Nisip. One day, we were gathered in a conference room at the war department, discussing the latest situation on warships. Nurvig e'Sfero, the industrial leader in charge of warship manufacturing, was to give a report.

"How much progress have we made on the warships?" I asked.

Nurvig didn't look happy, judging by his droopy eye tentacles. "If we want to replicate the three old ships, it will take us one year to build the infrastructure needed for their manufacture. And we're having problems manufacturing the hull material. It is a composite of titanium, carbon, polymers, and ceramics—almost as strong as carbodurium, but not as resilient. No records survived from our ancestors about making the stuff."

"Can you substitute other materials? How about carbodurium?" I asked.

"We don't have the technology to make carbodurium in quantity," said Nurvig. "Let me restate that: We can make carbodurium, but we don't have the technology to macroatomically weave it."

"Weave it?" asked a Sferogyl.

"The carbodurium structure is nano-tubular," said Nurvig. "It has to be, for lack of a better word, woven into the final shape or structure. That's why such large structures like warships can exist. There is almost no material expansion when exposed to temperatures from zero to 2,000 degrees. And it is the strongest and hardest material when impacted by anything."

"How about using titanium?" I asked.

"We could substitute titanium, but it would have diminished capabilities against proton blasts. We'd have to increase the power of the energy shields, which causes other technical issues."

Obviously, I didn't know what building a 300-meter-long spaceship entailed, but I had confidence that Nurvig knew what he was talking about. "Building something even bigger is out of the question?"

"Yes," said Nurvig unhappily. "We could build smaller, 100-meter ships with our technology, but when facing 750 fighters and twelve frigates, we will need at least 200 ships, as Xirxyg e'Sfero has assessed. I can't even begin to speculate how long it will take."

"You're saying size matters when facing a behemoth like *Mangle*," I said. "Or build more of the smaller-sized ships." A thought was churning in my mind, but it hadn't fermented yet.

"Definitely," said Xirxyg e'Sfero.

"How about raw materials?" I asked.

"We are in good shape with all materials, with the exception of uranium to build the busting balls," said Nurvig l'Sfero. "Nisip has a limited supply of uranium."

"Do you remember the asteroid 12G-Alpha?" Varna e'Sfero, who was sitting behind me, asked.

Nurvig turned so fast to face him he gave the impression of a spinning top. "Good point! That was the dumping grounds for depleted uranium fuel by an ancient civilization."

"Can you use the *Duck* or *Goose* to bring the uranium from the asteroid?" I asked.

"We certainly can," said Logrn. "I'll leave tomorrow to analyze the uranium over there."

The *Duck* was sent to recover the uranium from asteroid 12G-Alpha. This asteroid was orbiting the sun a few million kilometers from Nisip, and within one month, the *Duck* returned with the first 200 tons of depleted uranium. That was a stroke of luck, finding that cache of uranium. As the saying goes: Other people's trash was our treasure. The manufacturing of new flying balls tripled, producing a dozen units per week. The *Goose* was enlisted to bring uranium from the asteroid as well, and I was hoping to double our production yet again.

We had only thirteen months left until "annihilation" arrived. I convened a special war meeting to analyze the situation and actions to take.

I began the meeting. "Nurvig e'Sfero, what's the status on the warships?"

Nurvig sighed. "We haven't made any progress on the material manufacturing processes for the hulls. We are doing well in building the infrastructure to build *Eagle*-size ships concurrently, and in some cases, we are ahead in the manufacturing of other systems, including the NLS engines."

"When would be the latest date that you need to know if the hull material issue is resolved and you're ready to manufacture the hulls?"

"Two months, after which we have to go with standard materials for the hulls." Nurvig looked depressed.

"Unfortunately, each one of our ships, although bigger, would be only as capable as each of the Maggotrolls' frigates, which are one-third in length and more maneuverable," said Xirxyg e'Sfero.

Not good, I thought.

"How many busting balls could we manufacture by the time the invasion begins?"

Nurvig, who was in charge of manufacturing of them as well, cleared his throat. "Our forecast is 600 units of the flying type."

"Together with the old ones, we'll have 817 balls," I said, thinking aloud. "And 217 are not flying."

"Should we convert the others for flying?" Logrn asked.

"Perhaps. But first I'd like to know what's the status of the military force buildup."

"We've applied all the information from our ancestors' files, and we've currently enlisted over 100,000 officers." Seeing my disappointed expression, General Kland raised one hand. "The pace will accelerate. The recruits were taken from our police force to build up our officer body. We will be able to double our armed forces every month from now on. We will reach three million soldiers in six months, and more after that. Large-scale maneuvers and simulated battles will begin in two months."

"That's good. How about weapons?" I asked Xirxyg e'Sfero, the weapons manufacturing leader.

"We began construction on ten proton cannons," he answered. "They are placed strategically on the planet. Each cannon has ten muzzles arranged at ten km radially around the proton accelerator. We will have them operational by the time the attack begins. And we'll have as many fake proton guns placed around the real ones."

"How about weapons for the troops?" I asked.

"We're on track to have one million explosive projectiles guns and five million laser guns. Also, 300,000 personal missile launchers, and 100,000 field laser guns and rail guns. Also, ten thousand mobile proton guns. We will have three million sets of personal armor for the soldiers."

"General Kland, knowing what your future army and arsenal might be, how are you doing in simulated war games against our enemy?"

"Yes, Logrn e'Sfero and his teams have developed very realistic software for simulated battles. Several thousand soldiers are using the games in the field in real and virtual battles. Millions of future soldiers who currently are needed as workers use the games in the after-work hours to train."

"We developed simulated flying battles against *Mangle*, the frigates, and fighters," said Logrn proudly.

"Fantastic, Logrn e'Sfero," I said, seeing some progress on most fronts. "General Lantolan, the news should please you."

"It sure does," said General Lantolan. "So far, we have over 500 pilots taking turns to fly the 200 flying busting balls we received. By the way, our pilots call the flying busting ball, the FBB, and GBB refers to the ground balls."

"Those are fitting names," I said. "However, General Kland, besides sharpening our military skills, we'll need to constantly reassess our weaknesses in fighting the enemy. The situation of our forces, weapons, and skills are fluid at this time."

"Very much so," said General Kland. "We may find out that we have too much of some weapons but not enough of others."

"We will have the computers conduct games based on what our enemy could be doing," said Logrn.

I could sense that the morale had improved among the participants. Of course, the games might tell us that we didn't have a snowball chance in hell of winning.

Twelve months before the invasion, we had another special war meeting. By that time, I had become the war program manager, and this time, the subject of the meeting was the war games.

"What results are you gathering from the war games, General Kland l'Sfero?" I asked.

General Kland looked stressed. "We have only a ten percent chance of winning, and with devastating losses. Without warships to counter the *Mangle*, it will be a bloody war. However, if *Mangle* did not exist, we would have a ninety percent chance of winning."

"Hmm. Their warship is the linchpin," I commented.

"That, and the twelve frigates and 750 fighters," said General Kland. "Their warship will blast us from space. The frigates and fighters will give air support to their invading forces."

"But we have our FBBs," said Logrn.

"That's why we have a ten percent chance of winning," replied General Kland. "Without them, we'd have no chance."

"Would more FBBs increase our odds?" I asked.

"Yes," came an emphatic reply from General Kland. "But it will not get better than fifty-fifty. The problem is *Mangle*, which we can't destroy without similar warships of our own."

The news was gloomy among the participants, forecasting that, even after all the effort they were pouring in to defending themselves, they would lose.

"They'll be hesitant to kill you," I said. "Their goal is to take you as slaves and preserve as much of the planet and infrastructure as possible."

"It seems to me," said Glave o'Sfero philosophically, "that the Maggotrolls stand to have a one hundred percent loss, if all of us die and Nisip turned into a sandy wasteland."

Masada came to mind. What would the Sferogyls have to lose? They'd die as slaves anyway—why not just kill themselves upfront? "You are not considering that option?"

"Why not?" Glave proposed. "If all the members of our society are armed to fight and set up to die rather than be taken alive, what's left for the Maggotrolls?"

"In that case, everyone will lose," I said sadly. "But before considering the self-annihilation option, let's see how we can improve our odds of winning. There is another strategy we can use." Everyone looked at me. "You need to start leaking the misinformation to your population that we're building several dark-universe spacecraft to attack Vestrallum. Those spaceships will be manned by suicide crews, and each spaceship will be armed as a planet buster, intent on destroying the entire planet."

"Why would we spread a lie?" General Kland asked. "We won't be able to carry out that threat."

"It's to spread fear," said Glave o'Sfero. "We're willing to die and willing to destroy Vestrallum, even if we won't be around. A no-win situation."

Chapter 23. The Battleship Nisip

"Any other ideas?" I asked.

"We've exhausted all the alternatives," said Xirxyg e'Sfero.

"Perhaps," I said. "But, when stuck in the mud, you must leave your boots behind."

A few, who might have had that experience, chuckled.

"Nurvig e'Sfero, what is the progress on the hull material?" I asked.

Nurvig looked ill. I'm sure that he felt personally responsible for not overcoming the hull-material obstacle. "I don't have any hopes that we can be successful."

Some of the participants gave small cries.

"Maybe those warships without the right material are our boots," I said.

"What do you mean?" Logrn asked.

"Those ten destroyers will be just ten tin cans that even their fighters will be able to obliterate," I said. "Why build them? Why spend the material, the labor, and the effort for something that won't stand a chance in battle?"

"We should not build them?" General Kland wondered.

"We should not," I answered. "Instead, we should build as many FBBs as possible." I looked around, and I swore I could see their minds spinning out of control.

"I fail to see how that would help us." Logrn said. "We have little chance as it is."

"Let me put it another way. Imagine that we could have a warship as big and capable as *Mangle*," I said. "General Lantolan, would you tell us of a typical engagement between two capital warships?"

"Well, we might start with a salvo of proton bombardment, from tens of thousands of kilometers away, and so would they," said Lantolan. "Not much damage would be done, since the distance and energy shields will protect each warship. The next phase would be to launch the auxiliary task forces—the frigates and fighters—to attack and destroy the other capital ship. The fighters engage each other or attack the frigates, which will approach the enemy warship to fire missiles and proton blasts. Each warship will defend itself with its own firepower and missiles. The winner would be the warship that has more auxiliary forces left undamaged, or whose missiles and proton blasts inflicted more damage on the other warship. The outcome would be flee, surrender, or be destroyed."

"Would the warships engage in direct battle with each other at close proximity without the use of the auxiliary forces?"

"They could, if they're crazy or desperate, but the chances of one ship or both being badly damaged or destroyed is guaranteed. Warship-to-warship combat is the last act of desperation."

"You're saying that the fighters, destroyers, and frigates in this case, will be doing the fighting, and the warship will act as a base and command center," I said.

"Yes, but we shouldn't underestimate the warship's proton cannon power," answered General Lantolan. "It will destroy many of the frigates and fighters attacking it."

I wasn't sure if they understood what I was getting at. "In that case, we already have a capital warship." I saw a lot of confused faces. "It has more and bigger proton guns than *Mangle*. And it has fighters."

"Where is it?" asked General Lantolan.

"We're standing on it and its name is Nisip."

Everyone gasped.

"But Nisip is a planet," said Logrn. "And the FBBs are not exactly fighters. We don't have frigates."

"A planet is the biggest warship there is," I said. "The FBB is a fighter that is hard to obliterate. If we don't have frigates, how many FBBs will be needed to annihilate a frigate? Or how many FBBs can we build instead of a frigate?" I had my arms up, shaking them to get my point across.

It clicked. The realization that they were not in such bad shape seemed to reinvigorate them. Slowly, everyone attending saw the new paradigm.

"When you defend a planet, the planet itself is a warship," I said. "Let's not try to build weapons that don't work, but let's build weapons that we know will work," I concluded. "Nurvig e'Sfero, if you stop the production on the ten destroyers, how many busting balls could you produce?"

"At least a thousand more."

"How about making an effort to build two thousand balls? Do we have enough spent uranium?"

"We do, even for two thousand. Would that include converting the old balls to flying?"

"If we need to, but the GBBs can be used for ground defenses. If the enemy lands, their transport ships will unload millions of Maggotrolls on Nisip." I crossed my arms. "Now, we need to find problems with the strategy I'm suggesting. And also, what would be the solutions to those problems?"

"I realize that the FBBs are sturdy, but they, too, can be destroyed," began General Kland. "And the FBBs don't have offensive weapons."

"The only thing that could destroy a ball is a direct hit from *Mangle*'s super gun proton blast," said Logrn. "Or maybe the frigates' proton blasts. The other firepower won't affect the FBBs, unless the fire can be focused and sustained against a single ball. The missiles can be avoided or be smashed in head on collisions."

"But you see," said General Lantolan thoughtfully, "when the enemy warship discovers that we can smash them with the FBBs, which for them will resemble fighters at first, they will unleash their own fighters. Also the guns from the frigates will be a formidable danger."

"I realize that all an FBB can do is crash and destroy the other craft," I said. "But that's the intent, anyway. The FBB doesn't do it with firepower but with its mass. The FBB is an offensive weapon, a uranium missile. If you put an enemy fighter against one of our FBBs, which one will win?"

"Our FBB, of course," said Logrn. I motioned to him to elaborate. "An FBB cannot be destroyed by the fighter's fire power. The FBB will have to smash into the fighter, which at first would be easy because of the surprise factor, but after that, the fighters would keep their distance. We'll need to develop a game strategy to overcome the enemy fighters' avoidance."

"But which one is more agile?" Xirxyg asked rhetorically. "The FBB is able to achieve a maximum speed of 10 km/s. But it can achieve that speed extremely fast. The enemy fighter, even with antigrav engines, won't be able to do that, because of the craft's slower acceleration due to the lack of antigrav shells in the cockpit. Of course, after a while, the fighter's speed will surpass ours. That is a shortcoming for the FBBs."

"How do you know that the fighters don't have antigrav shells in their cockpits?" I asked.

"The whole fighter has to be spherical inside and outside, not to mention that it would affect its weapons," replied Xirxyg.

"Then we have the acceleration advantage up to a maximum speed of 10 km/s," I said.

"Absolutely," said General Lantolan. "But, after the enemy discovers that we have only fighters, their fighting strategy will change. Their fighters will retreat and their warship will fire its big cannons at our balls. Who knows, they may hit more than one ball with one blast. Their proton beam can diverge to over one meter in diameter and still be effective."

"I don't think it will be able to hit more than one ball at a time," said Logrn. "But unfortunately, the targeted FBB will be destroyed. The pilot in that ball won't have any way to know that it had been targeted and to take evasive actions."

"If the FBBs can be targeted," said General Lantolan. "The FBBs should always be moving in short random and erratic flight patterns."

"Hitting an FBB with the big proton gun is like shooting a fly with a cannon," I said.

"Yes, a lot of energy wasted for a ball," agreed Logrn.

"It could be," said General Kland. "There is another issue that bothers me. Our pilots have diminished monitoring capabilities and cannot communicate with each other while the VAL is active. How are they going to attack the warship as one fighting group?"

Even I agreed that was a problem. "Logrn e'Sfero, can the ball change colors?"

"Yes, to any color or pattern. It can even become almost invisible. Why?"

"Can it become luminescent?"

"Yes, it can. But it will become easier to target."

"We need to communicate," I said. "Develop a language by using external luminescent colors or patterns to inform the other balls how to attack, defend, lure the enemy, and so on."

"That would work," agreed Logrn. "Of course, the onboard computer will have to do the communications and reduce the time of being luminescent."

They were on the right track.

"Good, now back to the proton beam," said General Kland. "If a warship fires at another warship, the proton beam will be narrow, under ten centimeters. But if they fire at a squadron of fighters, the beam could be wider and sustained longer."

"What if we give the impression that we are one massive warship?" I asked.

"By flying in tight formation?" someone asked.

"Yes, or by coupling with each other," I said. "What if we could create a giant but hollow cone or even a disk? The enemy would see a large warship. The tactics would change to warship-to-warship battle." I raised a hand to overcome objections from a few. "I know the balls cannot fire back, but the enemy will blast a narrow and intense beam. But within the formation, the FBBs should be flying in a close enough formation to give the impression of a hull, but at the same time in a random pattern to avoid as much as possible the enemy's fire. When they are close enough to the *Mangle*, the FBBs would disperse and attack like a swarm of wrecking balls. The enemy and its computers will not be able to react fast enough. By the way, Logrn e'Sfero, if the FBBs line up and act like a spear, let's say, could the point FBB draw additional outer layer protection from the ones behind?"

"We will have to examine that and the linking of balls, if it can be done," said Logrn.

"That would change all our battle tactics," said General Kland.

The talking, the analyses, the preparations, the training, and the simulations continued, refining the strategy of using the FBBs as fighters. The manufacturing of FBBs increased, and by the time the enemy fleet's arrival was expected, the Sferogyls would have built 2,223 FBBs.

The entire Sferogyl population was on a war footing, and by the time the Maggotrolls arrived, the Sferogyls would have more than ten million soldiers on the ground. Provisions were stashed away, medical supplies were distributed, the planet went dark, and most of the non-essential population hid deep underground, waiting for the enemy.

Chapter 24. Waiting

Varna, Turnd, and Bovern were with me in my suite; the adults having a beer and getting accustomed to the new reality of imminent war, and Bovern drinking milk. The lights in Tandalo and all the other cities were off. All the buildings' windows, including mine, were draped with opaque curtains, just in case the spy satellite could penetrate the oculi camouflage. Even the bubble cars in the streets had dipped headlights. There was an eerie quietness and darkness in the city.

The enemy had not been sighted yet, but suspense was thick in the air. Near every city, a decoy projection was set up on the ground to give the impression that all was well on Nisip and its cities, and that the Sferogyls were unsuspecting of what was about to happen. When *Mangle* would appear over Nisip, normal sapient beings would panic and flee, therefore the Sferogyls set up fake remote-operated transporters, creating a lot of dust, to give the impression of fleeing population from the cities. With the Sferogyls seemingly fleeing from the population centers, the planet would appear to be ready for the taking.

Everything that the Sferogyls could think of was set up to entice *Mangle* and the other four transporters to get as close as possible to Nisip, so that the firing of the ground proton cannons would be as effective as possible. The element of surprise was essential to being victorious.

"Tim Andrus, have you been through a war before?" Bovern asked.

"Yes, Bovern k'Sfero," I said, thinking that in my human life I had

164

not, but as a god most likely I had. However, I'd seen news and many war movies, and that would suffice as experience.

"Are we doing the right thing, Tim Andrus?" Varna asked.

"I believe you are. You have the right to defend yourselves, even if that costs a lot of lives, on your side and theirs."

"A lot of my friends are in the spaceforce, flying FBBs," Turnd said. "Varna and I are meeting on virtual flying battles every night. We are volunteers on standby, in case we're needed."

I got the hint. "Would you like to be a pilot, Turnd l'Sfero?"

"Yes, Tim Andrus," he said, without seeming to give it a second thought.

"How about you, Varna e'Sfero?" I asked.

"It would be an honor to join our spaceforces as a regular, Tim Andrus."

"Me, too," said Bovern.

"Bovern k'Sfero, you're too young to fly an FBB," I said.

"I can help in other ways, Tim Andrus."

"Yes, you can. Listen, I appreciate your company, and by now I know my way around. You should help your fellow Sferogyls instead."

"But that's not up to us, Tim Andrus," said Varna e'Sfero.

"I'll talk to Glave o'Sfero." We toasted to a successful future.

And I did talk to Glave o'Sfero that night. He agreed that if I didn't need Varna and Turnd, they should join the spaceforce, if they qualified, but that I should keep Bovern to help me with chores. Luckily, Bovern was not upset about staying with me.

Next morning, we said our good-byes, and Varna and Turnd left for the spaceforce conscription center, with a recommendation from me. Later that day, I found out that they were admitted as active pilots.

When I arrived in the war room, everyone was at their stations, busying themselves with idle work while awaiting the enemy's arrival. There were large holo-screens around the room, depicting selective images from the ground and space. Everything was unnervingly quiet.

"What's taking them so long?" General Kland wondered aloud.

"The exit from the dark universe is plus or minus three light days from the arrival position, General Kland," said Logrn. "They may have already arrived in our solar system and are approaching Nisip at high speed, but not necessarily at NLS. It may take as long as five to six days for us to detect them."

"It's been six days already," said General Kland. "The suspense is killing me."

I smiled and suspected that everyone, no matter the solar system, feels like a fish in a blender when waiting for the imminent act. Dark times were ahead of us. I busied myself and reviewed the situation of the military forces again.

The 217 GBBs were integrated with the Army, and for all practical purposes, they represented the armored division. The Army had ten million soldiers. It sounded like a lot, but four million colonists, mercenaries, and soldiers would invade Nisip. The Sferogyls conducted simulated battles based on what they knew about the enemy's forces, weapons, and tactics. And they did well in simulations. The unknown was what would happen in the actual battles. The enemy had a mind of its own, and based on its assessment of the Sferogyls' resistance, it would change its strategy as needed. The fog of war would engulf us all.

Our ten super-proton cannons, with ten muzzles each, were ready. The only problem was that they were test-fired into empty space, but never at a real target. How good the guns would be against *Mangle* was a big unknown. I crossed my fingers that they'd at least deter their warship from approaching Nisip too closely to use their proton cannons effectively.

The spaceforce was made up of over 2,200 FBBs and was organized in five Birds. One Bird was the Special Forces Bird. The other four Birds, each having around 500 flying balls, were assigned to the four major cities: Tandalo Bird, Marjon Bird, Dengholan Bird, and Sferogug Bird. Each Bird was further divided into Wings, Groups, Squadrons, Flights, and Elements. Each Element had three FBBs.

A few months back, I had requested my own FBB. It was specially built for my anatomy, although it was the same size as the others on the inside and outside. It was a meter and a half in diameter externally and only one meter in diameter internally, and it weighed twenty-six tons, much larger and heavier than the GBBs. The ball opened like a cut tennis ball when squeezed, and once I climbed into the ball, it would close and seal at the atomic level on my verbal command. The outside skin didn't give any indication of an opening. Inside, I could sit in a relatively comfy chair with armrests, but I had to cross or bend my legs; it wasn't exactly the cockpit of a fighter jet. Afterward, I requested a headrest, not for safety but for comfort. Needless to say, there was no harness to strap myself in with, since the ball had its own gravity, and I was not subject to inertia movements. However, I had an energy shield helmet to protect me against energy discharges from outside or inside.

When flying, it was as if the world around me were moving, including Nisip and other craft. I was the center of the universe. The ball had noise suppressors, so it was very quiet inside, even if it were impacted by enemy fire. I requested several warning signals and other sounds to correspond with the action during battle, such as a beeping sound when I was tracked and locked on by missiles, rail guns, or plasma. The sound for proton hits was like hail on a tin roof, and for lasers, like a buzz of a saw cutting through wood. It seemed that the other Sferogyl pilots liked those features and requested them for their FBBs as well.

Unfortunately, laser or proton fire was undetectable, since it arrived at the speed of light, although the aftereffects of those shots were readable and displayed on the cockpit screens, identifying the source of the fire; again, it would be after the fact, but it was better than not knowing who had done the shooting, in case you'd survive. The missiles, projectiles, and even plasma blasts could be identified prior to impact, and the onboard computer displayed them and took corrective maneuvers to avoid them if one was dead center against my FBB.

In the cockpit, which was the inside of the ball, holographic displays occupied 180 degrees around me, showing me the outside on 360-degree spherical coordinates. In other words, I could see all around me on those screens with very little movement of my head. Up, down, port, starboard, forward, and rear were relative terms to my FBB. Nisip was not up or down, only a number based on an analog clock position on my horizontal plane and a degree inclination on my vertical plane. And the positions changed every time my craft moved. Because of the VAL, the craft had only visual monitoring and no other sensors, such as radar, energy disturbances, or gravity field distortion readings.

The displays were intelligent visuals, displaying not only what I could see with my naked eye, which would be very little, but visuals monitored by the onboard computer, identifying and magnifying the targets as needed. Many of these images were digitized, and flight parameters were displayed around the objects surrounding my FBB. Since most of the FBB motion would be erratic, the computer stabilized the images to a steady motion and kept track of the targets such that I would not get dizzy, confused, or lose the targets. Orange vectors, or arrows, showed safe paths, while purple vectors showed incoming attacks, whether it was a craft or a missile. These vectors represented by arrows were either longer or shorter, depending on the speed at which the object was coming at me. The craft around me were represented by different-sized dots, depending on their size. Orange was friendly, and purple was the enemy. Because of speeds during battle and to prevent vertigo, numeric coordinates and vectors replaced the images.

I participated in training exercises and virtual games. All exercises were conducted on the dark side of Nisip to avoid being spotted by the enemy's satellite. It was a thrill every time I flew in space. My displays showed in ultrahigh definition the serene and brilliant sky, until the action would begin. Contrary to the sci-fi movies I remembered seeing in the past, once the fighting began, the images on the displays were too fast to react to by verbal or manual commands. The FBBs around me—and future enemy fighters—would move so fast, and distances increase or decrease so rapidly, that each craft could disappear into the darkness of space in the blink of an eye. There was no such thing as visual sighting, maneuvering in position, and dogfights. Two craft flying at each other at 10 km/s or 20 m/ms appeared and disappeared in two milliseconds—a blink of an eye took 300 milliseconds. Thank God for the onboard computer, operating at nanoseconds and taking the right actions, since one millisecond was a long time in actual combat. That's when the vectors came into play to guide me on my flight paths, speeds, and directions. My responsibilities were to plan ahead, acquire targets, and make the best intuitive decisions. The onboard computer performed most of the flying, without me even knowing it.

The FBB's motion was based on X, Y, and Z coordinates, and spherical coordinates as well. Two joysticks with three activation buttons each—three for three fingers on each hand—controlled the craft's direction and motion at slow speeds. At first, it felt as if I were playing a musical instrument, but I learned all the control sequences to fly my FBB with dexterity and precision, using three fingers of each hand, just as any Sferogyl pilot would. The craft executed verbal commands as well, in case my fingers got tired. All this was feasible at one second or longer reaction time; at less than a second, the onboard computer took over. All I had to do was select the target and the rest would happen—fast. The vectors and dots, not the images, were my friends in combat.

While in space, the antigrav engine provided normal gravity, and only when I disengaged the engine did I become weightless. I preferred the onboard gravity better, especially when other FBBs changed directions on a dime at full speed around me. Becoming dizzy and throwing up was inevitable without the active onboard gravity.

The FBB had limitations. Its fuel—neutrons—lasted only four hours, although recharging was fast. When the fourth hour ended, recharging at the ground bases was mandatory. The ball traveled at a maximum speed of 10 km/s, the escape velocity of Nisip. Any FBB had to stay close to Nisip, to use the planet's gravity to push or pull itself. An FBB could accelerate from Nisip and never be able to return, unless it encountered another mass-object with enough gravity to bounce back. The shortcomings in maximum speed were compensated by the ability to fly at full speed, 10 km/s, and reverse direction at an incredible acceleration. An FBB was hard to pin down.

I was part of a special three-FBB Element. Needless to say, I requested that Turnd and Varna be part of my Element. They were thrilled to fly with me. And Bovern was even happier that we were back together.

Anu had told me not to fight, but I had to fly in one of these balls, and it was an exhilarating experience. Maybe I wouldn't have to engage the enemy.

A few more days passed without any sign of the enemy. Most of the time, I was in the command center, helping, if I could, with the simulated battles from behind holographic displays, or on my balcony, drinking beer with Varna and Turnd when they were not on duty and discussing events of the day or the past. Bovern drank snail milk and listened, fascinated, to our stories.

In the command center, the atmosphere was more relaxed, and some Sferogyls wondered if the enemy would ever come.

But then, a purple light began pulsing and a buzzer sounded: Enemy sighted.

Chapter 25. The Battle Begins

The deep space sensors identified the enemy armada trailing Nisip in orbit around the sun. It was composed, as we knew, of the four transport-cargo ships and one battleship-carrier. The twelve frigates were deployed, making the entire fleet look foreboding. They were decelerating quickly, and their speed matched Nisip's when their position reached 200,000 kilometers from the planet. An hour later, the armada split into four battle groups. Four frigates escorted three transporters. Surprisingly, one transporter did not have any frigates as an escort. The four battle groups moved toward Nisip.

The ETA was three hours at their current speed. As they got closer, the transport ship battle groups approached Nisip from four directions, each heading eventually toward one of the major cities on Nisip: Tandalo, Marjon, Dengholan, and Sferogug, as expected. It was curious that *Mangle*, with all its firepower, was farther away from Nisip, behind the invading transporters. Common logic would say that the heavy hitter would be the first to clear away any opposition. But that wasn't the case here.

"What's their strategy? What are they doing?" General Razvij called from Dengholan.

"We planned for this scenario," General Kland replied. "But with *Mangle* or the frigates in front. Any ideas why they're deploying the transporters first?"

"They're exposing their weak front, the transporters, to draw fire from us," I said. "Since they haven't detected any warships opposing them, they're suspicious of ground fire."

"Our proton cannons are standing by," said General Sarmal

l'Sfero.

"Stand by until the fire order is given," said General Kland.

Our super proton cannons were waiting patiently. All we could do at this time was watch tensely as the enemy ships approached Nisip, soon to be within shooting range.

Suddenly, the silence was broken by a transmission on all channels from the Maggotrolls:

"Attention, all Sferogyls. This is the warship *Mangle*, part of the Maggotroll assimilation force. The Maggotroll Empire has decided to assimilate Nisip and all its population. There is no need for alarm. You'll be treated gently. Do not resist or fight our expeditionary forces that will descend on your planet shortly. Should you resist and fight us, there will be dire consequences for your actions. Your leaders' response is demanded within one hour, starting from now. The lack of a response will be considered an act of resistance and therefore cause for immediate attack. You have sixty minutes."

I thought bitterly, *They didn't say 'Resistance is futile,' as the Borg said in the* Star Trek *series.* Oh well, that was a different part of the galaxy, I guess. The message continued repeating at five-minute intervals, in case we didn't get it the first time, while the countdown decreased accordingly. I wondered what the *Mangle*'s captain and his staff was thinking, observing the quiet and nonresponsive planet. Their monitoring showed everything was normal up to their second message. But with fifty minutes to go, a storm of communications erupted on Nisip. Soon after, ground transporters and trails of dust radiated out of every major city. The Sferogyls gave the impression of fleeing in panic. In reality, the civilian populations of all the major cities were sheltered deep underground. Only military and emergency teams were left in the cities.

But the Maggotrolls were not stupid. The Maggotrolls knew that the Sferogyls, just like any population under assault, would panic and run for safety, so they continued approaching the planet as planned, not taking any rash actions, while transmitting their surrender message. There was still no reply to their demands from Nisip.

The Sferogyl General Command wanted to give the impression of a complete breakdown of leadership and panic on Nisip. We wanted to lure them as close as possible, and so far it was developing as planned.

I watched the tense faces of my rotund friends. Many officers at their stations were communicating in terse sentences with other command centers all over Nisip. Everyone hoped the Maggotrolls would not suspect the blasts coming their way until they were too close for comfort. The farthest, but still effective, range for our proton cannons was 50,000 km from the surface. The closer they were to Nisip, the greater the impact they would receive from the surface blasts. But *Mangle*, although approaching with the rest of the ships, stood behind and beyond that range, while sweeping the planet with its sensors to gather information. We were confident that there was no detection of our weapons and energy storage batteries.

The Maggotroll command must have been very sure of their superiority and defensive shields, letting the transporters approach the planet with only frigates as military defenses. A more aggressive scenario would have been to bombard Nisip into submission. But they wanted the goods intact, as much as possible.

A display in the war room showed the distance and time expected for at least the transporters to be within firing range and the percentage kill potential based on the distance from the surface. Our proton cannons were fully activated, the protons spinning at high speeds in the acceletrons, and standing by. The kill stats were climbing, as they passed the thirty-minute mark from ETA and getting closer to Nisip.

Their forces were dispersed into five separate groups, the four transports and *Mangle*. All craft were approaching Nisip with their bows toward the planet, as if they were gravity bombs in free fall.

The anxious faces of the military officers in the war room, none of whom had ever fought in a real war, were unsettling. They were responsible to monitor and conduct the battles about to begin in less than thirty minutes. There were hundreds of these officers, sitting in their bowl chairs, watching the holo-displays, and waiting for the "commence firing" order. Would they perform as trained?

The last transmission from *Mangle* ended and the time clicked to zero, but General Kland held the fire order. The three transporter groups and the escort frigates began descending into Nisip's upper atmosphere, with their bows pointing down toward the ground. They should assume a horizontal position after they entered the atmosphere. Not all the transporters entered the atmosphere at the same time. The fourth transporter lagged behind and stopped above the upper atmosphere, hovering over the capital. *Mangle* came by the side of this transporter to provide support. That was a problem. Under *Mangle*'s protection, that transporter was safer from our destructive firepower. But that's what war was all about: chance, confusion, opportunity, and unpredictability.

"Attention, all zones. Aim at the transporters. Fire!" ordered General Kland.

There was a large hologram allocated for each battle theatre. The holograms showed quick bursts of proton energy from the ground cannons hitting the enemy ships. Shafts of superheated air were left behind, before the proton blasts exited the denser atmosphere. In an instant, the transporters were engulfed in flashes of plasma caused by our proton blasts, dissipating against their energy shields. Each of our proton cannons fired at six-second intervals, rotating from muzzle to muzzle to dissipate the firing heat. The firing continued, despite the enemy's shields holding. The intent was to weaken the shields, make them fail, and then strike at the hulls of the transporters and kill the enemy.

"Why are our proton guns not penetrating the shields?" demanded General Kland.

"Our guns are at full power, General Kland," said General Sarmal from his station. "Their shields are stronger than we anticipated."

Then it dawned on me why the ships were pointed with their bows down to the surface. "General Kland, the enemy ships are exposing their bows only," I said over the intercom. "The bows have a smaller surface, and they must be armor hardened. Probably each ship is channeling all its energy to the bow area to withstand our proton blasts."

General Kland understood. "Attention, all guns. Fire at all enemy ships on the broadside, if in range." Additional but farther away proton cannons began blasting at the enemy.

Both the transporter and *Mangle* over Tandalo were hit, but their shields held without damage. *Mangle* began firing with its heavy proton cannons at the location of our gun muzzles with an incredible precision, destroying each nozzle. Each blast left a large crater in the ground. Luckily, the neighboring ground muzzles were not destroyed, and they took their turns to fire at the enemy. Unfortunately, *Mangle* was not fooled by the proton gun decoys and never wasted its firepower on them.

In the other three battle theaters, the frigates began systematically attacking and firing on our ground proton cannons as well. Their fire was even more deadly because of the proximity to the muzzles. And then some good news: One frigate was pulverized over Sferogug. But the other three frigates hit the rest of the muzzles in that region, putting them out of commission. Implosions could be seen where the proton raceway's vacuum was breached.

There were stressful moments among the officers, trusting ten million Sferogyl soldiers on the ground not to start firing prematurely. The plan was to let the transporters, if not destroyed, approach within five km of the ground before attacking them with additional ground fire. Our ground forces were seeing the failure of the big proton cannons to make a dent in the transporters. But they had to wait. Their firing would alert the frigates to their positions, and they would be destroyed in turn.

Another frigate was disabled over Dengholan, and it crashed to the surface. But the good news didn't last for long.

A broad announcement was made in the command center, "Enemy fighters deployed to assist the transporters."

"Launch the FBBs," ordered General Kland.

"Each Bird except Tandalo's are airborne," announced General Lantolan.

Considering how easily the enemy annihilated our not-so-super proton cannons, the FBBs were our only hope now. I wished that the transporter over Tandalo would hurry and get down for the FBBs to attack it as well.

As each transporter reached the five km altitude, they leveled off for landing, and our ground forces opened fire on them. The frigates took evasive actions and responded with their own fire against our ground forces. Their proton blasts made the ground explode and destroyed some of our mobile guns, which were remote-controlled from deep underground. At this time, the casualties were minimal on the ground, other than the loss of the destroyed weapons. From mobile ground launchers, dozens of missiles fired up at the three transporters and exploded in nuclear fireballs. Some of them caused holes in the transporters' hulls, signaling their inevitable demise. The frigates and newly arrived enemy fighters recognized the new threat and began descending aggressively toward the missile launchers, which quickly took shelter underground. They would resurface from other holes in different locations and begin firing their missiles again.

From nowhere, warships appeared above the horizon and headed toward the enemy frigates. They were our FBBs attacking in the formation called "harpoon." Five FBBs formed the tip of the harpoon, followed in a line by forty-five others making up the shaft, screeching through the thin air at 10,000 km/h. The frigates' energy shields knocked away the leading FBB, but as each ball following the one in front bounced off, the following ball hit a focused area in the same spot on the shields.

The first frigate to be hit and penetrated by the FBBs was the one over Marjon. Looking on a detailed hologram, I could see that there were at least five FBBs that smashed through the frigate's hull, after which that frigate dissolved in a fiery explosion. Pieces of it began falling in flames toward the ground. Numerous FBBs randomly attacked the transporter ship over Marjon. Although the transporter was armed with defensive guns, they were no threat to the storming balls banging on its shields. One FBB managed to crack the shield of the transporter, penetrated the hull, and hit one of the transporter's antigravity engines. Three kilometers above the surface, the behemoth began spinning, as the remaining antigrav engines tried to counterbalance the descent.

The craft's shuttles began exiting from the cargo bay, to save as many colonizers as possible. The energy shields had to be turned off around the cargo bay to allow the escaping shuttles. Those gaps in the shields invited the FBBs to attack mercilessly. The descending transporter was at an altitude of two km, and it evacuated as many of its bailout shuttles as it could. Some parts of it were on fire, and the smoke emanated from many other sections of the transporters. Soon, individual colonizers started jumping out of the craft, using old-fashioned parachutes—which made sense, because they were within the atmosphere, but it was a surprising development for a space invasion. In spite of the frenetic evacuation, there must have been hundreds of thousands of colonizers who remained on board as the transporter's captain tried valiantly to prevent a free fall to the ground.

"All guns, fire on the wounded transport and its shuttles!" shouted General Jongen, who was in charge of Marjon.

The barrage of fire from the ground intensified, and it didn't take long for the transporter to rip apart, while falling to the ground with its hundreds of thousands of colonizers still on board. War is cruel—kill or be killed. The remaining three frigates, stormed by the FBBs, decided to flee rather than attack our ground forces.

"Our first victory against the Maggotrolls has happened over Marjon!" an announcement blared in the command center. Marjon was saved.

But there were three other transporters that were faring better. Waves of more fighters stormed out of *Mangle* to the defense of the transporters attempting to land at Sferogug and Dengholan.

The transporter under the protection of *Mangle* began descending. New fighters from *Mangle* sprang toward Tandalo to attack the ground defenders. Red laser beams, visible in the atmosphere, fired from the fighters, while surface-to-air missiles shot up from the ground to destroy the fighters, crisscrossed the sky above the capital. *Mangle* fired its massive proton cannon at the Tandalo decoy first. Surprisingly, it had fooled *Mangle*'s sensors, but not for long, and soon it began firing at the defense ground forces.

"Commence Operation Warship!" shouted General Kland.

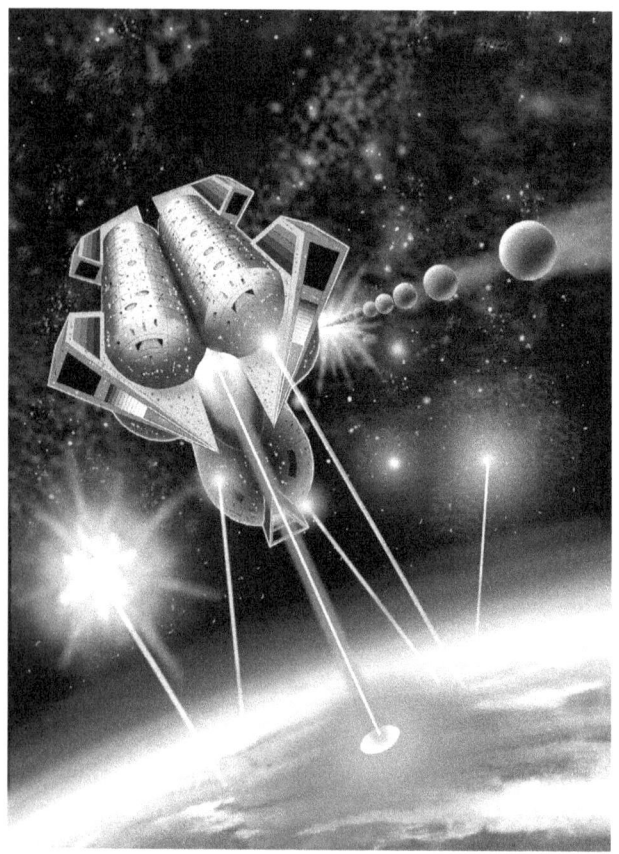

Chapter 26. The Ground Battles

The transporters that were headed to Sferogug and Dengholan managed to land without crashing, although both of them were damaged from our missiles and mobile proton fires. Most of their shuttles landed as well, taking defensive positions on the perimeter of the landings. Armored vehicles, resembling shiny turtles, disgorged from the transporters' bays. A swarm of colonizers in battle gear followed right behind them. The ground battle around those two cities began. Each city had fifty-some GBBs, opposing the invaders.

The frigates assigned to the transporters, along with the newly arrived fighters, began attacking the Sferogyl ground defenders, while the FBBs attacked the frigates in arrow formations. Flying inside the atmosphere and traveling at supersonic speeds, some FBBs engaged in dogfights—or, better said, cat and mouse fights—and the enemy fighters took casualties. Within the atmosphere, the FBBs had a definite advantage, being faster, more maneuverable and agile.

However, more pressing matters stopped most of the fights when the call was given for the FBBs to assemble for Operation Warship. On their way to the rendezvous place, many FBBs formed several harpoon formations and attacked any frigates they encountered. They punched holes through three of the frigates, destroying them. The other frigates retreated into space for safety, leaving the ground invaders only with fighters' support. But the fighters could not put even a scratch on the remaining FBBs, and slowly many more were destroyed or fled back to *Mangle*.

In the meanwhile, the GBBs around Sferogug and Dengholan were rolling, attacking the Maggotroll ground defensive positions with impunity. At Dengholan, a GBB platoon managed to reach the landed transporter. First, they destroyed part of the landing gear and after the transporter collapsed to the ground, askew, the GBBs crisscrossed its underbelly, making the ship unable to ever fly again. The enemy was running scared from those satanic balls that ran over them without compassion.

General Razvij signaled the GBBs: "Priority targets are the heavy weapons and armament, not the colonists." It seemed the GBB drivers were having too much fun running over the Maggotrolls. Soon, the GBBs were causing havoc among the attackers' armored vehicles, guns, and missile launchers. Visual assessment of the battlefield was impossible because of the dust, smoke, and explosions, but digital renderings of the battlefields gave our defensive ground forces a clearer view, and they adjusted their attacks for maximum destruction of the enemy forces.

Six Wings of FBBs, almost 1,500 of them, assembled below the horizon into their fighting formation. Because there were not enough FBBs to form a fake but large impression of a battleship, an ingenious method was developed to attack *Mangle*. The FBBs formed a circle around the warship on its equatorial plane and approached the target at a maximum speed of 10 km/s. It was a matter of seconds before the hundreds of FBBs in the ring would impact *Mangle*.

The warship did not wait; it took evasive action. It could not retreat into space without leaving the transporter below unprotected. Instead, *Mangle* moved down toward Nisip. The fast-shrinking FBB ring moved down with it. The upper atmosphere and the ship's proximity to the ground reduced *Mangle*'s maneuverability. From the ground, the proton guns and missiles from around Tandalo began firing at *Mangle*. The fighters and four frigates attacked the FBB ring to protect *Mangle*, but to no avail. Nothing seemed to destroy the devilish cannon balls flying toward the big craft. The gun turrets on the warship's hull began moving frenetically to take optimum positions, and they began firing at the invading ring. Salvos of missiles and laser jets were unleashed from *Mangle* to destroy the FBBs. The laser firing was not visible in space, but the command computer digitally simulated those jets. Some were short pulses, while others were of longer duration.

Fifteen hundred FBBs came on radial trajectories against the battleship. At the last instant from impact, *Mangle* energized its antigravity engines and fled into space, leaving its transporter, fighters, and frigates behind to fend for themselves. The space battle didn't last long, and the surviving frigates and fighters retreated toward *Mangle*, already a million kilometers away.

Near Tandalo, the transporter landed safely and began evacuating its forces to attack the city. Dozens of FBB squadrons came down from space to join in the ground battles around Tandalo, Dengholan, and Sferogug. The enemy ground forces were left without air support and were smashed by GBBs or FBBs. The enemy's laser and proton fires, visible in the atmosphere, were intense, but nothing seemed to stop our hellish balls.

It looked good for our side.

Soon, the air battles diminished in intensity, and many of the FBBs had to retreat to their bases for neutron refueling. The GBBs continued rolling on the ground, smashing the enemy's vehicles and weapons. Unfortunately, the enemy figured out a way to stop the rolling balls. They used their proton guns to create a maze of trenches. Those slowed the GBBs down, and some even got stuck and had to sink underground for protection. The enemy blasted at the ones stuck temporarily in the trenches with proton gunfire and managed to destroy some of them.

Although the air battles came to a lull after hours of fighting, the ground battles continued unabated. The Sferogyls divided their ground forces to fight around the clock, pulling exhausted forces behind the defensive lines and replacing them with fresh soldiers. The relentless attacks exhausted the Maggotrolls, and they retreated behind their newly formed defensive lines.

At Dengholan, the Maggotrolls' defenses were near collapse. They took refuge inside their damaged transport ship, managing to raise a protective energy shield. It was unknown how many survivors there were. At Marjon, the last resistance from the surviving Maggotrolls was extinguished, and tens of thousands were taken as prisoners.

At Sferogug, the battle continued, and the Maggotrolls were in better shape to resist the Sferogyls' attacks. The Maggotrolls created a large, crisscrossing network of trenches around their base, slowing down the GBBs. They placed many of their proton guns on higher elevations and blasted the attacking Sferogyl soldiers. Their transporter, with its active energy shields, protected itself and the Maggotroll soldiers taking shelter inside it.

At Tandalo, the Maggotrolls were victorious. They captured the almost deserted capital and even some satellite neighborhoods farther away from the capital. Their transporter was in near-intact condition, and they moved it for protection into a large bowl of a suburban city of Tandalo. They took over 100,000 Sferogyls, who had remained in the city as emergency teams, as prisoners. Sferogyl troops encircled Tandalo, but not much fighting was taking place for fear of harming the prisoners.

Chapter 27. After the First Battle

The day after the invasion began, we gathered in the war room to assess the situation.

"Marjon, report status?" General Kland asked from the command center.

"This is Marjon, General Jongen l'Sfero reporting. There is only sporadic firing from entrenched or fleeing Maggotrolls. Another night is coming, but the mopping up operation continues until we capture or kill them all. The transporter is full of dead Maggotrolls, perhaps as many as 700,000 colonists. We're considering setting it on fire for health reasons. We took almost 50,000 prisoners, and there are 75,000 wounded. So far we've counted 110,000 colonists dead on the ground from the initial ground fighting. The rest of the Maggotrolls fled or are entrenched in small caves in defensive positions, and have most of them surrounded. We lost only one GBB and one FBB. We have 6,000 casualties, and another 21,000 wounded. We're two million strong, and spirits are high. Standing by to assist the other cities."

"Excellent, General Jongen l'Sfero. Marjon did well," said General Kland. "We will return to the subject of assistance and reinforcements shortly. Dengholan, what is your status?"

"Dengholan reporting. General Razvij l'Sfero, speaking. The enemy has assumed a defensive position, mostly behind the energy shields of their transporter. We took 40,000 Maggotrolls as prisoners and destroyed most of their heavy weapons and armored vehicles. We've assessed that as many as 200,000 Maggotrolls are dead. We have them encircled and contained outside Dengholan. The trenches they dug slowed down our GBBs, and they became less effective against the Maggotrolls. We lost or are missing seven GBBs and two FBBs. We have over 25,000 casualties and another 50,000 wounded. Our troops are resolved and confident of a quick victory. We are making plans for an assault at nightfall. We will have to use all the FBBs we've retained, and we request as many FBBs as possible to join us in the forthcoming battle. We have two million soldiers, we don't need any other ground enforcements, and we hope this will be over in a few days."

"Very well, General Razvij l'Sfero. Dengholan's battle shall continue. We will inform you shortly of how many FBBs we can spare," said General Kland. "Sferogug, what is your status?"

"This is Sferogug, General Pantongev l'Sfero reporting the status. The situation on the ground is quiet at this time. Just as at Dengholan, the transporter is shielded, sheltering most of the enemy troops. They were successful in setting defensive positions on the ground around their transport ship and have several heavy proton guns located on higher elevations. We did not take any prisoners, but we estimate over 90,000 dead. As for the wounded, we think they have either retrieved their wounded to safety or killed them. We suspect that they may have a dozen space-fighters inside their transporter when they took refuge from our FBBs. We lost or are missing four GBBs and three FBBs. We have over 75,000 casualties and another 60,000 wounded. Our troops are in a resolute mood and eager to restart and win the battle. We are making plans to use heavy proton cannons from Sferogug's factory, which the workers have just finished assembling. We have two and a half million soldiers, and no other reinforcements are needed, except for more FBBs."

"Another good report, General Pantongev l'Sfero. The answer will be forthcoming about how many FBBs we can spare," said General Kland. "Tandalo, what is your status?"

"General Kland, General Alvuteran l'Sfero reporting for Tandalo. Unfortunately, we did not fare as well as the other cities, because *Mangle* protected this transporter. Tandalo is partly destroyed by *Mangle*'s proton cannons, and the colonists have occupied the rest of the city. They hid their transport ship and it is shielded now, making it difficult to destroy it. We didn't lose any GBBs, but we lost two FBBs. We had heavy casualties, over 150,000 dead, and another 200,000 wounded. Yes, we need reinforcements, especially ground soldiers. As you know, the enemy took prisoners in Tandalo, and the new count is 132,218. Because the enemy is mostly underground in our capital, the upcoming battle will be slow and bloody. Our strategy at this time is containment and later to destroy them with neutron bombs."

"Containing the enemy is the best for right now, General Alvutern l'Sfero," said General Kland. "I'm sorry about your losses."

"It was mostly from the proton blasts from *Mangle*," said Tandalo's general. "We will need more GBBs and FBBs as well."

"FBB Force, report your status," said General Kland.

"This is FBB Force, General Lantolan l'Sfero reporting. First, I'll start with our losses. Besides the FBBs lost as reported by the other theatres, we lost 31 FBBs in space. Altogether, we have 2,185 operational FBBs. We destroyed six of their frigates, and by latest count, we've destroyed 97 fighters. The ring formation threw them off. *Mangle* lost precious seconds, unsure what to do, and it's licking its wounds right now. Before it retreated, several FBBs had managed to penetrate two of its three hulls. One of the hulls has three distinctive holes in it. The other hull has just one hole and a dent. The FBBs are either on patrol or are back at their bases for refueling and refitting, and fresh pilots will fly the FBBs to new attacks on the ground targets. The soonest *Mangle* can arrive in orbit to resume its attack is at least four hours. Just let me know when and how many FBBs you need at each battle theatre."

"Thank you, General Lantolan l'Sfero," said General Kland. "General Sarmal l'Sfero, please report the situation of our super proton cannons."

"General Sarmal l'Sfero reporting. Only two of the guns are intact. Three were completely destroyed. The other five have various degrees and types of damage to the muzzles. We are in the process of repairing what we can with the spare parts on hand or cannibalizing parts from the guns that cannot be repaired. We expect to have seven guns operational, and we estimate twenty-eight muzzles to be functional. Logrn e'Sfero and his team have come up with a new configuration for the proton slug to include a bundle of electrons in its core. The proton blasts' efficiency will increase by 45%."

"Thank you, General Sarmal l'Sfero," said General Kland. "I'm surprised how ineffective our super cannons were."

"So were we, General Kland. We have powerful guns with the capability of shooting 3,000 kg-proton-mass blasts and a focus of less than 10 cm in diameter. But since we never fired at a shielded real target, the results were less than satisfactory."

"General Sarmal, do the best you can to get as many muzzles as possible back online and improve their efficiency," said General Kland. "Overall, considering the damage we inflicted on the Maggotrolls' ships, we've had light losses in our FBB Force. I'd like to thank all our fighting forces. So far, well done, and our victory is almost certain. I want to thank Tim Andrus for suggesting the ring formation and for training several pilots for each FBB as back-ups to sustain a continuous flying presence and to increase our rate of attacks. Continue your attacks as soon as you have your FBBs back up."

The overhead hologram displayed the stats of losses and what survived, for the enemy and us. It was just cold accounting, and looked good in some areas, but not so good in others. The Maggotrolls lost 32% of their colonizing forces, which was positive for the Sferogyls.

"I have a concern, General Kland," I said. "If the catastrophic crash of one of their transporters is put aside, we lost as many soldiers as they did. I think those colonists are mercenaries." Puzzled eyes turned to me. "They are not mere farmers or miners, but hardened fighters."

"Meaning?" General Kland asked.

"The Sferogyls have a physical disadvantage," I said. "Maggotrolls are hominidal in shape, and they can lie flat on the ground, minimizing their profiles. Sferogyls cannot. And in the images I saw from the fighting, the enemies were wearing armored reflective suits for protection against laser fire."

"We need to be more cautious when engaging the enemy in battle," said General Kland thoughtfully.

"Not all our soldiers have armor, and we try to keep those soldiers sheltered as much as we can," said General Razvij l'Sfero. "I recognize that not being able to minimize our profiles is a weakness for us. We'll reanalyze our tactics and protection."

"And we need FBBs to give us air support," said General Pantongev l'Sfero from Sferogug.

"The FBBs have done considerably better than the GBBs," I commented. "The enemy has figured out how to neutralize the GBBs. How difficult is it to make them airborne?"

"I think it is easier to build them from scratch," said Logrn e'Sfero.

"Let me clarify," I said. "Not for space flight but just for above ground, in the atmosphere?"

"That's easier. Especially if we keep them under a 100-meter ceiling," said Logrn e'Sfero. "Any comments, Nurvig e'Sfero or Xirxyg e'Sfero?"

"This is Xirxyg e'Sfero. That is correct—we can modify each ball within a day."

"Then we need to do that," said General Kland. "We'll have to replace ground drivers with pilots, and we have a good number of extra pilots."

"We'll begin immediately with the conversions," said Xirxyg e'Sfero.

The reinforcements of FBBs began swarming the enemy encampments at Dengholan, Sferogug, and Tandalo, with the biggest concentration of FBBs against Sferogug and Tandalo. The enemy deployed energy shields around all their strong holdings and did not suffer much damage, despite two more days of continuous attacks from our FBBs.

A new threat soon appeared. The enemy had figured out that the more intense the proton blasts, the worse for the FBBs. They teamed several of their proton guns to concentrate the blasts against one FBB at a time. The strategy worked, and we lost nineteen FBBs within hours after the enemy had begun the new strategy.

It appeared that the only advantage we had was vanishing.

Chapter 28. Destroy the Enemy

Later that day, when I returned to my suite, I found Turnd and Varna waiting for me.

"What's up, guys?" I asked amicably.

"Bovern k'Sfero has disappeared, Tim Andrus," said Turnd, shifting his weight from one foot to the other.

"What do you mean, 'disappeared,' Turnd l'Sfero?"

Varna cleared his throat. "While you were away, he volunteered to assist with a delivery of food to our front lines near western Tandalo. His convoy was ambushed by the Maggotrolls."

"Was he taken prisoner?" I asked, feeling a knot in my stomach.

"Although there were casualties, his body was not found," said Varna. "We hope he was taken prisoner."

Poor kid! He wanted so much to do his part in the war, and now he was a prisoner. I felt sad for the little Sferogyl.

After two more days of nonstop battles, my distress over our lack of progress and Bovern's abduction made me restless to do something. Although our visual information was adequate, I felt I was missing something about the field situation. I requested of General Kland, who directed me to General Lantolan, that my FBB Element be allowed into the field, and he approved it. You had to go through the chain of command, even on Nisip.

Together with Turnd l'Sfero and Varna e'Sfero, who were

itching for field operations as well, we embarked on our FBBs and flew to Sferogug. There was a constant layer of dust and smoke from FBB impacts and the firepower discharged by both sides. In the dusty atmosphere, the laser guns were almost useless, and only proton, missiles, and rail guns did any damage. We circled the battlefield from a distance for a better view, and although our forces surrounded the enemy, the Maggotrolls were well protected behind their energy shields. Our FBBs adjusted their tactics to avoid the concentrated proton blasts by moving more erratically toward their targets. Unfortunately, the FBBs bounced like ping-pong balls off the enemy energy shields when they tried to ram them.

The enemy managed to adjust its shields for maximum protection. I was sure that *Mangle*, still under repairs one million km from Nisip, had refurbished its shields to do the same. Here at the Sferogug battle, if any of the FBBs could penetrate the shields and stay inside, it would be unstoppable. I signaled my escort to circle above, while I descended to the ground level. I had only visual capability, since the onboard computer was programmed to monitor flying objects, not static ground-based weapons. From there, I flew at only a meter above the ground at the speed of sound and approached one of their proton gun emplacements.

The gunners may not have been aware of my approach, and I was too fast for them to react, while they were looking up in the sky for targets and feeling secure behind their shields. During my training, I had smashed through many barriers but never against an energy field. I was flying at the speed of sound and aiming for the ground line where their shields originated. I didn't know if I would bounce off, or if I would be spread like peanut butter inside my cockpit, but I wanted to test penetrating underground, under their shield-bubble. The dusty view around me turned dark instantly after I hit the ground. Quickly I pulled up, just to find myself coming out of the ground flying toward the sky, leaving an explosion of dust behind me.

I wasn't sure if I had hit the energy shield while underground, but I came out a good 400 meters beyond the gun emplacement. I signaled immediately to my escort to spread the word about my maneuver. Without wasting any time, I came down and flew at ground level at great speed toward the same target, and when I was near it, I slowed down to 100km/h. I punched the ground near the shield's edge, and I came up inside the shield's bubble from underground.

"Surprise, surprise, boys and girls!" I laughed. The gunners couldn't fire their proton guns at me from inside the bubble—they would have annihilated themselves. But I had the smashing power of a wrecking ball, so I destroyed the gun. The gunners were nowhere to be seen. I couldn't get out through the energy shield unless I went underground again. Instead, I decided to wait, to let the dust settle.

Energy shield tunnels connected all the gun emplacements and all their strong points, including their transport ship. I was in, like a bull in a china shop, and the best china was the transport ship, where the energy shield generator resided. I spotted the shortest distance tunnel to the transporter and gunned my FBB toward it.

It was so terrible of me (not!) that on the way to the transport ship I wrecked two more proton guns while flying supersonically at ground level. It must have sounded like hell from my speed and the sonic boom I created. I went through the ship's hull as if in a blur, and due to my antigrav engine, I stopped on a dime inside the ship. I was in a utility room of some kind, with the walls covered in multicolored conduits. Behind me was a round hole. That's where I had come from.

The dark blue and scaly interior of the ship was alien indeed, and I had to orient myself and find the generator, but I didn't know what it looked like in the first place. The Maggotrolls opened laser fire on me from three different directions, ending my wondering.

I began doing wheelies in the ship—imagine a ball bearing inside an eggshell. I popped out in several places from the ship, but I went back inside for more damage. And damage I did. Maggotrolls were exiting the ship in a panic through the holes that I created.

My wrecking continued through the hibernation chambers filled with the sarcophagi in which the colonists spent their time traveling here. Not all the sarcophagi were empty. The Maggotroll command had kept some of their crew, probably the ones incapable of fighting, in hibernation. At least they didn't suffer when my ball smashed through them.

The other FBB pilots flying above noticed what I had done and followed suit. They got in through the underground, but we had to be cautious not to smash against each other. I'm not sure who smashed the generator, but when it happened, it was as if the lights had gone off. Literally, the lights went off, and emergency lights began pulsing, intermittently illuminating the insides of the wrecked transporter.

I thought, *My job is done here*, and I propelled my FBB up through the ship's hull, the roof, and stopped at about two km up in the sky to observe the mayhem. There must have been over 200 FBBs doing a demolition derby against the enemy's ship, armored carriers, proton guns, and other weapons. There was only death and destruction down below. Vehicles and the enemy troops that survived were fanning out from the ship, running for their lives, but to no avail. The FBBs were crushing them, and the Sferogyl soldiers were cutting them down with rail-gun fire.

"Command Center, this is Tim Andrus," I opened communication after I disabled the VAL on my FBB.

"Come in, Tim Andrus," General Kland replied.

"Sferogug enemy base is in shambles."

"Acknowledge that. Well done, Tim Andrus," said General Kland.

"General Lantolan ordered to emulate your tactic at Dengholan and Tandalo. The enemy camp near Dengholan is in the process of being destroyed. The transport ship near Tandalo has been rendered inoperable as well. However, inside Tandalo, the enemy is still holding their ground."

The ground invaders were destroyed, along with all their transporters. The exception was Tandalo, still being held by the Maggotrolls. We were almost victorious.

Aside from Tandalo, we had a remaining problem.

Mangle.

Chapter 29. Space Battles

A week passed, and finally the alert was given. *Mangle* was moving toward Nisip to renew the assault. What surprised us was its appearance. *Mangle* had become three distinct warships, as the cylindrical hulls separated. Instead of one target, we were faced with three, and each one had a powerful proton cannon under its belly where the dark universe tunnel had been.

Their trajectories were aiming for Marjon, Dengholan, and Sferogug, the victorious cities. It seemed they were coming to exterminate those habitable locations, although now deserted by the Sferogyls. Three-quarters of their ground invasion force was nonexistent, and they could not conquer Nisip with the colonists left in Tandalo. Nor did they have the necessary transport ships to escape or take slaves. However, Mangle's three units were a danger. Big danger.

We were in the command center, observing and dreading what was coming our way. The large overhead display projected the trajectory of the three ships advancing toward Nisip, along with the final destinations and a time countdown to confrontations.

"General Kland," an officer said. "One of the ships has deviated from its course and is now heading for Tandalo. Marjon is no longer in danger."

"Tandalo?" I heard several officers wonder.

"That's curious," said General Kland. "Why Tandalo? It is already occupied by the Maggotrolls."

"It's coming for us," I said. We were 134 km away from Tandalo and two kilometers underground.

"They've discovered our command center location?" asked General Kland. "Nurvig e'Sfero, can they destroy us?"

"It will take 10 hours of proton blasting to destroy this center," replied Nurvig. "But after two hours, we will experience unpleasant tremors."

"Then we have two hours to destroy that ship or evacuate," said General Kland, establishing the operational timetable.

"Understood, General Kland," said General Lantolan. "We'll use eight Wings to attack them. The ship coming toward Tandalo is in the best shape, and we gave it the codename, *Mangle 1*. The ship heading for Dengholan is *Mangle 2*, and the last ship heading for Sferogug is *Mangle 3*, which is the most damaged. Three hundred fighters escort *Mangle 1*. *Mangle 2* and *3* have 200 each. They also have two frigates each."

I looked at the hologram of each ship. They were approaching with their bows down as before, except for *Mangle 3*, which was approaching with its aft. It seemed the bow of *Mangle 3* had sustained irreparable damages. "General Lantolan, can we assess how much repairing they did on *Mangle 3*?" I asked.

"Structurally very little, Tim Andrus," said General Lantolan. "The energy shields are at full power, though."

"Even in the damaged areas of the bow of number *3*?" I asked.

"I'll inquire, Tim Andrus," said General Lantolan. "They're attacking us with their best protected side. Magnify the *Mangle 3* bow." On another hologram, we saw the bow of the ship. Structural repairs were made in a hurry or not at all. We could see some of the ship's interior trusses.

"General Lantolan," said an officer. "Some of the energy shield emitters are missing and others seem to be broken."

I focused on the emitters, which looked like rivets on a steam engine, but at a larger magnification, they were in the shape of mushrooms, many of them broken. These emitters-receivers created the energy shields protecting the craft. They were in a hexagonal pattern, resembling a honeycomb, if they were not missing or broken off. Their absence made the energy shields weaker, even allowing holes in the shield. That was the ship's Achilles' heel.

"By splitting into three ships, *Mangle* has split us into three smaller forces as well," said General Lantolan, who had conferred with some of his staff. "General Kland, I request to attack the weakest ship, *Mangle 3*, with six Wings, and *Mangle 2*, with two Wings. Leave *Mangle 1* for last."

General Kland exchanged communicating whistles with some of his staff. They all seemed to be in agreement. "General Lantolan, attack as requested. Prepare to relocate to our secondary command center. Nurvig e'Sfero, maintain the same level of energy in this center to disguise our move."

"General Kland, General Lantolan, I request to be airborne with the Special Forces," I asked.

"Considering the progress you've made in the battle of Sferogug, Tim Andrus, your request is granted," said General Kland.

"I agree, Tim Andrus," said General Lantolan. "Would you like the leadership of the Special Forces?"

"Thank you, General Lantolan, but I prefer to operate independently with my Element."

"Request granted, Tim Andrus," said General Lantolan.

Everyone in the command center began departing for the secondary location, which was a more decentralized center than the current command center. I departed for my FBB at one of the underground bases, where I would join Turnd and Varna. Anu had said not to fight, but I had already disregarded that advice. Besides, I was perfectly safe inside my ball.

On my way to the base, I kept an eye on the situation in the sky. *Mangle 3* approached Sferogug without any visible opposition from us until it reached 1,000 km from Nisip. From below, 1,500 FBBs advanced vertically in a corkscrew formation of 15 km in diameter. The Maggotrolls were surprised the first time by our ring formation, and we hoped they would be surprised again as we spiraled toward *Mangle 3*, while the ship was inside our corkscrew. Its 200 fighters and two frigates seemed to be overwhelmed by a spiral of 1,500 balls from hell, but it began firing randomly with proton blasts at the FBBs.

The fighters had their missile launchers replaced with proton guns, which were almost the length of the fighters. They had learned that missiles were not effective against the small, erratically flying balls. Now, the fighters had four proton guns, and they were firing madly at every FBB they encountered, but for the time being without much impact. The lack of casualties against the FBBs was odd, considering that each fighter could shoot four proton jets against a single FBB. They didn't concentrate their four proton guns on a single target, as the ground fighters found to be effective against the balls. Could that have been for lack of energy?

Mangle 3 joined in with its guns, trying to destroy our FBBs. They knocked a few out of their formation, but those FBBs quickly joined back in at the end of the spiral. The enemy's firepower lasted briefly as the corkscrew passed by *Mangle 3* in less than a second.

The last FBB at the bottom of the corkscrew changed direction on a dime and dove toward the bow of the ship, followed by the next one on the spiral. They might have expected a swarm attack against their hulls, but the FBBs attacked sequentially on the weakened ship's bow. When 1,500 FBBs hit the same spot on the shield, inside *Mangle 3* it must have felt like a continuous jackhammering for a few seconds. By hitting the same spot, the emitters in that area would overheat from the energy drawn by the field and eventually fail. The continuous impacts caused a permanent plasma cloud around that area. *Mangle 3* took evasive maneuvers and its fighters came after the FBBs. By the end of the fourth second and 1,000 FBB blows, the weakened shield cracked and a wave of FBBs broke through, but they were stopped by a secondary energy shield, which didn't last, and hundreds of FBBs penetrated the bow of *Mangle 3*.

Just as the last FBB exited through other sections of the ship's hull, *Mangle 3* came apart. Large pieces of the ship surrounded by smaller debris ejected in all directions, and a dust cloud obscured for a moment the spot where *Mangle 3* once was.

It was a surprisingly easy victory.

I was in orbit below the dismantled ship, and my Element raced immediately to *Mangle 2*. When we arrived, 500 FBBs were attacking *Mangle 2*. This ship had one wound in the middle of the hull, the perceived weak spot in their shield. *Mangle 2* held, and it concentrated several turret laser guns at one time on the same attacking FBB. They had destroyed seven FBBs already. The FBBs regrouped and attacked again in the harpoon formation from both sides of the hull. They didn't crack the shield, and we lost four more FBBs.

After *Mangle 3*'s demise, almost 1,500 FBBs joined in attacking *Mangle 2*. Less than 200 fighters and the two frigates joined the fighters from *Mangle 2* for its defense. Their strategy was to scatter the FBBs and prevent them from striking the ship in concentrated attacks. The four frigates stood at a distance and took orchestrated proton shots at the FBBs, destroying many of them.

Mangle 2 must have sent a distress call, because soon 300 fighters from *Mangle 1* joined in the fight. Still, the enemy fighters were outnumbered almost three to one by the FBBs, and instead of firing their four proton guns on each FBB, the fighters kept firing single shots. That may have been due to the proton supply available for their guns. That was good for us, and so far there were no casualties among the FBBs from the fighters. Consequently, many enemy fighters were smashed. Several hundred FBBs, not involved in crashing the fighters, assembled in tight formations and attacked *Mangle 2* with a renewed effort.

As the fighting formation orbited Nisip, a signal was given by the central command to clear the area around *Mangle 2*. The operational ground super proton cannon fired, but incredibly, *Mangle 2* held—but just barely, judging by the diminution of the reactant plasma cloud. The window of opportunity to fire on *Mangle 2* passed as the planet rotated, but the guns took a last salvo at the enemy frigates, and two of them blew up. The big cannon from the surface did a good job this time. *Mangle 2* was left with only two frigates to defend it.

Our FBB forces regrouped and renewed their attack on *Mangle 2*. The situation had improved for our side in the battle against *Mangle 2*, so I decided to check on *Mangle 1*. My Element of three FBBs arrived twenty minutes later where *Mangle 1* was orbiting. There were only a handful of fighters and two frigates serving as escorts. My onboard computer displayed orange vectors of possible attack paths against the few enemy craft. At the moment, we were outnumbered, and so I proceeded cautiously, checking the purple and violet vectors of incoming fighters and possible proton blasts from the frigates. The laser shots from the fighters that hit me, which I never saw coming were identified as buzz saw sounds by the onboard computer. The longer the buzzing, the worse for my FBB. I had to get immediately out of the fighters' tracking and firing, and my erratic and random movement accomplished that.

Mangle 1 opened fire on Nisip with the massive proton cannon at its bow. The blast hit the ground at the spot where our command center was suspected to be. A massive crater was left behind, and some of the ejected rocks from the blast reached orbit. At that rate, it would take less than 10 hours to blast a hole down to the command center. But I could be wrong; as the hole got deeper, there was more dirt to dislodge.

The enemy realized that they were six fighters and two frigates against three FBBs, so they advanced toward us with confidence. The prudent choice for us was to retreat, but we took too long to make that decision and found ourselves encircled by them. Although there were only six fighters attacking us, they did not approach us head on, but they looped around us, while firing their lasers and proton guns. They split into three pairs, attacking each one of us, and by luck or planning or a correction of their proton supplies, each fighter began firing all four proton guns at once, although at less intervals between shots. They definitely had a proton supply or energy problem. We began taking dramatic maneuvers and making erratic movements to avoid the blasts. My computer was displaying pulsating purple vectors, the possible firing directions from each fighter that engaged me, and I found myself on the defensive. My cockpit buzzed repeatedly from laser hits, and the continuing sounds of hail striking a tin roof told me when I was being hit by proton blasts as well. Occasionally, blue filaments of electricity dissipated in the cockpit when my FBB was exposed to prolonged proton blasts. I felt as if I was inside a toaster with bad short circuits.

Mangle 1's turret guns on its hull were blasting at us with a complete disregard for its few fighters' safety. Soon enough, several of the laser guns from *Mangle 1* hit one of its fighters when, by chance, Varna moved out of the way just in time. My onboard computer flew in the most erratic fashion it could manage, and I saw two fighters chasing me. Dumb shits! I reversed instantly and one of them rear-ended me. Needless to say, my busting ball won, and the fighter's debris flew by.

There were only four fighters remaining, and instead of harassing us, they regrouped. The three of us were in the center, the four fighters were at twelve o'clock, and a frigate each was at four o'clock and at eight o'clock. According to my computer, the enemy fired all their proton guns in unison and hit Turnd dead center. His FBB disintegrated from the impact of two-dozen proton blasts. I took instant evasive action so as not to be the next victim, but Varna flew head on to the nearest fighter and obliterated it. He must have been mad at seeing his friend, Turnd, die; instead of retreating, he attacked the fighters ferociously.

The enemy discovered how to destroy us—via concentrated and massive proton fire—and we couldn't survive by just taking evasive actions. I joined Varna and went on the attack.

Mangle 1's big proton cannon hit the planet again. To my surprise, the remaining three fighters turned tail and ran back home to *Mangle 1*, while the other two frigates fired on us. Varna and I followed the fleeing fighters. To allow the three fighters inside *Mangle 1*, the ship had to open its shields. And we hoped to follow them in, on their tails. The three fighters fired their rear rail guns and lasers at us, while their atomic propulsion engines were at full power to distance themselves from us, but there was not enough time to accelerate away. We went through the opening in the energy shield together with them. It happened in an instant. We were in, and heading for the hull.

Unfortunately, not so.

Mangle 1 had another plan for us. The fighters didn't turn off their energy shields and smashed into the inner secondary shield. The fighters bounced back and forth between the fields, turning into shredded metal. A few milliseconds later, we smashed in the shield as well, and bounced back and hit the interior wall of the outer shield, but unlike the unfortunate fighter pilots, our gravity shells in conjunction with the active VAL protected us. Needless to say, this happened so fast that my computer took care of the flying. We were trapped between two energy shields and in trouble.

Mangle 1 had another surprise in store for us. It deployed proton guns on its turrets, most likely of the same power that the fighters had. When a gun—proton, plasma or laser—is fired, the shields must be opened to allow the beam to go through, otherwise the blast will be redirected against the ship. *Mangle 1* was determined to kill us by blasting their newly deployed turret proton guns and holding the outer shield closed, even at the risk of damaging their own outer shield emitters. It was like shooting fish in a barrel, and we were the fish. Even if we didn't take a direct hit, the protons between the two shields would accumulate, bounce around, and slow us down, eventually making it even easier for them to blast us.

The two of us began a rapid and random motion inside our encapsulation, as if we were electrons around an atom's nucleus. *Mangle 1* was the nucleus, and it wanted to transform us into quarks. That thought caused different colors to flash before my eyes and it left a bad taste in my mouth. We began an agonizing minute of random bouncing, getting buzzed by lasers and grazed by occasional proton blasts, which ozonized the air inside my ball.

I felt as if my luck had run out. Would Anu be able to resurrect me? He had told me not to fight!

Mangle 1's massive proton cannon fired again just as I was coming toward the jet. Going through it was instant obliteration, and I was flying too fast even for my computer to react and stop.

Chapter 30. Hell in Space

God was with me. At the last moment, as if in a dream, I stopped in front of the deadly proton jet, which the onboard computer was indicating was there. From the corner of my eye, I saw on a screen the inner energy shield ocular opened around the proton jet. Without any more deliberation, I turned full speed toward the ship, squeezing between the proton jet and the shield's rim.

I made it to the other side of the second shield and didn't even stop to thank God, but I continued at full speed parallel to the proton jet toward *Mangle 1*. The proton blast stopped just before I punctured through the hull near the nozzle, blasting debris down the cannon's barrel. I deviated my trajectory slightly and began crashing through the acceletron's electromagnetic helical coils wrapped around the cannon's barrel, until I blasted right through the proton generator and continued traveling along the longitudinal center of the craft, smashing into other machinery and equipment that I couldn't identify.

I tried to keep a high speed, busting through bulkheads, storage compartments, and equipment of any kind that stood in my way. Sparks and explosions and steam and escaping gas and round holes were left behind me. My FBB cancelled any noise from the impacts, and I was glad about that, because otherwise I would have gone deaf and then would have had to file a report with the galactic OSHA. However, the inside of the ship was not made of sand, but hard alloys. At times, I just crawled through some of the bulkheads. Furthermore, the ship's internal gravity robbed some of Nisip's gravity, and I couldn't accelerate as much.

Inside, the Maggotrolls were running for their lives, as a meter-and-a-half ball busted through walls or speeded up through the corridors. There was artificial gravity inside the ship, judging by the curving cross-corridors, but it didn't much matter if I rolled on flat corridors on the longitudinal axis of the ship or on the bending corridors across the ship. I accelerated when rolling in corridors and slowed down when I hit metal and composites, whether they were bulkheads or agglomerations of tubes, cargo, weapons, stuff, or machines, which packed the inside of the ship.

Occasionally, I was shot at with laser fire, but they were handheld devices unable to singe my FBB. When some stupid or desperate Maggotrolls stood their ground, as if their armor would have made a difference, I ran over them, like a bowling ball blasting pins in all directions, and turned them into minced meat. The smarter ones got out of the way and then chased me while firing their lasers down the corridors or in the newly created corridors I had just made. Hatches were closing frantically to stabilize the internal atmosphere in the over two-kilometer-long vessel. I'm sure I punctured the hull in so many places that the gases were leaking in space from many parts of the hull. This was the way to kill the monster—from inside.

And then something unexpected happened.

A giant flash engulfed me.

The holographic displays inside my ball went dark, even my energy shield helmet became opaque, protecting my eyes from instant blindness. A tremendous noise reverberated through the walls of my ball and deafened me, in spite of the noise-cancelling protection. The temperature was rising fast, and I became weightless. That was as bad as it could get, and I hoped that my antigrav engine was not fried. Before I could figure out what to do, the power came back on in fits and starts until it stabilized. The temperature normalized. The displays, one by one, came alive, showing me the outside images. *Mangle 1* was no more. I remained, which was good, at the center of what must have been an explosion.

A big explosion.

I was a bit stunned but fine, not believing that I was alive. I regained my calm and my wits, and thanked Sferogyl technology for having helped me survive a neutron explosion or something similar, judging by the outside radiation readings. I must have busted one of the ship's neutron magazines. Once free from the energy encapsulation, the densely packed neutrons escaped. Although it didn't feel like a lot of time had passed since I had gotten in, I must have wrecked the inside of the ship for 14 minutes, just enough time for the neutrons to decay into protons, electrons, and neutrinos. The result: The ship was pulverized in the process.

Varna survived as well, hanging around nearby, sending me signals, and inquiring about my status. One enemy frigate was dead, although intact, orbiting with no visible energy left in it. The explosion probably short-circuited its power banks. But the other frigate survived and decided to challenge us head on, firing its bow proton guns, a dozen missiles, and several laser guns at us. We flew toward the frigate in a line formation, dodging the missiles, lasers, and protons. I was leading, with Varna behind me.

Nevertheless, many blasts ricocheted off us, and a few seconds later, the bow's pinchers flanked us. At that worst possible time, my FBB experienced intermittent power shortages, and I feared the loss of my antigrav protection, expecting either to bounce away, rejected by the frigate's energy shield, or get smashed to a pulp from the negative inertia upon impact. But I plowed right smack into the middle of the frigate's 'mouth,' its bow.

The frigate's energy shields must have been down. Varna's FBB went through the hull right behind me, and we came out of the frigate from different sections of its body.

We had killed the frigate. It was dead, but it did not explode. It kept going on its trajectory like a dead fish, tumbling slowly, and occasionally blue arcs escaping from its hull. Whatever one of us had hit, it was deadly for the 106-meter-long frigate. The ship had no power, and the interior atmosphere gushed out into space, carrying with it unidentifiable stuff and even bodies. I wondered if there were survivors and if they were in safe compartments or even escape pods. There was nothing I could do for them at the moment, and no pods launched out from the frigate.

I signaled to Varna with color pulses, and together we flew back to *Mangle 2*'s battle. The fight was going on, and to my disappointment, the enemy fighters had reorganized and ganged up on one FBB at the time, blasting it with all their proton guns. The debris were strewn in an immense area, pieces of broken fighters and lifeless FBBs cracked like broken eggs. Light signals received by my computer informed me that there were as many as 400 FBBs destroyed.

The enemy had two frigates left intact and almost 400 fighters. I wasn't sure if our FBBs and perhaps even the enemy fighters were aware that *Mangle 1* had blown up, but I'm sure *Mangle 2*'s command knew it, and they opened proton fire on Dengholan. I signaled to our FBBs that *Mangle 1* was destroyed, and the good news seemed to reinvigorate their assault on *Mangle 2*.

My light signals attracted the attention of two enemy fighters, who attacked Varna and me. One of the enemy fighters forgot to get out of the way, and Varna's FBB shattered it. I checked to see if the pilot was smashed like a bug on the front of Varna's ball, but there was no trace of him. I chased the other enemy fighter, and I was surprised when it fired the proton guns backward at me. Not only had they replaced the missile launchers with proton guns, but also the guns were bidirectional. There were very few fighters engaging us head on, but they were able to outrun us, and they kept on firing proton and lasers at us, no matter if they were attacking us or fleeing.

Our FBBs kept making new formations and attacking *Mangle 2*. It was just a matter of time before we would destroy it, but in the meanwhile, it was blasting Dengholan with proton jets from its massive cannon, while we were taking casualties from the fighters and frigates. Varna and I went straight to the vicinity of the proton cannon's discharge opening, waiting for an opportunity to sneak in through the oculus in the energy shield. *Mangle 2*'s command spotted us, and they were not going to make the same mistake as *Mangle 1*. The enemy command dispatched as many fighters as they could spare against us. We must have drawn ten fighters each, firing their proton and laser guns at us in unison. It was getting "hot," and we had to take quick evasive actions to prevent our annihilation.

Whenever we were away from the big proton cannon's discharge tunnel, *Mangle 2* fired at Dengholan. We were in a bind. We had to fly constantly around that area to prevent the cannon from firing, while at the same time moving superfast to avoid the fighters and *Mangle*'s turret gunfire. We were joined by other FBBs trying to protect us, and soon there was a storm of hundreds of FBBs and enemy fighters, firing, dodging, chasing, and smashing around the bow of *Mangle 2*. The ship's big cannon blasts stopped, but not for long, and it restarted firing its cannon regardless of who was in front of the proton blast, destroying its fighters and FBBs alike.

It was hell in space.

Soon I realized that the fighters formed an orbiting ring around the proton exit area. We charged ahead, smashing as many as we could. It was a dangerous gamble, as some of us would pass through the proton tunnel of death. Every time I found myself going through that zone, I prayed the gun wouldn't fire right then, but I was lucky only so many times.

It fired and grazed my rear, while pulverizing everyone following behind me. It was a horrific experience, as the entire cockpit crackled with blue electric tendrils, zapping me, too. My FBB was infused with quadrillions of quadrillions of protons, which were hungry for many more quadrillions of quadrillions of electrons. And the electrons did not wait for a second invitation. They migrated from all my systems to join the protons, creating new atoms of hydrogen. My ball vented those gases, thank God, because it would only take a spark to cause a hydrogen-oxygen explosion in the cockpit.

I found myself in a blackout. My displays were blank again and I couldn't see out, and even if I could, it wouldn't do me any good. I didn't have control of my FBB. I didn't know if my ball's VAL was active, giving me some protection in case I impacted something. Until my neutron generator recharged my electrical batteries, I was a sitting duck. Not sitting, actually, but drifting into deep space at thousands of kilometers per hour. My destiny was either being blasted by the enemy's proton or laser fire, crashing on Nisip, or getting lost in space. In any case, time was not on my side. If I reached the point of no return, I wouldn't be able to use Nisip's gravity anymore to pull me back in. But I was a god. I should be able to perform a miracle.

I shouted, "Let there be light!"

To my astonishment, my FBB came back to life and I regained full control again. Coincidence, or my godly powers? I'll leave that for another day to ponder.

I returned at full speed and smashed into *Mangle 2*'s force field. I bounced back, just to see two fighters blasting me from opposite directions. I didn't have time to teach them a lesson, and so I flew back into the storm of craft in the big proton cannon's discharge area, joining the mad wasp dance going around. I didn't know if the fighter pilots had been told why they were there, but they hung around while slowly dying from us smashing them. At the same time, the Sferogyl soldiers around Dengholan were dying, too, from *Mangle 2*'s massive cannon proton blasts. I was fairly sure that Varna knew how I had gotten through the force field of *Mangle 1*. However, the other FBB pilots did not know, and we did not have time to send communication codes with the information.

Varna was flying close when the cannon opened fire again. He was in the right location and squeezed in along the proton beam. He got into the gun's muzzle, and then the proton cannon blasted again. I saw Varna's FBB disintegrate in an explosion that ripped the gun's muzzle apart.

Varna was dead.

The explosion blew a hole in the force field, and several dozen FBBs, along with me, took advantage of that and rushed in. We began putting holes in *Mangle 2*. It didn't explode like *Mangle 1*, but it lost its energy shields shortly after that, and the rest of the FBBs around the hull attacked like piranhas, leaving parts and pieces—not to mention Maggotroll bodies—where *Mangle 2* once was. Hard cheese, I'd say, for *Mangle 2*. After we were finished with it, it resembled Swiss cheese for sure.

The remaining enemy fighters—perhaps 300 of them and soldiers in escape pods and one frigate—fled the scene, landing in the Tandalo area, taking refuge with the remaining soldiers and mercenaries on the ground.

We had won the war. It was the end of the Maggotrolls' invasion, at a cost of millions of lives on both sides. Even more painful were the deaths of my friends, Varna and Turnd. It was a bittersweet victory. We were so close to ending this war, but my Sferogyl friends died in the last minutes of battle. Sadness overcame me. I would miss them.

Chapter 31. Undorkhan the Brute

After I landed back at my base, cheering Sferogyls surrounded me, lifted me up in the air on their thin arms, and paraded me around. In their minds, I had delivered them from slavery. Kegs of beer were uncorked, and everyone drank and cried and cheered and drank some more.

Later on, I checked my FBB, thankful that it had protected me so well. Besides scratches and pits from the lasers, it had a black gash where the big cannon's protons had hit me. The ball was operational, but I couldn't imagine it being shielded in that area any more.

After the obligatory second round of several steins of beer, I left the happy-crying party and returned to the command center. General Kland and Logrn e'Sfero burst into tears when they saw me. It was emotional. They had known Varna and Turnd since they were children, growing up in the same pod. I told them how they had perished as heroes, and they cried again, and to my surprise, they went down on their knees and kissed my hands in appreciation for what I had done for them.

However, there was another ground battle to be won in Tandalo, and we returned to our tasks in the command center.

Jurmalan m'Sfero, a soldier, was assigned as my security detail. When he saw me, he went down on one knee. "It is an honor to serve you, Tim Andrus."

"Thank you, Jurmalan m'Sfero. At ease, soldier," I told him.

"First, I need to find a young Sferogyl, and for that I need a vehicle to go to the Tandalo front."

He saluted and took off to requisition the vehicle.

In the meantime, I issued a request to locate any Sferogyls who had witnessed Bovern's abduction in the western Tandalo battle zone, and I received information about a few soldiers who had witnessed the ambush. Without delay, Jurmalan and I jumped into the manually driven ground vehicle he had acquired, which resembled a bobsled on five pairs of fat wheels capable of accommodating four Sferogyls. The vehicle could be driven from any of the passengers' seats, and I sat in the front for a clear view, while Jurmalan drove from the seat behind me.

Although the common method for Sferogyls to travel was underground, there weren't any underground roads leading to the front lines, so we followed a dirt path made by previous vehicles. As we approached the front lines, we could hear occasional explosions and the whooshing of missiles or FBBs. The closer we got to the fighting, the more the landscape changed for the worse. The ground was puckered with craters from explosions and had long black lines of singed earth from the laser fires. Carcasses of armored vehicles lay discarded like turtles all around us. Piles of charred Maggotroll bodies piled up here and there. The stench of dead and scorched bodies, burned craft, and spilled chemicals was overpowering. The Sferogyls set on fire many of the dead Maggotrolls to prevent the spread of diseases, and plumes of acrid black smoke polluted the sky.

We passed a GBB that seemed to have exploded from the inside, probably caused by proton blasts. Occasionally, the power generator in some wrecked vehicle was either smoldering with black toxic smoke or spraying blue tendrils of electricity in the air or on the ground. A crashed enemy fighter nearby, with its proton tubes pointing toward the sky, resembled an antiaircraft gun. The battle had never stopped and continued around the clock all around us.

We arrived at the rear of the front line. Jurmalan asked for the location of the soldiers who had witnessed the ambush, and he drove in the direction given.

When we arrived there, the soldiers recognized me, as all the Sferogyls would, and each went down on one knee. "It is an honor to meet you, Tim Andrus," they said as one. They were dusty, bloody, and haggard on their return from battle.

"Thank you. At ease, soldiers," I said. "I came to talk to you about Bovern k'Sfero. Anyone knew him or saw what happened to him?"

"Yes, I know Bovern k'Sfero, Tim Andrus," said one of the soldiers. "He volunteered to help with the supply convoy to the southwestern front line."

"But Bovern k'Sfero is a kid," I said.

"He volunteered. No one forced him, Tim Andrus."

"That's true." I sighed. "Tell me what happened when the convoy was ambushed?"

"The route the convoy took was secure, far behind the rear lines. Out of nowhere, several Maggotrolls opened fire on the convoy. We don't know if the Maggotrolls were advanced scouts or lost in battle, but after killing our soldiers in the convoy, they ordered the civilian volunteers to drive the trucks to their lines."

I looked intently at the soldier.

"Bovern was not among the dead ones," he said.

"Then Bovern could be alive." I was hopeful.

"The Maggotrolls did not release the names of any prisoners," said Jurmalan. "As far as we know, they don't even want to talk to us."

"Where are the Sferogyl prisoners being held?"

"In the center of the city, last I heard."

"Maybe the Maggotrolls think that'd be the only chance to survive, by taking hostages," I speculated.

"I don't know, Tim Andrus," said the soldier.

"Have we taken Maggotroll prisoners recently, soldier?"

"Yes, two days ago, we took one prisoner, Tim Andrus. He was flying low in a shuttle and we shot him down. We took him alive."

"Where is he being held? I need to talk to him."

"I can take you there."

"Soldier, you just came from battle. You need to rest."

"It's all right, it's on my way, Tim Andrus." The other soldiers voiced their eagerness to accompany us there for protection.

We followed them through newly dug underground tunnels, passing by a field hospital where the injured were treated. I'd seen the battles, the killings, and the wounded on holo-displays, but seeing the wounded in flesh and blood, a lot of dark-red blood and cracked shells, was unsettling. As I passed by the ones who could talk, each thanked me for saving their people, and I thanked each one of them for their valor.

Captain Rezekne l'Sfero saluted smartly, and he took me immediately to the enemy prisoner camp to see this new Maggotroll prisoner by the name of Undorkhan. Although I knew what the Maggotrolls looked like, seeing them in person, they were downright intimidating—tall, bulky, and ferocious-looking. The Sferogyls kept them in cells cut out of the stone along tunnels. From behind thick bars, the prisoners gave me murderous or curious looks as I passed by. They probably hadn't ever seen anyone like me, pale and with a head full of dark hair, and they wondered what I was. In spite of my greater strength, super-duper suit, and instant blades coming out of my suit, I was glad they were behind those bars.

"That is Undorkhan, Tim Andrus." Captain Rezekne pointed to a mean looking, giant Maggotroll dressed in brown fatigues. He must have been at least two-and-a-half meters tall and almost one meter wide at the shoulders. His hair was orange and spiky in two manes on his flat, baldhead, as all Maggotrolls were bald from the forehead to the back of the neck. His electronic studs were removed from his earlobes, showing just black holes.

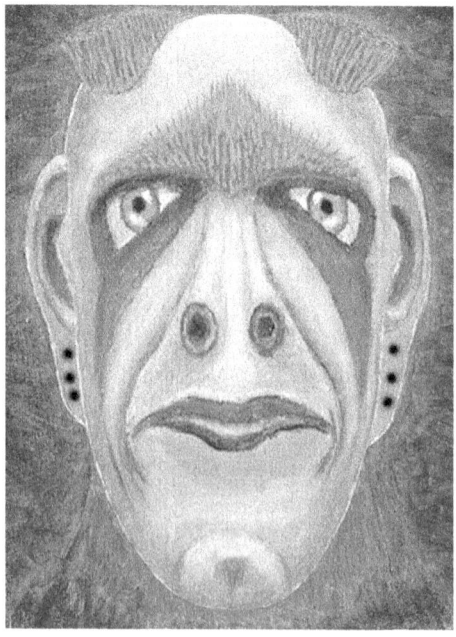

He was alone in his cell and held on to the bars, staring at me with narrow, mean eyes from under his orange unibrow. Frankly, considering his light-blue skin color, even darker blue shadows under his orangey eyes, and dark blue lips, he looked like a beast. Political correct not.

"I'd like to talk to him, Captain Rezekne l'Sfero."

"Certainly, Tim Andrus." Captain Rezekne took me closer to his cell. The cell's five-centimeter-thick bars were reassuring. I sensed that Undorkhan felt superior and wouldn't volunteer any answers to my questions.

"From what hole did you crawl out of?" Undorkhan asked in a deep voice. "You're no Sferogyl, unless you've lost a lot of weight and grew a neck." I heard some chuckles from nearby prisoners.

"My name is Tim Andrus, and I came here to ask you some questions," I said calmly.

"What kind of ugly species are you?" Undorkhan asked disgustedly followed by a malodor of decaying flesh emanating from his breath. Suddenly his appearance changed; his eyes widened, and as if coming to a realization, he said, "The rumor among the blimps is that they have a god among them. Are you that one? You don't look like much of a big shit."

"Maybe I am that one."

"Yeah. Easy to pretend you're a god when I'm behind these bars. I bet you'd shit like any other hominid if I got my arms around and squeeze you."

"I want information about Tandalo."

He spat dark-blue phlegm in my direction. His eyes narrowed again, probably to scare me. What kind of god would I be if I were scared of him? I had to prove myself to myself. And to him.

"Captain Rezekne l'Sfero, I'd like to step inside his cell and have a face-to-face chat with this prisoner."

"Tim Andrus, this is not advisable. He's twice your weight."

"I'd say more like four times, but that won't be an issue." I said all that without taking my eyes from the brute. He didn't blink. I winked at him. I hoped that confused him regarding my intentions. He pulled his head back slightly, the corners of his lips bent down in disgust.

Captain Rezekne l'Sfero spoke into his communicator, and half a dozen soldiers came running, armed with energy blasters.

"Tim Andrus, please change your mind. He is dangerous."

"Don't worry. I take full responsibility. Please open the gate."

"Prisoner Undorkhan, step to the back of the cell, sit down facing the wall with your hands on your head," ordered Captain Rezekne l'Sfero, raising his gun.

"With pleasure, Captain." Undorkhan retreated with a satisfied smirk on his face and sat down as instructed.

The soldiers kept their guns trained on Undorkhan, not believing that they'd see Tim Andrus go in with that monster. Captain Rezekne pressed a button on a box around his belt, and the iron bars parted in half, allowing me to walk in. The bars slammed behind me after I was in.

In the blink of an eye, Undorkhan jumped up and twisted in the air to face me. His tubular nostrils flared with loathing, anticipating the kill. His eyes were on fire with hatred and, at the same time, disbelief at seeing me alone with him in the cell. The other Maggotrolls who could see us began shouting encouragement for him to rip my head off and shove it somewhere.

"In my world, we shake hands when we meet someone. What do you do on Vestrallum?" I asked coolly.

"We pound people into the ground." He charged at me headfirst like a bull.

Time slowed down, and I saw him as if he were moving in slow motion toward me. Was my fear giving me the impression of time slowing down, or was it my bionanobots? There wasn't any time to solve that mystery, so I extended my right arm and punched him in his hairless forehead with my fist.

Undorkhan's body—actually, his head first and then the rest of him—was propelled backward. The back of his head reached the wall first, while his feet were last. He came down and lay at the bottom of the wall like a giant brown burlap sack.

I looked at my fist with satisfaction. He weighted 400 kilos easily, and he lay in a lump. That much power wasn't mine. That had to be the bionanobots, or maybe my suit. Or my telekinetic powers. It was good to be a god.

There was total silence in the prison corridor, and I turned around to see what had happened. The other prisoners who could see us stared with their mouths open. The Sferogyl guards lowered their guns and gaped as well. Jurmalan looked amazed. I supposed, after what they had just witnessed, the myths about me would expand exponentially.

The first sound I heard came from Undorkhan, who was bleeding from the back of his head, blue blood trickling down around his neck. The wall was smeared with blue blood as well. I pushed him with my foot, and he rolled onto his back. My four knuckles were imprinted on his forehead in dark blue dents. He opened his eyes and slowly focused on me, trying to make sense of what had happened.

"It would have been a lot easier to shake hands," I told him, cracking my knuckles.

"Wha-, wha-, what in hell happened?" He looked around, disoriented.

"Instead, you preferred to pound me into the ground. Did you enjoy it as much as I did?" I lifted him up and sat him against the wall. I pulled up a stool and sat down in front of him. "Shall we talk?"

Chapter 32. Undorkhan the Canary

I was hoping that he would sing like a canary, but instead the dumb brute lunged at me again. This species was slow to learn and required another lesson. I obliged him and pounded on his head, using my other fist like a hammer. He leaned backward against the wall, lost consciousness, and then began sliding sideways into a gravity-friendly position. I turned and looked at Captain Rezekne, shrugging as if in disbelief at what had just happened. Judging by his smirk, Captain Rezekne seemed to appreciate the pounding Undorkhan received.

I grabbed a clay carafe from a shelf and poured water over his face. He woke, groaned, and slowly pushed himself up into a sitting position. He touched the back of his head and saw the blood on his hand. He then touched the top of his head, where a bump was growing like a volcano, and moaned. That brought him back to his senses. He looked at me with fear and hatred.

"Let's not repeat that, as I may kill you next time," I said in a gentle voice.

He nodded. Potential death restored him to reason.

I sat down on the stool. "What is your rank?"

"Colonel."

"Military or mercenary?"

"Military."

"Are there mercenaries in Tandalo?"

"Most of the invasion force."

"How many?"

Undorkhan hesitated. I raised my right fist.

"Eight hundred thousand."

"Tell me about the Sferogyl hostages."

"What?"

"How many are they, where are they, and are they kept in fair conditions?"

"Yes, they are kept in fair conditions. We have over 130,000 of them. We keep them in that ball building, the Assembly House."

"Did you identify them, register them?"

"We ID them with a number, painted on their bellies and backs."

"Are there any kids among the prisoners?"

"Kids?"

"Young ones, smaller ones," I clarified.

"There are smaller ones." He paused, as if thinking. "There was a small one we caught recently. Some of us wanted to use it as a ball."

I felt my blood pressure rising and had to control myself from not ripping his head off so I could use his skull as a ball.

"But mature Sferogyls rose to protect him," he added quickly, noticing my change in mood. "We had to shoot some of them to quiet them down. Afterward, we stopped. Dead Sferogyls are not worth anything."

"Do you know his name?"

Undorkhan shook his head. "We don't care about their names. We ID them with numbers, like I said."

There was a good chance that it was Bovern, I thought. "What do you intend to do with the prisoners?"

"We hold them for ransom."

"What do you want?"

"Let us go."

"Go where?"

"Away from here."

"Do you realize that all the Maggotroll transporters were destroyed?"

"*Mangle* is out there."

"*Mangle* has been destroyed, too."

"No!" he said incredulously. His eyes opened round, shocked by the news.

"You were taken prisoner before *Mangle* returned to face its demise. Only a few fighters and their pilots survived."

Undorkhan dropped his head into his hands. "We're stranded here."

"For at least one-and-a-half years," I said. "Holding out will not help you anymore. You must surrender."

"And what will the Sferogyls do to us?"

"If the Maggotroll Empire wants to rescue you, they'll have to pay for the death and damage you caused, and send transport ships to bring you back."

Undorkhan sighed. "If *Mangle* was destroyed, we'll have to start negotiations. But that's not up to me."

"But it can be," I said. "You can open the communications with your higher command."

"I'll do what I can." He looked at me as if he were seeing me for the first time. "So it is true. You're the god the prisoners were whispering about."

"Maybe."

"It's our bad luck that you came to their defense," said Undorkhan bitterly.

"What can I say? There is a god after all." I stood up. "Who's your commander?"

"Orbyzykhan the Great."

Interesting—Anu had mentioned that name before. "I'll leave you in the good hands of Capitan Rezekne l'Sfero. And do the right thing—convince your Orbyzykhan the Great to open a dialog."

I had gotten what I wanted, so I left. On my way out, I passed near a cell, and an even bigger Maggotroll, but dumber, tried to grab me by the throat. He howled like a beast in distress when I pulled his arm out of his shoulder socket. That was for them trying to use Bovern as a ball.

Once outside, I opened a communication channel. "General Kland l'Sfero, this is Tim Andrus. I think I convinced one of the Maggotrolls, Colonel Undorkhan, to help us open communications with the enemy."

"Outstanding," the general said. "Hopefully, we'll be able to stop the bloodshed."

"There is another thing, General Kland. I think Bovern may be among the prisoners."

"Good, good, Tim Andrus. How are the prisoners being treated?"

"Supposedly well. They are being kept in the Assembly House."

"In the center of Tandalo."

"Are there any tunnels that reach that structure?"

"I'm looking at a map. Yes, there are tunnels, but they lead to other structures. None to the outside of the capital."

"How about the pillars around it? Isn't the structure surrounded by four pillars, which support the ceiling?"

"I don't understand, Tim Andrus. They're solid rock."

"Could your people quietly core a shaft from the top through the center of one of them to reach the hostages?"

"I'll have to ask Logrn e'Sfero. I'll get back to you, Tim Andrus."

If the Sferogyls could excavate a shaft and reach inside the Assembly House, we might be able to rescue the hostages—of course, without alerting the Maggotrolls, as we'd jackhammer the solid rock.

On our way back to the command center, Logrn contacted me. "Tim Andrus, we would be able to dig a hole at the center of the western pillar by using acid and then vacuuming the sand left behind. It will be a slow process, but it would be a quiet process."

"Thank you, Logrn e'Sfero. But wait, I just realized this—why wouldn't you use a GBB?"

"Of course. You're right. We'll look into that digging possibility."

232

Back at the command center, I found out that the Maggotrolls were receptive to starting a dialog. Now would come the lengthy negotiations, while we dug the shaft to rescue the hostages. Or so I thought, until Glave o'Sfero contacted me.

"Tim Andrus, the Maggotroll command is ready to talk, and they want you to conduct the negotiations."

"Me? How do they know about me, Glave o'Sfero?"

"Somehow they found out about you, and they would feel reassured if a god negotiated with them in good faith, Tim Andrus."

"Sure. I'll be glad to help. When do we start?"

"As soon as you get to Tandalo."

"To Tandalo?" I said, disbelieving. "Glave o'Sfero, are you saying that they want me among them?"

"Yes, Tim Andrus, that's what they said." Glave o'Sfero cleared his throat. "And here is the bad, or good, news. They told us they have Bovern."

Chapter 33. Start of Negotiations

"That's good news," I said happily. "Glave o'Sfero, do you know if he's well?"

"They said he's well, Tim Andrus."

"How did they find out that it was Bovern I was interested in?"

"As you requested, Undorkhan contacted the higher command to open negotiations. He told them about the encounter he had had with Tim Andrus, the god, and how peculiarly interested you were about the little one. He stressed his impression that you wanted to see all this mess settled peacefully."

"But I never told him Bovern's name."

"I'm afraid the Maggotrolls put two and two together and got to Bovern, Tim Andrus. They're using Bovern as an incentive for you to go there. They want you."

"Of course. Remove the god from the equation, and they might win," I said.

"My thoughts exactly, Tim Andrus. You are not obligated to go. Bovern will be a hero, if he were to die, just as many hundreds of thousands have died already."

I sighed. What kind of a god would I be if I let Bovern be tortured and killed? A cowardly god, and that wasn't me. "I'll go."

"You don't have to, Tim Andrus. Think it over."

"I've already thought it over. I'll go meet them, Glave o'Sfero."

General Kland and Logrn e'Sfero approached my station in the command center. They looked somber.

"As Glave o'Sfero said, you don't have to go in person, Tim Andrus," said General Kland.

"Contact them audio-visually first," said Logrn.

"They specifically want me to go there. I don't want Bovern hurt." I thought for a second and then said, "However, I want to talk to Bovern before I go, to see if he's well."

Half an hour later, a channel of communication was opened, and I could see Bovern sitting by a Maggotroll. On either side of me stood Logrn and General Kland.

"How are you, Bovern?" I asked, scrutinizing his features for distress.

"Tim Andrus, it is you! I'm well. I heard that you were coming to get me."

I smiled. A kid is a kid, no matter where in the universe. "Yes, I'll come get you, Bovern k'Sfero."

Logrn and General Kland talked to Bovern as well, after which the Maggotroll sitting next to Bovern took over the conversation.

"I am General Ambronkhan," he thundered. "We request that you, Tim Andrus, come here in person to negotiate with us."

"Why do you want me to come in person, General Ambronkhan?" I asked.

"We trust a god more than a Sferogyl," he replied. "We feel that if you were among us, you'd be a fairer negotiator."

I sensed Logrn and Kland's uneasiness. What if the Maggotrolls were to take me captive? The Sferogyls may not want to take that risk and let me go.

"I assure you, General Ambronkhan, I'd be a fair negotiator, no matter where I'd be."

"Your presence here is mandatory." General Ambronkhan patted Bovern's head with his large hand, as if to say, "*If you value Bovern's life.*"

"You realize, General Ambronkhan, you are not in a position to make any demands."

"On the contrary, Tim Andrus, we have over 130,000 reasons and Bovern, and for negotiations to start, your absence is nonnegotiable."

I leaned back in my chair and displayed a stoic face. They wanted me badly. One part of me said, *Don't go. It's a trap.* The other said, *You cannot cook an omelet without breaking eggs.* Sometimes risks are necessary.

"Very well, General Ambronkhan, I will come." I terminated the communication.

"This is highly suspicious, Tim Andrus," said General Kland. "I don't trust them. They want to take you hostage to increase their leverage."

"I agree, Tim Andrus," said Logrn.

"I agree, too, but let's say, hypothetically, if I were to be taken prisoner, what would you do?" I proposed.

"We have three choices: negotiate, negotiate while fighting, or fight," said General Kland.

"And what would the result be, General Kland?"

"The only reason we don't attack with all we have is because Sferogyls are being held hostage," he replied. "However, this won't be a standoff. One way or another, we will destroy them. We cannot have this situation continue while the Maggotrolls prepare to return with reinforcements."

"Therefore, you'll continue your fight, regardless of what happens to me."

"Yes, we will," said General Kland. "But your safety is our concern, Tim Andrus."

"A god cannot be imprisoned or harmed."

There was a long silence.

"We appreciate your assurances, Tim Andrus," said General Kland.

"Before I leave, let's plan for the possibilities that could ensue, from negotiations going as planned to me being taken prisoner, or even being killed." I said.

"Killed?" said Logrn in shock. "But you said—"

"I'm a god and I've died in the past, and I've been resurrected. Not to worry," I said. "Depending on what happens to me, you must take specific actions as if you knew of the situation. That will keep them guessing."

We worked out the details, the best we could foresee, and I was ready to go.

Jurmalan drove me to the western underground entrance of Tandalo. He wanted to come with me, but I forced him to turn back, and I walked by myself to the Maggotrolls' checkpoint. Two dozens Maggotrolls—armored, helmeted, and armed with lasers—formed a corridor for me to pass through. An officer was waiting for me at the other end, and I approached him. The officer removed his helmet, and it turned out he was a she—a female Maggotroll officer.

"I come unarmed." I raised my hands and passed through a weapon-detection ring in front of her.

"Welcome, Tim Andrus. I'm Lieutenant Katrinakhan. Follow me, please." She turned on her heel and walked into the city along one of the boulevards. If it weren't for the occasional vehicles and Maggotrolls going back and forth, Tandalo would be a ghost town. I followed her, flanked by a dozen soldiers. When we arrived in a small plaza, she pointed and said, "There is Bovern."

Bovern stood across the plaza, waving at me, and I smiled, seeing him unharmed. He began walking toward me and I did the same, but after a few steps I sensed something odd. A force field engulfed me suddenly, suspending me in midair.

Bastards! They entrapped me in a force field from which I couldn't escape. What was worse, Bovern had disappeared. It must have been a hologram to trick me to walk toward him without paying attention to the trap. I was caught, immobilized, and I could do nothing about it.

Chapter 34. Timurud

"What's the meaning of this?" I asked indignantly, struggling inside the force field bubble, unable to go anywhere.

"Orders, Tim Andrus," Katrinakhan said.

It was what it was, and at the moment there was not much I could do about it. One thing I couldn't afford to do was to look scared. A god never fears. I relaxed, somehow, while held in the cocoon of the force field. I was curious to see what they would do next with me. Demand the Sferogyls' surrender? Even they couldn't hope for such a ridiculous outcome. But maybe in their world, that's how business was carried out: Take high-value captives and negotiate for whatever you want.

Maybe.

As my force-field entrapment pod was whisked through the city on a ground transporter, I realized the Maggotrolls had no intention of surrendering. They were fortifying the city for a long resistance. What were they thinking? What gave them hope? Was it just desperation, or did they have something else up their sleeves?

Katrinakhan and the guards were traveling in the Sferogyls' bubble vehicles, although many of the cars had the clear canopy knocked off to provide room for the Maggotrolls' bulk. We arrived at one of the larger towers near the Assembly House's sphere. They kept the hostages nearby for protection. Cowards.

A minute later, I was shoved inside a meeting room of sorts— no, make that a poor imitation of a throne room. There was a large chair, the throne, at the opposite end and several smaller chairs on either side of it. I should have studied more about the Maggotrolls' society, culture, and customs. Too late now. I was going to have a crash course in their way of doing things.

Maggotrolls of all statures, dressed in light armor but without helmets, were gathering, and as they passed my bubble, they looked at me with loathing. From their appearances, they didn't look to be noblemen or courtiers, more like mercenaries, low-life entrepreneurs, or land speculators. I presumed that the most important of them sat on the chairs on either side of the throne in some pecking order. Ambronkhan came in without checking me out and sat in the chair to the right hand of the throne. He must have been important, considering his seat location.

The big honcho, Orbyzykhan, was not there yet, probably waiting so he could build up the suspense. Katrinakhan stood by my encapsulation, not showing any emotion. In spite of being a Maggotroll and resembling a bluish corpse, she was attractive, somehow. Her orange eyes were very expressive. When they were hateful or afraid, her eyes would narrow. Katrinakhan's eyes now were rounder and softer, not reflecting any unease toward me. Instead of manes her hair was braided in two rows.

"Katrinakhan, what's going on here?" I asked, trying to stand up the best I could, but without much success.

"You will meet our supreme leader, Orbyzykhan the Great."

"Never heard of him. Is he important?" I played dumb.

"He's the King of Vestrallum, you moron. Don't worry, he's heard of you." I detected a mischievous undertone, as her eyes narrowed slightly.

Ignoring the fact that she had called me a moron, I asked, "Are you a mercenary or a regular soldier?"

"I'm a soldier, a first lieutenant, in the second regiment, fifth battalion, third company of the expeditionary force of King Orbyzykhan the Great." She straightened up proudly.

"How old are you? You seem to be very young."

"Thank you. I'm of the appropriate age to serve as an officer."

"Are you married?" I asked.

She snorted.

"Do you have a boyfriend?"

She rolled her eyes.

"You prefer women, I gather."

She snorted again.

"How would you like to have a drink with me after all this is over?"

She turned her head and looked at me with disgust. And I thought she was attractive. "You know, I'm a god," I said. "You'd better watch what you say or the looks you give me, or else—"

"Or else what? You're entrapped inside a force field, *god*."

I was sitting crossed-legged in my containment field, and to show her my lack of concern over my current situation, I folded my arms behind my head. "I'm amusing myself." I leaned back, and rolled backwards ending on my head with the butt in the air. Embarrassing. I struggled to gain a more dignified position.

She looked at me and smirked. "We'll see how amused you are when we shrink the force field around you until you resemble a Sferogyl."

I sure hoped my suit would protect me.

Then I heard growls. Two animals resembling two medium-sized lions came in. They had manes like lions, but the rest of their bodies and tails were covered with scales, like those of a fish. They were hideous creatures and their manes were not made of hair but of sharp quills, similar to those of a porcupine. Without delay they charged at my bubble, and I had to steel myself to not scream and jump but look cool instead. Not that I could jump anywhere. That was the beauty of the force field—it didn't let you out, but it didn't let anyone or anything else in, either. They circled my bubble until a command was given. They retreated to the throne and lay down near it like two obedient house pets.

Judging by how everyone bowed, Orbyzykhan was making his entrance from behind the throne. At first glance, he didn't look that great. He was rather short for a Maggotroll, only two meters tall, but with a superior demeanor. Meanness showed in his narrow, slanted eyes. He was in light combat armor, and a blue cape draped around his shoulders. He slumped in his chair and glared at me. I showed him my best unreadable stone face.

"Tim Andrus. Finally," he said, with a sigh of relief.

I was confused. Who is this Maggotroll who knows me and has so much interest in me? "I'm sorry, but I don't remember meeting you in the past."

"He doesn't remember meeting me in the past." He roared with laughter, and everyone in the room did the same. He stood up and came close to my bubble, scrutinizing me carefully.

"Orbyzykhan, what is the meaning of this, taking me prisoner? I came here in good faith, as agreed with Ambronkhan. Please explain this breach of protocol."

"Protocol? Hmm. I would have given an entire planet to get you sealed in a force field, just the way you are now. But instead of paying a fortune to capture you, you walked willingly into my trap for the love of a small Sferogyl." He burst out laughing again.

243

Once the laughter had died down, I said, "I don't find this amusing at all. Release me immediately. The Sferogyls will have no mercy on you after this act of barbarism."

"Tsk, tsk, tsk. Well, maybe from their and your perspective, you think you've won. Far from it!" he shouted. "We never intended to negotiate with the Sferogyls. But thanks to Colonel Undorkhan, we discovered, beyond any doubt, that a god is helping the Sferogyls. And this god cared about small Sferogyls. We interrogated all the small Sferogyls and discovered Bovern to be the right small Sferogyl. So we asked little Bovern about a god among them, but he played ignorant. Maggotrolls can make stones talk, and Bovern told us everything we wanted to know and then some about you."

"You miserable creature!" I tried to move forward in my force field, but the space around me shrunk and I found myself with my head between my knees. Katrinakhan must have shrunk the field to counter my insult and fury. "I hope for your sake he is unhurt," I said through clenched teeth.

"Have no fear, Tim Andrus. He's fine, in a round cage suspended from the ceiling in my office." He kept circling me with his hands at his back. "Feeling a little bit tight in there, god? Don't worry. I will not reduce you to a blob of meat, blood, and bones. I have great plans for you." He gave me a knowing look, which didn't encourage me. "As I was saying, Colonel Undorkhan told me your name, and Bovern confirmed it. But Bovern did so much better. He described you. A god taking sides with my enemy is no trifling matter. But a specific god among my enemies was of great interest to me. I've been looking for you for over one hundred years, and now I have you." He clenched his fists and inhaled with satisfaction.

"Who the hell are you, and how do you know me?"

"Tim Andrus, that's your name, isn't it?"

I did not respond.

"I'm really curious why you use an alias. Why not go by your real fucking god name?" he shouted.

I stared at him from under my eyebrows. Could this Maggotroll know me from way before?

"Because you knew you were going to fight me," he pounded his chest, "and you didn't want to reveal your real name so you could surprise me. Isn't that true, god Timurud?"

Chapter 35. Given to the Dogs

There was a gasp of surprise among the Maggotrolls in that room. Orbyzykhan knew my real god identity. I couldn't tell if that was bad or extremely bad.

"You devious son of a bitch!" He turned into the color of an indigo boil about to burst.

Now I understood why Anu didn't want me to reveal myself to the Sferogyls as Timurud, except to Glade o'Sfero. Whatever Timurud did, it was obvious that he had helped a great many and consequently pissed off many others. Anu's strategy worked, and Orbyzykhan came to invade Nisip underprepared.

"Face it, Orbyzykhan, you lost and are stranded on this planet. Negotiate, and the Sferogyls might be lenient," I said.

Orbyzykhan circled around me, cracking his knuckles. "I came with only one warship, because I wanted to beat one of my rivals to the punch. I knew that my firepower was not enough. *Mangle* was not enough to conquer a planet, even Nisip with the old technologies the Sferogyls possess. But, a second warship, the *Mauler*, will arrive here within days. My sister, Princess Groznikhan the Beautiful, commands *Mauler*, and she is a superior captain to the loser who commanded *Mangle*."

"The Sferogyls will maul your *Mauler*," I said sarcastically.

"Not a chance. Although, I admit those balls gave us a hard time. Unfortunately, we discovered too late a sure way to destroy them."

"But then, you're still holed up down here facing millions of heavily armed Sferogyls surrounding you, thirsty for revenge. The FBBs will smash you into cosmic dust."

246

"FBBs? That's what you call the balls? The FBBs will be no threat to us. We know how to destroy them now. Unfortunately, as I said, we figured that out too late and couldn't save *Mangle*."

"I'm kind of curious—how are you going to destroy such a perfect weapon? It withstood a neutron explosion."

Orbyzykhan swallowed bitterly. "Simple and genial. Counteract the ball's atomic layer frequency. Unless they have a variable frequency all these balls will be flying naked. Even laser shots will be able to destroy them."

The fool divulged such critical information. If I could only inform the Sferogyls to modify the FBBs' VAL to variable frequencies!

"We figured out your little trick, and the Sferogyls are working as we speak to modify the FBBs to variable frequencies." I raised an eyebrow and bobbed my head as if to say, how about that!

Orbyzykhan narrowed his eyes to mere slits. That must have been unwelcome news. "You are bluffing. Just like the Sferogyls spreading false rumors of sending suicide missions to destroy my Vestrallum."

"Huh. You think so? But what if it's true?" I said.

"If it's true?" Orbyzykhan wondered. "Well, for one, you don't give your enemy heads-up information about an oncoming attack. Vestrallum was informed, and if there are such attacks coming, they'll be prepared."

"Very well then, you got me," I said, as if defeated. "What do you intend to do next?"

"I'm going to amuse myself by torturing you," he said with an evil smile.

"Lord Orbyzykhan, with all due respect," General Ambronkhan said in a trembling voice. "Is it prudent to mistreat a god?"

Orbyzykhan turned quickly and stared at him. It was a good question that he had to think about. "General Ambronkhan and all our esteemed entourage, it is time you learn the truth about the gods. The only way gods can deal with us mortals is by assuming a flesh and blood appearance. In their spiritual form, they are harmless. In their mortal appearance, they can be tortured and killed, and there is no repercussion for it, unless they come back as mortals and then you kill them again, until they learn their lesson. And that's the last I'll say about this." He gave a stern glare to his general. Orbyzykhan had a point, which didn't look good for me.

Orbyzykhan glared at me with a seething expression. "Not to worry, I won't kill you. You are a treasure of knowledge about advanced technologies, which we will squeeze out of you. And afterward, you'll continue to live a long, miserable, caged life to pay for what you did to my family and, specifically, to my father." He spoke so forcefully that drops of spit erupted from his dark blue mouth.

"What are you, a sore loser? It was war, that's what happens in war." I had no idea what had happened and what I had done to his father, but I figured it must have been bad.

"Yeah, it was war. If it weren't for you, my father would have died after a long and satisfying life. And we wouldn't have lost all our capital warships and our kingdom, reducing us to paupers."

That must have hurt, whatever I did to them. But knowing that I had another life on Earth, not as Timurud, what he said must have happened a long time ago.

"How old were you when all this happened?" I asked.

"My sister and I were in our twenties."

I gave him a puzzled look.

"After the defeat, my sister and I were taken as hostages by a less sophisticated civilization, and we traveled at near light speed. The Maggotroll Empire aged one hundred years. We aged ten years. It might have been a little bit of luck. By the time we returned, the bastards who had taken over our kingdom had turned soft and forgotten how they had gotten their fortunes. Short story—they died, and I regained my kingdom of Vestrallum and got back into the good graces of the emperor."

"What made you attack Nisip and the Sferogyls?" I said.

"What's the matter? Are you obtuse, or have you lost your marbles?" He placed his hands on his hips, leaning into my force field. "Vestrallum was their planet, and that's how our dynasty began in the Maggotroll Empire, thousands of years ago."

"After thousands of years you're still coming after them?"

"No, it is not a personal vendetta, just business." He waved his hand dismissively. "It just happens that they would come in handy, mining diamonds for us. Nisip would be added to the Maggotroll Empire, for which the emperor would be thankful. I would be awarded Nisip to add to my kingdom, and I could keep a good share of the mined diamonds. Wealth and imperial expansion would continue." He paced around, with his hands behind his back, trying to look royal.

"However, when it comes to you, Timurud, it is pure vengeance," he said, grinning wickedly at me. "It's about time you get on your knees, kiss my boots, and ask for mercy."

The force field shrunk slightly and rotated me into a kneeling position facing the floor. I felt that was as far as they could squeeze me before I was crushed or my suit reacted against the force field to save me.

"By the way, I forgot to mention," I said, looking down at the stony floor. "Everything you've just told me, the Sferogyls have heard as well." It was a bluff.

"Is that true, Ambronkhan?" Orbyzykhan asked.

"He's lying," said Ambronkhan. "There is no transmission leaking outside this chamber. And definitely not from within the force-field bubble."

"Pity. You cannot detect telepathy," I said.

"What?" Orbyzykhan shouted. "You're lying! You wish you could do that."

"I did. Why do you think the Sferogyls ceased fire? Now that they know what will happen, they're retrenching to prepare for a new assault. Also, they've got the information about the frequency, and they'll modify the FBBs to destroy *Mauler*."

"Is that true, did the Sferogyls cease fire, Ambronkhan?" he hollered at his general.

"Yes, they did, my supreme leader," he replied. "But we cannot be sure why they did so."

That was the prearranged plan with the Sferogyls. If I was taken prisoner and they didn't hear from me within an hour, they would stop their attacks against the Maggotrolls. Unfortunately, I wasn't able to inform the Sferogyls telepathically about what Orbyzykhan had told me, but I knew I planted a seed of doubt in his mind.

My force-field bubble rotated to face him. He was breathing heavily, his round nostrils flaring, furious at what I had said. "Let the dogs teach him a lesson." He walked back to his chair and gave a hand signal to the animals.

The force field enlarged and became a dome. I bounced off the floor but stood up quickly, regaining my dignity. The two dogs were ushered into the dome, and they leaped at me. I deflected each one sideways with my arms. They landed on their feet, growling and snarling at me. Killing them was a simple matter, but if I killed them too fast, I'd be constricted again in a tight bubble. I needed time to figure a way out of the force field. At the moment, it was a dome, and I knew that there wasn't a force field under the floor. But would I have enough time to dig a hole?

The two dogs moved away from me, planning to attack me from two sides. With their manes of quills raised into spikes, with their mouths full of piranha teeth, and with the sharp spurs on the backs of their feet, they were not only hideous but deadly, too. I had to trust my suit would protect me and not be shredded into pieces. I moved sideways, inspecting the floor, and then I saw my escape: a brass ventilation grate on the floor nearby.

It was outside the dome, but not far from the edge. Some Maggotrolls were standing on it, spitting insults at me and encouraging the dogs to attack. One dog attacked me first, and a split second later the other did the same, from the opposite side. I was quicker than they were, and I jumped up and away from their snapping jaws. I had to play with them until I could figure how to move the dome. The disc that generated the force field was in the middle of the chamber. I had to move it toward the grate.

I began an intricate dance with the beasts, and as if wanting to kick one of them, I kicked the disk. The darn disc was heavier than I thought, but I nudged it. The dome moved and knocked down some of the spectators. In my struggle I lost my balance, giving one of the dogs a chance to jump on my back. It was trying unsuccessfully to bite me on the back of my neck. My force field helmet protected me. The other grabbed me on the forearm, and while I shook him, I advanced toward where the grate was.

I hurled myself forward and fell onto the grate with one dog on my back and the other now biting my leg. Screaming and faking panic as I was "mauled," I extended a blade from each wrist and cut the grate. Under my weight and that of the dog on my back, I collapsed through the hole in the grate. My upper body was below the force field dome now, and freedom was at the other end of the ventilation shaft. Except that the dog on my back was preventing me from squeezing into the shaft, and the other one was pulling me out of the hole. Without pity, I extended the spikes on my back and pushed up. The creature's lungs were perforated; it didn't have enough air even to squeal. I crawled in, peeling the dead dog off my back against the opening's edge, while pulling myself deeper inside and dragging the other dog after me. To finish the second dog, I rolled on my back and extended a long blade from the bottom of my foot through its mouth and body. That one squealed before it died.

Liberated from the beasts, I raised barbs on my forearms and claws from my boot tips and crawled in the vent shaft to escape. By now the Maggotrolls had figured out what happened and began sounding the alarm. The other end of the vent duct was too far, so I cut a hole in the duct's metallic wall and dropped down onto a ramp way. Through doors above and below, several soldiers burst in, searching for me.

I was trapped.

Chapter 36. Camouflage

I wished I could disappear. So I did the next best thing and jumped up to the corner of the ceiling over the ramp way, implanted hooks from the tips of my boots and my hands into the walls, and ordered my suit to camouflage, blending in with the ceiling and the wall. I became a chameleon.

Several soldiers in attack mode streamed in from above and below, blasting their laser guns at the ventilation duct. Because they were tall, the Maggotrolls walked hunched over, up and down the ramps toward my hanging spot. I congratulated myself for clinging on the corner between the celling and wall. Had I clung on the ceiling, they would have bumped their helmets into me.

They stopped under the vent duct on either side of the hole through which I had made my escape and stared at the blackened laser holes in the duct. From the soldiers' assessment, I was either inside that duct, dead, or I had escaped up or down on one of the ramps before they arrived. One and then a second one climbed into the vent shaft to find me. More soldiers burst in through the doors below and above and searched for me on the other floors. Patiently, I stayed in my corner, contemplating my next move. There was a lot of commotion on the floors below and above me, and only two soldiers remained on guard under the hole in the vent duct. The time was ripe to make my move.

While still camouflaged, I retracted my hooks from my boots and I swung from my claws upward toward the two soldiers' location. The search noises didn't dampen the scratching I made with my claws, and the two soldiers became alert, positioning themselves back to back with their guns pointing at possible danger. I admired their defensive tactic and complimented them with a long blade going through the chest of one and exiting through the chest of the other. I twirled the blade to increase the hole and make sure the air was free to escape from their lungs so they didn't scream. They collapsed to the floor in a sitting position, pinned back-to-back by my blade, if not dead then dying soon. I retracted the blade and left them sitting in a growing pool of their blue blood.

Per my command, my suit took the configuration of their suits, and in an instant I was one of the soldiers, except I had a hole in the front and back left from my blade—a minor detail. I acquired their laser guns, inspected the trigger mechanism, and set it for continuous stream. And then I jumped up back into the vent tube. Moving as quickly as I could, I crawled back into the throne room. The Maggotrolls had removed the two dead dogs from the vent hole, for which I was thankful, and I crawled up to the floor above. The room was not completely empty. Several spectators and soldiers were talking and looking at the dogs' carcasses. A Maggotroll soldier crawling up into the room through the grate opening was no reason for alarm. I came out and everything would have gone well if one of the soldiers hadn't talked to me, pointing to the hole on my chest.

Since he had his helmet on, I couldn't hear him. But he expected me to hear him via my helmet comm. My helmet was a holographic display with no ability on my part to hear what he was saying. The simplest thing I could have done, from his point of view, was to remove my helmet if the comm was out and ask him what he wanted. Instead I raised both my laser guns and, spinning in a half circle, I cut everyone around me in half.

Not all died. Some soldiers in armor were only injured, and two of them opened fire on me. My suit held, although the camouflage vanished. I could have started a laser fire battle with the soldiers, but it would have taken time to kill them with the laser guns, and I didn't want to linger. I threw the guns away and assailed the standing soldiers, cutting them in half with my blades. There were black guts, gore, and blue blood all over the room. The ones who were not dead were moaning or screaming, so I let them be, while I fled in the direction from where Orbyzykhan had come into the throne room.

My goal was to find Bovern. Orbyzykhan had said he was holding him in a cage suspended from the ceiling in his office. I suspected his office was behind the throne. There were three doors, and none had any markings. I stood back and analyzed them, looking for some clue to which one was his office door.

"Don't make a move, Timurud." Katrinakhan held a laser gun to my head. She didn't have her helmet on.

"Katrinakhan, what a surprise." I said, calmly turning toward her. "Can you tell me where Orbyzykhan's office is?"

"Down on you belly, you rat, or I'll blast you!"

Quicker than she could blink, I reached for her gun and pointed it upward. She pulled the trigger, shooting the ceiling, before I pulled it from her grasp. With the other hand, I grabbed her by the throat and lifted her. I had no problem lifting her, but since she was taller than me, she ended up on the tips of her boots. She hit me wherever she could reach, and I squeezed my hand around her throat until her eyes bulged round and she turned even bluer. Killing her served no purpose currently, so I let her drop after she stopped hitting me. While she was gasping for air, I tapped on the controls on her left forearm.

"Where is Orbyzykhan's office?" I asked her computer.

Technology is wonderful and dumb. The computer gave me instructions to go through the center door to a second secure door, where I had to enter a passcode to get access to the foyer.

I lifted Katrinakhan by the throat up to her knees. She struggled to get back on her feet, but I kicked her feet out from under her.

"You have two choices—live or die." Her eyes were wide with terror. "Do you have the passcode to the office?" She shook her head, as much as she could. "No? Then you die." I squeezed her throat and then she nodded.

It took her a moment to catch her breath, but not for long. I squeezed her throat again. "Now listen here, Katrinakhan, only gods can die and be resurrected. Once you are dead, you'll stay dead. If you ask me, it is better to stay alive. What will it be?" I let her go and she slumped to the floor.

"Don't kill me," she pleaded through a rasping voice.

"I will not, if you cooperate. Get up."

She stood up and I pushed her toward the center door. She opened the door and we advanced through a corridor toward the second secure door. I observed my surroundings. This corridor seemed to have been built recently by the Maggotrolls, as part of Orbyzykhan's security measures. Katrinakhan waved her hand over the keypad. Blue warning messages appeared on the keypad. She nervously waved her hand again.

"They changed the pass—"

A blast of plasma blew both of us back all the way through the first door. That was unexpected, and luckily for me, my suit protected me. Katrinakhan was not so fortunate. Her suit barely protected her, but her unhelmeted head was charred.

Chapter 37. Bovern

Alarms began blaring after the plasma blast. It seemed that Katrinakhan wasn't aware that the codes had been changed after I escaped, and only Orbyzykhan's essential assistants had received the new codes. She was not one of the essentials. As additional security, anyone tempering with the code, like Katrinakhan entering the old code, would be incinerated. Orbyzykhan wasn't taking chances with friend or foe.

In the meanwhile, I was still outside the office where Bovern might be. As I recalled, the corridor seemed to have been made by the Maggotrolls, not the Sferogyls. Maybe the walls were not security protected? They seemed to be thick, but my blade could cut through it. I went out, picked up Katrinakhan's gun, and went in through the right-hand door, which led into a room with many holo-monitors. It was a security monitoring station, and I could even see myself on one of the displays. Surprisingly, the room was empty and no one sounded the alert, but that wouldn't be for long. Using the laser gun, I blasted all the equipment.

I deployed the longest blade I could and punched it through the left wall. It went through like butter, without any electrical sparks or plasma blowouts, and I cut a hole large enough to access behind the security door. After kicking the slab inward, I climbed through the opening. Bright lights began flashing. This was not the time to debate what the lights meant, so I stormed inside and through the next door, after blasting it with Katrinakhan's gun. The room I entered was round and had many sofas along the walls. The absence of bowl chairs told me that this was a Maggotroll room.

In the center of the room there was a metal spiral staircase, with steps ascending to the level above. That was a Maggotroll stairway. I approached cautiously and took the stairs up to the level above. This room, again round, was dimly lit. No one was inside, but it seemed to be Orbyzykhan's office. A spherical cage hanging from the ceiling confirmed that.

"Bovern, is that you inside that cage?" I asked, approaching it.

"Tim Andrus, you came!" said Bovern excitedly from the cage, which was not much larger than the kid. His arms and legs were sticking out through the bars.

"Are you alright?" I asked, while searching for booby traps.

"Yes, I'm alright, but be careful. The cage is set to electrocute me if any unauthorized people tamper with it."

"Hmm. Did you see how the cage is disarmed?"

"It is from a device on the desk over there, but it is palm-imprint activated."

Short of having Orbyzykhan's hand with me, it would be impossible to disarm the cage. I had to free Bovern and the time was short. "Are there any other entrances to this room?"

"I don't know," Bovern said. "Orbyzykhan came here only by the spiral staircase."

The first thing to do was to block anyone's access into here while I figured how to get Bovern out of the cage. I went to the spiral staircase and chopped it with my blade. Most of it collapsed down below. Then I dragged the desk and flipped it upside down, covering the hole. Through one of the half-round windows, I saw down below a lot of hubbub and more soldiers running toward the building. Enforcements had arrived.

"Lights," I commanded to see better the contraption-rigged cage.

Commotion started in the room below. The soldiers were down there already.

Above the cage, there were multiple wires coming from the ceiling, wrapped around the cage's chain. Cut any of them, and Bovern would be fried. There was no time to figure out which one was which. I had to cut the chain and the wires in the fastest motion I could muster. I pulled a cushy chair under the cage. Then I flipped a credenza on its end and positioned it near the cage to give me fair reach to the chain and wires above.

"OK, Bovern. I have no choice but to cut the chain and wires. There will be some electrical discharge, no matter how quickly I cut them. Be prepared. After that, the cage will fall on the chair below. It is a cushioned chair and will dampen your fall a little. Ready?"

"I'm ready, Tim Andrus. Cut it." He retracted his arms and legs, transforming himself into a ball.

Several laser shots from down below penetrated through the wood desk, which caught on fire.

I extended my blade and swung as fast as I could to cut the chain and wires. Blue electrical arcs discharged from the wires and the room went dark, due to the short circuit I caused.

"Bovern, are you all right?" I jumped down and raised the cage from the chair.

"Yes, it wasn't that bad." A few tendrils of smoke rose from his round body.

"Stay low." I cut the top portion of the cage, reached in, and pulled little Bovern out. "How do you feel?"

"I'm hot."

The only light in the room was coming from the burning desk, and smoke was rapidly filling the room. I grabbed a glass container with water from another credenza, and I poured the water over Bovern to cool him down.

He spluttered and said, "What did you do that for?"

"To cool you down. Close your mouth and nose." I poured the rest of the water over him, and steam started coming from his shell. The small amount of electricity had heated him up noticeably. I grabbed him by the hand and dragged him into the bathroom, placed him in the sink, and opened the faucet.

"It feels good," he said. "I feel much better."

"Good. Stay under the pouring cold water until I get back."

The soldiers below were dousing the room with fire retardant to put the fire out. In a short time, they would be climbing into the office. There was no time to waste. Several swords were mounted on the wall, including their leather belts. I took the leather belts and made a harness to carry the truncated spherical cage. In the bathroom, Bovern was having fun with the water.

"OK, time to go," I said. "Get inside the cage."

"Why?"

"I'll have to carry you as we make our escape."

As Bovern got inside the cage, he argued, "But I can run and roll fast."

"Sure, but not as fast as I can do it." I strapped the cage to my chest, although I would have preferred to carry him on my back, but there he would have no protection from the laser fire behind me.

Now, if I only knew how to get out of there. Just as I was debating my escape, several Maggotrolls came down by ropes outside the windows and opened fire, shattering the windows. I returned fire and all of them fell down from my shots. Looking out and up through the window, I saw a few Maggotrolls staring down from the window above. I shot at them. One even fell out. I dropped the laser gun and exited through the window, grabbing one of the ropes hanging from above, and I climbed up. The soldiers below fired at me, and I was hit in the back several times. My suit, my second skin, protected me well—I felt nothing too painful. As far as I could remember from my youth, I never was able to do acrobatics and rope climbing as I did now. But then, I didn't have bionanobots in me. Luckily, there were no other live soldiers left in the room above, so I climbed in.

Down in the plaza a voice boomed, "Fire the cannon and blast him."

This was a deadly moment. I had to get out of this place immediately. With my blade drawn, I burst through the door and exited onto another ramp way. Three unlucky soldiers, who seemed to have just arrived, presented no resistance to my blade. I cut through them like paper. I ran across the landing to another door, which I shredded, and got into that suite. A large explosion detonated behind me, probably from the cannon. I turned my suit to camouflage, blasted a back window, and climbed down along the wall, using the protrusions available here and there and the claws extending from my boots. I didn't remember ever rock climbing, other than climbing trees when I was a kid, but now I was as agile as a monkey.

No one saw us as we came down. My camouflage worked as long as I stayed near the wall. There were hundreds of soldiers on the ground, looking up at the fire escaping from the windows of the building we had just been in. I moved sideways with my back out toward the soldiers to maintain my camouflage and managed to get away from the building, switching to invisibility.

With all the fires above, we were not noticed. I ran away from that location faster than an Olympic athlete on Earth, and with Bovern in a cage attached to my chest. I didn't even break a sweat. Behind us there was a terrible cacophony of sounds and blasts and explosions. I wasn't sure if they knew where I was, or if they had followed my trail. Although invisible, I ran carefully along the shadowy passages until I came across a manhole—actually, a Sferogyl-hole.

I pulled the cover off and climbed down into the underground drainage tunnel and ran down a stream to the sewer processing plant. Every city in the galaxy must have one of those plants, and I was right. The water reclamation plant was deserted; I couldn't blame the Maggotrolls for not sticking their noses in there. Who wants to fight around cinnamon-smelling shit? I spotted the effluent and ducked under the discharge pipes.

"What are we doing here?" Bovern asked.

"Getting you out of here," I said.

"How?"

"Along one of those pipes." I pointed to myriad pipes going down through the ground.

"Eww, it smells."

"Sorry, kiddo. But it's not that bad. This is treated waste, and it is the only way I can think of to get you out of here, so you can tell General Kland about the new warship, *Mauler*, coming our way. Let Logrn e'Sfero know to change the VAL on the FBBs to variable frequencies."

"I'll do it," he said proudly.

I selected one of the effluent pipes, shut off the upstream valve, and cut off the pipe downstream of it. To eliminate more of the smell, I opened a fire hose I found nearby and flushed water at full blast down the pipe. It was a small measure to clean the leftover grime from inside the pipe.

"Do you remember what I told you to do?" I asked.

"Yes, tell General Kland and Logrn e'Sfero about the new warship, *Mauler*, coming our way and to change the VAL on the FBBs to variable frequencies."

"You got it. You'll need to get into a ball and roll down the pipe to where it discharges outside."

"I'll do it." He rolled in a ball.

"Take care, Bovern, and good luck." I dropped him inside the pipe, which was slightly larger than his round body. He disappeared in the dark pipe like a pea down a straw. I hoped he'd be OK and that he would inform his compatriots about what I had told him.

Unfortunately, I was too large to go out through one of those pipes. But I could fight my way out in another location. Or maybe while inside Tandalo, I would create havoc among the Maggotrolls, and perhaps even liberate the Sferogyl captives—although saving 132,000 Sferogyls was almost impossible while surrounded by one million armed Maggotrolls. I hoped Logrn was making progress digging a shaft down the pillar near the Assembly House.

While invisible, I sprinted out of the treatment plant toward the Assembly House. As I got closer, I noticed the silence in this part of the city—more so than usual. What was going on? Where were the Maggotrolls? I advanced cautiously. The dawn was approaching and soon there would be daylight coming through the oculi. The silence around me rang alarm bells.

Suddenly, from somewhere, I heard a noise that grinded on my nerves. It was as if someone were dragging a metal table on the concrete pavement. I stopped and listened carefully, trying to identify the sound and what the Maggotrolls were planning.

Then it dawned on me. The Maggotrolls had let out a Coshmar to hunt me.

Chapter 38. Coshmars

A Coshmar was a living nightmare, a half-intelligent beast that was created in the lab to do one thing: kill. And now specifically, to kill me. The Maggotrolls had retreated to safety and sicced a Coshmar on me. But was there only one or more of them?

The last time I had seen such a creature I was just a defenseless head on a fuzzy ball. Now I was Timurud, with bionanobots and a super-duper suit on me. There was a reason why they unleashed the Coshmar: It was able to sense, smell, and hear me. My invisible skin was not going to help me much against that, but it was better than nothing.

I stayed put, waiting for it to come to me. Moving like a cat from hell, following my scent, it approached me from the treatment plant. It stopped, looking in my direction with red burning eyes. It was ugly even in the dark! No doubt it had infrared vision and was seeing me right through my invisible suit.

Suddenly, something landed on my back and flattened me against the ground. It took the breath out of me, and before I could recoup I was flung into the air toward the red-eyed Coshmar I saw earlier, which was waiting to sink its teeth into me. I extended two blades from my wrists and oriented my body to hit it head on. The creature must have sensed the blades and got out of the way. I hit the pavement instead.

Quickly, I was back on my feet, and I saw what had hit me and threw me into the air: another Coshmar. There were two of them, and they were circling me, snapping their tails. No doubt, they sensed my blades and kept their distance, planning their next move by communicating through shrieks that would waken the dead. I relaxed and heightened my inner senses. From that moment on, I had to be as agile, as powerful, and as quick as I could possibly be.

Something told me to jump laterally, and I did. Into the spot I was standing a second before, a third Coshmar dropped, slashing the air with its claws but keeping its insect wings half deployed. Now I had to fight three bestial creatures armed with sharp teeth and claws. All three were male and looked formidable. The only good thing was, they were not any bigger than I was. I hoped there were only three of them.

Offense is the best defense. Quick as lightning, I attacked the new arrival, which was nearest to me. Instead of jumping out of the way, the creature opened its wings to fly away, but my blade cut one of them in half. It howled, making a sound I'd never heard before, resonating in my solar plexus. I didn't take the time to savor my handy slice, and kicked it out of the way to attack the one behind it. The third one leaped toward me from behind. Before it reached me, I slashed at the beast in front of me, managing to gouge its face, but the creature clenched my other hand at the wrist.

Knowing the one behind me was going to pounce on me shortly, I kicked back and extended sharp spurs. I felt one of my spurs hit flesh, and then more howling erupted. The one whose face I'd slashed managed to grab my other arm and tried to immobilize me, while at the same time it head-butted me with its spiky skull. I swear I felt some of its spikes near my eyes, but my invisible helmet protected me well. Another Coshmar swept my legs out from under me, and I fell down under two Coshmars who were gnawing at my protected face, while their claws slashed at my suit.

The two of them lifted me, holding me by my legs and arms. The third one, the one whose wing I'd chopped in half, bit me on the stomach. Unsuccessful, it moved to my crotch to take a bite. Bad idea. I extended a spike from my crotch and it lodged itself in its upper gum between its front teeth. Black blood exploded out of its mouth, as it shook its head to pull out of the spike. I imagined razor-sharp barbs protruding out of my arms and legs where the others were holding me. They dropped me, howling in pain. At the same time, the unfortunate one with a spike in its gum managed to break free, but not before both of its front teeth snapped out of its mouth, like two buttons popping from a tight shirt.

I lay flat on my back. Two of them were sucking blood from their hands in an attempt to stop the bleeding caused by the barbs. Breathing heavily, vapor was coming out of the mouth of the toothless Coshmar. They knew I was down. They felt me when they were trying to tear me apart or slash me or bite me, and were confounded by their inability to penetrate my skin. They could see me in infrared, I was sure, and figured out my hominid shape. I was supposed to be easy prey, but I was not. And they couldn't see what cut and punctured them every time they touched me. Doubt in their abilities to kill me was obvious from their hesitating stance.

I jumped to my feet, and this time they did not encircle me to start another attack. Instead, I attacked them and cut each of them with lightning slashes. They feared my blades, which they couldn't see, but they sensed them and felt the burns. It was not in their nature to retreat and run, and after a short moment of backing away, they repositioned for attack.

The one with a half wing went behind me and grabbed me by the shoulders. Just as I was trying to figure out how to kill it, the other two grabbed me by each arm and began flapping their wings. The one behind let me go and I felt I was being lifted. No way was I going to let that happen! I swung my legs up and slashed each one with blades coming out of the tips of my boots. The two shrieked and dropped me. It wasn't that high, but I didn't have enough time to correct my position to land on my feet. I fell flat on my back.

My suit hardened to protect me from the impact, but nevertheless the slam took the breath out of me, again. They didn't waste a moment and began kicking me, making quick contact and retreating, so I couldn't cut them. Darn it. Just when I thought I was winning, they figured out a way to bang me hard. I was disoriented and dazed from bouncing off the stone ground, not to mention somehow battered. A change of tactics was needed immediately.

I disengaged my invisibility cloak. The transition to visibility distracted them for a second, which was enough to extend my blade to maximum length and cut both legs off the Coshmar closest to me. The other two stepped back, as if in horror. I quickly re-engaged my invisibility cloak and jumped to my feet. The legless one was using his elbows to crawl away, while bleeding profusely and wailing in agony. The other two attacked me as one, but I was upright and fought back, slashing at the parts of their bodies closest to me. I was covered in their black blood, making my invisibility patchy. As we were fighting and moving around, I stumbled on the legless Coshmar and fell down backward on top of it. The other two began kicking me again, while the legless one under me held my upper arms. I extended my back spikes and killed him, but his arms clutched me with an iron grip.

I retrieved my back spikes, rotated my legs up, and pivoted backward, landing on my knees while still held by the dead Coshmar. Cleaver blades extended from my boots' soles, and I chopped off the Coshmar's arms, freeing myself, although with two portions of its arms hanging on me. The other two jumped on me, trying to disable me with quick punches and kicks. Occasionally, one took a quick flying leap, attacking me from above, while the other kicked at my legs. They were quick and had found a strategy that was going to tire me.

I had to end this, and so I flickered my suit between invisibility and light strobe camouflage. They stood and looked, hypnotized at the pattern changes between bright light and nothing. This was the moment. With one swift swing of my right arm, as the blade was extending to its fullest length, I decapitated both of them. Their heads bounced off the stony ground, while their bodies stood, waving their arms and fluffing their wings hideously.

And then I heard someone give the command, "Fire!"

A barrage of firepower blasted the two Coshmars still standing, the one on the ground, and me. Our bodies slammed against the nearest building.

Chapter 39. Run

They blasted us with a plasma blow. The Coshmars' body parts and guts were burning, strewn all around me and on the wall. My suit protected me, but the blast paralyzed me, although I had enough lucidity to change my suit to camouflage. Considering the smoke, vaporized blood, and flesh around us, I hoped they wouldn't find me. From all directions, soldiers, with their guns drawn, approached cautiously.

Even camouflaged, they were going to find me once they kicked the body pieces out of the way. I regained some feeling in my right leg, so I pushed myself along the bottom of the wall, away from the carnage. The soldiers kept approaching, and I was slowly moving out of the way. Another plasma blast and I would be an atom cloud. The feeling in my other leg returned, and I pushed away a bit faster with both feet.

Someone gave another command: "Fire again." There was a flash and the Coshmars' body parts were charred instantly.

They had missed me, but not by much. I could feel my arms now, and I reached up the wall, found an indentation, and pulled myself up. My strength and the feeling in my body returned as I struggled to move away. I pushed with my feet and pulled with my arms, clinging onto the creases of the wall. The soldiers stood meters away, waiting for the fires from the burning bodies to stop and cool down. I continued up the wall until my fingers found a ledge and I pulled myself up on it, lying on my belly and panting.

A soldier brought a fire disruptor and doused the charred remains to put out the smoldering remains of what was left of the Coshmars. White smoke engulfed everything for a time. Afterward, the soldiers moved in quickly, picking up charred parts and analyzing them before discarding them. They didn't care about the Coshmars. Pieces of me were what they were looking for. The soldiers on the ground, just meters below my ledge, didn't notice me as they searched. My camouflage saved me.

"What's the status, Lieutenant?" asked an approaching officer. I recognized Ambronkhan.

"We're still searching, General," said the lieutenant. "There are many charred body parts. Hard to distinguish between Coshmar and hominid."

"How many heads did you find?" Ambronkhan asked.

"One," said one soldier, lifting a blackened head attached to a neck and a shoulder.

Even charred as it was, it was easily recognizable as a Coshmar. The other two decapitated heads were blown away, but they had to be around somewhere. For the moment, that was good. But if they found the other two Coshmars' heads, they'd know I wasn't killed.

I was on the side of the building, well lit by the morning sun shining through the oculus above, and I doubted my camouflage was that good in full light. Luckily, they weren't using infrared detectors. Slowly and meticulously, I crept away along the ledge to the darker side, and once there I crawled up the building wall, looking for an escape.

"General Ambronkhan, I found another head," said a soldier. "It is a Coshmar."

"Any hominid body parts, Lieutenant?" the general asked.

"Not so far, unless it all turned to ash, General."

"It has cooled down enough. Scan the area with infrared," Ambronkhan ordered.

That was bad news, and I hurried until I reached the flat top of the building, which was not a tower-column building. I lay down on the roof to keep a low profile.

"The whole area is still too hot to detect discernable differences," said the lieutenant.

"Found another head, General. It is the third Coshmar."

"Scan the surrounding area!" shouted Ambronkhan.

A cordon of soldiers already encircled the building.

"Lieutenant, scan the building where the body parts were found," Ambronkhan ordered.

Bad news—as they scanned upward, they would eventually find the heat traces of my body as I climbed. I changed to invisibility and ran as fast as I could. I leaped to the roof of the other building and, without stopping, ran and jumped to the next one, outside the soldiers' encirclement. I looked back and knew that as a human I couldn't have made that 10-meter jump between the buildings. I was not out of danger yet, so I jumped to the next building, which was lower, and from that one to another lower one, and then down to the ground. I ran like hell along a hedgerow of violet vegetation and then across an open plaza, fully lit by the sun. If they followed me this far, my thermal traces would be gone, dissipated by the sun's heat.

The relative quiet that had shrouded Tandalo until now was broken by the restart of the fighting. The Sferogyls began the assault. Maggotroll soldiers, some on foot and some in levitating vehicles, went back and forth in a state of high alert. The Sferogyls seemed to attack on all fronts. In some cases, they broke the stone ceilings, and FBBs dropped in and began smashing the Maggotrolls. I knew somehow Bovern had made it. The Sferogyls attacked with all they had to capture or kill Orbyzykhan before his sister arrived on the *Mauler*.

In the chaos caused by the renewed battles, I ran, still invisible, toward the Assembly House, where the Sferogyl prisoners were being kept. Hundreds of soldiers surrounded the big round ball, crewing big guns, all pointing away from the ball. I ran behind a vehicle that passed me by and was heading toward the Assembly House. As long as the vehicle went to the entrance, the soldiers would part to let it go through, with me right behind it.

We passed through and I sneaked from behind the vehicle and ran to the entrance, where I discovered the Maggotrolls' handy work. Mercenaries this time, judging by their different uniforms, were rigging the lower part of the structure with explosives. As a matter of fact, they had brought more explosives in the vehicle I followed in there.

Chapter 40. Dig

Rigging up the Assembly House to blow it up was unexpected. The hostages were a good bargaining chip, and the Sferogyls could have been persuaded to make concessions. I hoped that these preparations were made as the ultimate act of defiance and not as an immediate action. Or perhaps they did this to get me to surrender or they would kill the hostages.

The last boxes with explosives were brought in, stacked in strategic places, and wired to remote-controlled detonators. To my surprise, the Maggotrolls evacuated the grand foyer and barred the doors from the outside. The Sferogyls in the great hall were left alone and unguarded.

Disconnecting the detonators would be a lengthy task, even if the devices were not booby-trapped. However, if Orbyzykhan did not intend to blow the building soon, a new alternative presented itself. I could enter the great hall and perhaps dig my way up through the stone pillar the Sferogyls were tunneling down from above. Logrn was digging from the top very quietly, and I could dig from the bottom, although noisily. I didn't think the Maggotrolls would hear it, with all the battle noises around them. Entering through any door was inadvisable, because of sensors. I ran up the spiraling ramp until I reached the highest entrance in the arena.

Next to the entrance, behind a column, I breached the wall and got inside under the bleachers. With great care, I cut a hole in a partition and peered in. Every seat was taken. The access ways were full, and even the bottom, the deliberation floor, was packed with Sferogyls. The light inside was dim, but visual sensors might be still spying on the hostages. I cut another hole between two eggholder seats at the ear level of two Sferogyls.

"Psst," I whispered.

The Sferogyl on the right asked the one on the left, "Did you hear something?"

"Yes, it sounded as if someone let out air," said the other one.

"Listen, you two. Do not turn around, just listen to what I have to say." The two Sferogyls turned slightly and their eye tentacles moved in the direction of my voice, but then they settled back into their original position facing forward. "This is Tim Andrus. I need one of you to go and get your leader. Do this quietly. Do not announce my presence. The Maggotrolls are watching. Go!"

The Sferogyl on the right did as I asked, and soon the other one left his seat, and two other Sferogyls sat in their bowl seats.

"Is that you, Tim Andrus?" the Sferogyl on the left asked. "I am Quantolan l'Sfero, and at my right is Honegrn e'Sfero."

"Yes, it's me. I am behind the bleachers."

"You came to rescue us?"

"That's my intention. What is your condition in here?"

"Bleak. Several of our elderly have died. What is the plan?" Honegrn asked.

"First, you need to know that all exits are barred and the first floor is rigged with explosives."

"Why?"

"I can only speculate, but in the meantime, I will try to cut an escape shaft in the western pillar."

"Why the western pillar?" Quantolan wondered.

"Logrn e'Sfero's team are using a GBB to dig a shaft in that pillar to rescue you. I'll core from below and hopefully we'll meet soon."

"How are you going to cut the shaft, Tim Andrus?" Quantolan asked.

"I have a blade that can cut through anything, Quantolan l'Sfero. Where can we gather to talk and plan further without being seen by the Maggotroll video-sensors?"

"Straight ahead of us on the third level is the exit to the restrooms, Tim Andrus."

"I see it, and I'll see you there." I moved quickly under the bleachers to the opposite side of the hall, where I cut a large opening and accessed the restroom area. Quantolan and Honegrn arrived shortly.

"Tim Andrus, thank god you're here to save us," said Honegrn. "How much time do we have?"

"I don't know. Your compatriots are on the attack. I managed to escape from a fraudulent negotiation trap, and the Maggotrolls are desperate to find me. We need to move as fast as we can."

"What do we need to do?"

"I'll be cutting the shaft going straight up inside the pillar, and the debris will need clearing," I said. "Also, you must make an improvised ladder to climb up and escape."

"We'll do it."

"One more thing," I said. "Can you get the people inside the hall to talk loud or sing to cover the digging noises?"

"Certainly."

Near the wide pillar, the Sferogyls made a Sferogyl-chain to move the chunks of rock and deposit them under the bleachers. From the hall, I heard a thunder of whistles. They were singing. I extended my blade and drove it into the stone at an inclined path first. My two-millimeter-thick and always one-atom-sharp reciprocating blade was marvelous. It felt as if I was cutting Styrofoam, except the chunks falling out were hard and heavy. The Sferogyls carried away all the rock and sand quickly. When cutting the vertical shaft, I was thankful again for my suit and force-field helmet. Besides the larger chunks, there was a lot of sand and dust that fell on me. To my surprise, the Sferogyls made two ladders from the rails of the ramps. That made it easier for me to climb up using opposite footholds and later for them to climb up. The shaft had to be over one meter in diameter to accommodate the Sferogyls, but I was making good progress.

Three hours later, I reached softer stone and the cutting speed increased, along with more sand pouring down every time I twisted my blade. I had no idea what was happening in the hall or outside it, but I kept cutting, hoping that I would soon hear the GBB digging down toward me.

Suddenly I felt a tremor and I listened. It was coming from above. I didn't know what was happening, but I could hear explosions vibrating through the rock. Was I closer to a battle center? Wondering wouldn't do me any good, so I kept cutting until my blade hit air.

One large laser gun pointed at me through the hole, until the Sferogyl above recognized me and greeted me happily instead. Earlier, the Sferogyls had heard someone excavating from below and stopped the GBB, while lying in wait for possible Maggotrolls digging up. Contact being made, I shouted down at the Sferogyls below and informed them that we had broken through. They applauded and whistled.

Logrn was waiting for me on the surface.

"Logrn e'Sfero, what a surprise!" I said.

"My surprise is equal, Tim Andrus." He pointed up to the dusky sky.

Mauler had arrived.

Chapter 41. The Rescue

"That's bad news, Logrn e'Sfero. *Mauler* came sooner than I expected," I said. "I gather you got my message from Bovern."

"Yes, we did, Tim Andrus. You don't know how thankful we are for the information you sent to us."

"How is he?"

"At first, very smelly." Logrn smiled. "But we cleaned him up well. He's a hero."

"That's good."

"Bovern said that Orbyzykhan is down here in Tandalo."

"That's correct," I said. "And his sister, Groznikhan, is commanding *Mauler*."

"That's bad news. She is more evil and cunning than her brother."

I looked up toward the slim sliver of reflected light from the warship. "You must attack *Mauler* right away, Logrn e'Sfero."

"We are preparing for that, Tim Andrus."

I turned my attention to the more immediate job at hand. "You need to extract the hostages quickly, Logrn e'Sfero. The Maggotrolls have rigged the Assembly House with explosives." I pointed to the well. "They made a ladder to climb to the surface."

"That won't be fast enough. We're going to vacuum them out, Tim Andrus. We'll use a larger vacuum than we used to extract the sand made by the digging GBB."

Vacuum them out? Sure, why not?

Teams of Sferogyls climbed down to give instructions to the hostages and prepare them to be sucked up to the surface. Afterward, they lowered a transparent, ribbed hose down the hole. The other end of the hose was connected to a catch chamber and beyond to a giant turbofan.

While Logrn and I stood by, waiting to see the vacuuming begin, I asked him, "Did you modify the FBBs?"

"We can't, Tim Andrus," Logrn answered. "There are only two resonant frequencies that we can use for the balls to function as intended. Variable frequencies won't work."

"Bummer," I said, disappointed.

The fan began spinning and soon I saw the Sferogyls coming up and along the hose, discharging them in the catch chamber. Four revolving doors dished out the Sferogyls from the catch chamber and deposited them on conveyor belts taking them to safety. The Sferogyls coming up were in their protective ball position and the whole setup reminded me of a giant bingo machine. At the other end of the conveyors, the freed hostages were escorted to emergency vehicles with purple flashing lights, and from there they were taken to makeshift hospitals.

"How fast are they being extracted, Logrn e'Sfero?"

"Three every second."

I made a quick mental calculation. "It will take twelve hours. Logrn e'Sfero, the extraction is not fast enough."

"This is the low speed, Tim Andrus. We'll accelerate soon."

The menace above in the sky attracted my attention again. "When did *Mauler* arrive, Logrn e'Sfero?"

"We detected it four hours ago, Tim Andrus. It settled into orbit one hour ago."

"Is this area camouflaged?"

"Yes, it is," said Logrn. "They won't see us."

I looked at the Sferogyls being brought up through the suction hose. The extraction rate increased, and most of them seemed to be in good shape in spite of the rattling and the speed of the recovery.

Logrn looked at a device on his suspender belt. "This is the maximum rate of extraction. We will finish in three hours."

"Did you send someone to take care of the explosives?"

"Yes, Tim Andrus, we have a team working to interfere with the blow up signal, and another team to set the video receptors in the main hall on a continuous loop. It will prevent the Maggotrolls from detecting the evacuation."

The suction/evacuation hose was whooshing, extracting the Sferogyls at high rate. That was as fast as it would get. Thousand of volunteers worked frenetically to extract as many hostages as they possibly could and bring them to the field hospitals. Darkness descended, and the dust caused by the operation obscured most everything within hundreds of meters. Strobes of purple lights flashed around us, giving the whole area an otherworldly look, even for Nisip.

Logrn and I departed for the command center in a flying craft, with several FBBs escorting us. In the distance, several enemy fighters took to the sky flying from Tandalo to *Mauler*.

"Did other enemy fighters depart before?" I asked.

"Not until now," said Logrn.

"Orbyzykhan has abandoned his troops, I bet, and he's flying to meet his sister," I said, pointing to the fighters. "How is the situation underground with the remaining hostages?"

"One hour to go," said Logrn. "Tim Andrus, are you worried about something?"

"If Orbyzykhan's troops feel that they have been abandoned, they may take desperate action."

"Or surrender."

"Not as long as *Mauler* is in orbit, Logrn e'Sfero."

Logrn was communicating with the team underground and I heard him shouting, "Don't let them in! Cut off the power!"

"What's happening?" I asked.

"The Maggotrolls are advancing on the Assembly House," Logrn said.

"They may want to separate the hostages into smaller groups."

"Why would they do that?" he asked.

"Better protection for their troops," I said. "Use the hostages as shields against your soldiers."

Logrn listened intently on his communicator. "Jam all frequencies. Prevent the explosion."

I opened communication with the command center. "General Kland, I suggest you send FBBs inside the Assembly House plaza. They must create a distraction until all the hostages are extracted."

Seconds later, our FBB escorts turned around and headed for Tandalo.

"What happened down there?" I asked Logrn.

"We're not sure," said Logrn. "The Maggotrolls were fighting with each other at the entrance of the hall." Logrn listened to his communicator and told me, "We managed to cut off the power. The FBBs have arrived in the plaza and are being fired upon by the enemy troops."

"How many more hostages to go?"

"Not many," said Logrn. "Because the power is off, the video feed is dark, and we don't know what the Maggotrolls are doing around the Assembly House."

It must have been chaos down there. The FBBs had never attacked inside Tandalo or so close to the Assembly House. If the Maggotrolls panicked, they could take desperate actions.

"The power has been restored," said Logrn. "The Maggotrolls bypassed the open circuits and now have live video feeds from inside the hall."

There was nothing we could do to help anyone, only witness the developments underground.

Logrn was listening to the reports when he erupted, "Increase extraction rate over maximum capacity!" He then looked at me and said, "The Maggotrolls broke into the hall after they saw it was empty. There are exchanges of gunfire between us and them near the evacuation route."

It's always hell at the last moment.

"Way to go!" shouted Logrn, listening on his comm. He lifted his arms up and said, "Everyone is safely out."

A giant explosion flashed behind us.

Logrn exhaled. "Everyone is safely out, but they blew up the Assembly House."

Chapter 42. Freedom or Death

We entered the command center, where everyone was busy at his or her station. *Mauler*'s hologram was displayed in the middle of the room. It was bigger than *Mangle*. Actually, it was longer by 50%. I read the stats: 1,500 fighters, 18 frigates. More laser and proton turrets as well added to its defense, and even more powerful proton cannons due to its length. We had only 1,527 FBBs to stop this behemoth.

"Tim Andrus, thank you from all of us for rescuing our hostages," said Glave o'Sfero.

"You're welcome, Glave o'Sfero."

"And thank you for returning to the command center, Tim Andrus," said General Kland.

"My duty, General Kland. Logrn e'Sfero told me that the FBBs' VAL couldn't be modified for variable frequencies."

"Unfortunately, that is true, Tim Andrus." General Kland sighed.

"We experimented to see how susceptible the FBBs are to harmonic frequency laser fire," said Logrn.

"And?"

"Disastrous, Tim Andrus. The lasers cut through an FBB's 25-cm shell in two seconds."

A two-note whistle preceded the broad announcement about to

be made: "Fifteen frigates were deployed from *Mauler*, orbiting in formation."

Mauler was getting ready to hammer us.

"We'll have to battle them as we did before, Tim Andrus," said General Kland. "We have analyzed what went well and what didn't go well in our last battles, and we'll adopt the best tactics."

"We have 1,527 FBBs in lower orbit awaiting for orders," said General Lantolan.

Another general announcement was made: "*Mauler* is due in range of our first ground proton cannon fire in three hours."

I didn't think we had three hours, even if our cannon could do enough damage. *Mauler* was not going to wait. Its first priority was to destroy the FBBs, our only offensive weapon.

A transmission on all channels shortly came from *Mauler*: "Attention, all Sferogyls. This is Orbyzykhan the Great on the warship *Mauler*. My sister, Groznikhan the Stunning, and I are here to conquer your planet. Unlike the last time, we will not be benevolent, and we are prepared to take what's ours or kill you all. You have five minutes to surrender."

As expected, Orby the not-so-great fled danger and returned to the safety of *Mauler*. What a coward. And what was that about Groznikhan the *Stunning*? Was she that vain?

A digital clock started ticking the countdown.

"Let the clock time out to zero," said General Kland. "Get in positions to execute FBB harpoons at the zero countdown mark."

Light signals were sent to all FBBs, and they started moving on their assigned positions. The tactic was simple: attack from different angles while being willing to sacrifice the front of the harpoon until we could penetrate *Mauler*.

A broad announcement was made: "Glave o'Sfero will address all the Sferogyls of Nisip on all secure channels in three minutes."

Will Glave o'Sfero give in and accept defeat and slavery, or fight to the death? Everyone in the command center was busy getting ready for the attack. There seemed to be no doubt that they would fight to the last Sferogyl.

An announcement came over the intercom: "Enemy fighters are being deployed."

I opened a channel to Logrn and all the generals. "Logrn e'Sfero, I have a question about the enemy fighters."

"Yes, Tim Andrus. What would you like to know?"

"Did you test the fighters' laser power against the FBBs?"

There was a pause. "We tested only with the warship turrets' laser power. The fighters' lasers are about 50% less powerful."

"And the frigates?"

"About 80% of the turret guns."

"Thank you, Logrn e'Sfero. Generals Kland and Lantolan, it seems to me that no matter how powerful the *Mauler*'s lasers are, if they don't hit the FBBs accurately, there will be no damage."

"I'm not sure I understand what you're saying, Tim Andrus," said General Kland.

"Do you want us to avoid attacking *Mauler*?" General Lantolan asked.

"Our FBBs' weakness is their speed of a maximum of 10 km/s in orbit. Therefore, let's stay in the upper atmosphere to diminish the power of *Mauler*'s laser guns. Following the turret lasers, the next powerful laser shots will come from their frigates and lastly from the fighters, but only at close range. Rather than attack *Mauler* and be destroyed by its powerful lasers, while being chased by their fighters, why don't we let their fighters engage us and destroy them before we deal with *Mauler*?"

"But *Mauler* is the real threat," General Kland objected.

"Yes, it is, General Kland, but *Mauler* has learned from *Mangle*'s demise. The FBBs destroyed *Mangle*, and if I were *Mauler*'s captain, I would avoid being attacked by the FBBs."

"General Kland, I think Tim Andrus has a point," said General Lantolan. "Attacking *Mauler* while being chased and fired upon by its fighters is perilous. The FBBs' erratic flight pattern gives us a greater chance of taking down their fighter force in the stratosphere."

"What do we do when the frigates attack or *Mauler* moves closer to Nisip?" General Kland asked.

"Avoid the frigates as well, if we can, General Kland," I said. "Let the enemy come to us."

While the generals conferred, another ultimatum came from *Mauler*. "Nisip, you have two minutes before you surrender or die."

The pressure was felt throughout the command center.

"But what about Nisip when *Mauler* begins blasting everything in sight?" General Kland asked.

"General Kland, this is General Alvuteran. We will be blasted anyway if we lose our FBBs. Nisip will have to hunker down."

"I agree, Generals," said Glave o'Sfero, who surprised us by listening in. "We will fight, but it will be our fight, not theirs."

"Very well. General Lantolan, send the signal to our FBBs to retreat into low orbit above the upper atmosphere," said General Kland.

A moment later, a broad announcement was made: "To all Sferogyls, stand by to hear from Glave o'Sfero."

"Greetings to all my brother Sferogyls in these grave times. This is Glave o'Sfero speaking. I realize that we thought we had won against our enemy, the Maggotrolls, but the empire sent another warship, more destructive than the first one, to take us as slaves or to kill us. This is a righteous fight against the enemy of freedom, and we will not suffer the same destiny as our ancestors. There will be only one outcome if we don't fight: slavery and slow death. If we fight, we have a good chance of winning, although many of us will die. I say that freedom is ours and cannot be taken away, as long as we fight to the last soul. God bless the Sferogyls and our fight for freedom."

As one, all the Sferogyls in the command center stood up and whistled their approval. It was the same all over Nisip. The Sferogyls would not capitulate.

The countdown clock turned to 0:00.

Chapter 43. Attack

The enemy spacefighters, 1,000 of them by the numbers shown on the general information display, descended toward Nisip. They were the primary line of offense, followed by fifteen frigates, and then *Mauler*. All the enemy craft were pointing with their bows toward Nisip in a classic attack formation, pointing their laser and proton cannons at us while minimizing their impact profile.

The fighters were coming fast and furious toward our FBBs, as I expected them to do. Their pilots seemed to be more confident in attacking the FBBs with their synchronized frequency lasers for harmonic destruction. We were 1,527 versus 1,000 of them at this time. Then to our surprise, *Mauler* disgorged a second wave of fighters, 400 more. We were practically even now.

"General Lantolan," said Logrn. "My team has calculated the penetration time of the fighters' lasers. It is five seconds over a focused area of 100 sq cm, and diminishing from there over a larger area. The frigates' lasers will cut through in three seconds over the same area."

What that meant was that if the laser beam were able to focus on an area of 11 cm in diameter, it would take five seconds to penetrate a 25-cm-thick plate of depleted uranium alloy.

A light-coded signal was sent immediately to all FBBs informing them of the danger from the fighters' lasers. Although it seemed good news that it would take five seconds to penetrate the hull of an FBB if it were blasted only within such a small area, the fact was that any laser blast achieving harmonic frequency with the VAL for even shorter durations would gouge the surface of a FBB. Better to not get shot at all, if possible. The information on the central holographic display showed that the FBBs began quivering at a higher rate in random patterns to avoid the laser shots.

The fighters advanced toward the FBBs at 100 km/s with their lasers already blazing. In a matter of ten seconds, they would be clashing with the FBBs. Besides the laser fire, the fighters had their missile launchers replaced by proton guns, which was a double peril against the FBBs. The fighters teamed together to pin a single FBB with their firepower, just as they did before *Mangle* was destroyed. The frigates moved aggressively right behind their fighters, and they launched missiles. The FBBs avoided being cornered by the fighters and survived the first salvo of laser fire, but the missiles launched by the frigates created space warps, and the FBBs were thrown out of their random movements. And suddenly we saw the first casualties among the FBBs. The enemy tactic worked: Shoot space-warp missiles at an FBB, send it flying on a predicted pattern, and then shoot at that FBB like a wolf pack.

Immediately, light signals were sent to our FBBs to be aware of the new tactics. Some FBBs flew head on against the missiles, and although the space was distorted around the FBBs, the predicted pattern became unpredictable and the fighters began missing their targets.

Other FBBs attacked the oncoming fighters head on, managing to destroy several of them. The losses seemed to even out, until the FBBs and the fighters were mingled together and only the skill of the pilots saved each one's skin. The fighters knew not to get too close to the FBBs, but at the same time the closer they got, the better their laser accuracy and power. The FBBs had only one weapon—crash into the fighters even if blasted by lasers and protons in a head-on collision.

After one hour of cat-and-mouse fights, each side had lost over 200 craft—mildly acceptable results, until the frigates engaged in the fight with their proton guns. An hour later, we had lost another 100 FBBs, while they had lost none of their frigates. The superiority shifted to *Mauler*'s advantage. It was getting intolerable.

I wanted to talk to General Kland about the best tactics we had learned from previous battles, but he was too busy directing the fight. Instead I contacted Logrn.

"Logrn e'Sfero, General Kland said he reviewed all our previous battles."

"That's correct, Tim Andrus."

"Did you analyze the data from when I punctured through the frigate's hull?"

"Yes, we did, Tim Andrus. We analyzed everything but did not see anything unusual. The energy shields at the bow of the frigates failed just before you attacked them."

"I would like to see the data. Logrn e'Sfero, would you join me, please?"

We gathered at my station, and Logrn brought up the data they had about the frigate demise. My FBB, followed by Varna's, approached the frigate without being repelled by its energy shields, and we consecutively punched through the frigate's hull.

"How do you know that the frigate's energy shields collapsed, Logrn e'Sfero?"

"How else could you have penetrated the hull, Tim Andrus?"

"Do you have energy readings from the frigate?"

"No, only the visuals," said Logrn.

"Only my FBB survived that battle. Did you analyze its data from that encounter?"

"We downloaded the data, but I'm not sure if anyone analyzed it, Tim Andrus." Logrn entered several requests, and the reply was that it was analyzed but nothing unusual happened.

"I'd like to see the data myself, Logrn e'Sfero, from the time after the neutron explosion."

He brought it up. "There are no data during the explosion. You went dark. After that, let's see," he said, and both of us stared at the additional data on the screen. "Nothing out of the ordinary."

"Superimpose all channels from my FBB," I asked. "Do you see here, one second before encountering the frigate's energy shield, my VAL stopped working? And then a fraction of a second later, it came back on."

Logrn raised a hand to his mouth, dumbfounded. "We presumed the frigate's shield malfunctioned. Instead it was yours, and Varna followed in your wake."

"I was lucky that during that second I was not hit. Without the VAL on my FBB, I had become impervious to the energy shield and I went right through, followed by Varna. I was just a cannon ball, which the shields could not deflect. But before I hit the hull, my VAL came back on."

"Yes, but how come you lost your VAL in the first place?"

"Because of the neutron explosion. The VAL malfunctioned at the right time and place. We have a new way to penetrate the hulls."

"By attacking without the VAL? We'll be killed," Logrn said.

"What if we keep the VAL on for laser blast protection until we reach the energy shields? Just before we get bounced back, we stop the VAL and we go right through it, and before we hit the hull, we re-energize the VAL and punch through."

Logrn took a deep breath. "I wouldn't dare have the pilots do this manually."

"Of course not. This takes split-millisecond control. The onboard computer has to sense the field, turn off the VAL, and just before hitting the hull, turn the VAL back on."

"Thank you, Tim Andrus. I have work to do." Logrn left hurriedly as he communicated with his team.

I looked at the battle status of hour three. *Mauler* was hovering above the battles, as if enjoying the show. The enemy lost another 100 fighters but not a single frigate. We lost another 100 FBBs. We were down to a little over 1,100 FBBs, and soon they would have to return to Nisip to refuel.

Chapter 44. Surrender

I began pacing around my station. The situation was deteriorating. But then our ground super cannon fired and destroyed two of the enemy frigates. In response, *Mauler* moved over our gun's site and blasted the muzzles in that area. As Nisip rotated, another ground cannon came into range and blasted three proton jets in fifteen seconds at *Mauler*. A plasma cloud formed on the blasted side of *Mauler*, but it dissipated quickly. One hundred fighters and six frigates descended toward that ground cannon, realizing that it was a threat they couldn't leave undestroyed.

General Sarmal held fire until the frigates were at the atmosphere's edge, and then he gave the command to fire. The cannon did its job and destroyed two more frigates. The remaining four frigates shot dozens of missiles at the cannon, destroying it and everything on the ground within tens of kilometers.

Surviving muzzles of the cannon that had shot at *Mauler* before opened fire again on the warship's side as it orbited away. Plasma ignited in response to the blast, which must have drained a good amount of energy from *Mauler*, judging by the lack of return proton fire on the offending muzzles. The ground-to-air defenses around the ground cannon opened fire to protect it from the frigates and fighters attacking it. The defenders managed to destroy another frigate and a dozen fighters before the missiles from newly arrived frigates obliterated large areas on the ground.

"This is a broad announcement from General Lantolan: All FBBs to return to the ground bases for refueling." The announcement flashed in color codes from different areas on the surface, calling them back, although the FBBs had another thirty-five minutes of fuel. What the announcement didn't disclose was the upgrading for the FBBs' onboard computers to attack *Mauler* in a new way. Logrn and his team succeeded in modifying the software for attacking *Mauler* as I had, by accident, the frigate of *Mangle 1*.

A diagram of *Mauler* appeared on the central holo-display. The fresh pilots who would take over the refueled and upgraded FBBs had been instructed on how to attack *Mauler* this time. There were eight targets: Its super cannons located in the dark universe tunnel at the bow and aft, and the six arrowheads. Those contained the NLS, and DU engines. If those engines were destroyed, *Mauler* would be dead in the water. It was our last hope. We had only 977 FBBs to defend Nisip.

"Congratulations, Logrn e'Sfero," I said over the intercom.

"Thank you, Tim Andrus. Your discovery of how to penetrate their energy shields was brilliant. And easy to upgrade."

"Just by chance, does *Mauler* have one single, fatal weak spot?"

"*Mauler* does not have such a weak spot, Tim Andrus. Even if its neutron storage magazines are hit, which are deep inside it, it wouldn't paralyze the warship."

"But how did I cause the neutron explosion on *Mangle 1*?"

"One of my associates finished the analysis of that explosion a few minutes ago. Even if you ruptured the neutron storage, there wouldn't have been the neutron explosion we witnessed. It was an onboard proton gun blast that caused a chain reaction when it blasted a proton battery."

"But who could have done that, Logrn e'Sfero?"

"Possibly a Maggotroll soldier who fired at you with a large enough proton gun and hit the proton bank instead."

"I see. So you're going to immobilize *Mauler* by destroying all its engines."

"That's correct, Tim Andrus. It was General Kland's idea. Do you concur?"

"Yes, I do, Logrn e'Sfero."

It was our last chance to survive this assault. There was nothing to do but wait. The clock showed minus-28 minutes before the FBBs would launch again. The refueling was quick, done in five minutes. What seemed to take longer was the software upgrading.

The enemy must have been surprised at the disappearance of the FBBs. They may not have known about the refueling, and in any case, it would have been executed in stages, where at least two-thirds of the FBB force would have stayed and fought during that time, just as their fighters would. The complete retreat of our forces could have puzzled them and left them wondering if we were defeated or planning a new attack.

It was quiet in space. The enemy frigates and fighters took new positions around Nisip, while awaiting new orders. Many of the fighters returned to *Mauler* for possible repairs and refueling. Frankly, I was surprised that *Mauler*'s cannons did not attack our positions without mercy. Maybe they still wanted many Sferogyls intact, as slaves.

A transmission on all channels came from *Mauler*: "Attention, all Sferogyls. This is Orbyzykhan the Great on the warship *Mauler*. You have been defeated. As a gesture of my magnanimous character, I am willing to spare your lives if you surrender unconditionally and immediately."

I opened communication to Glave o'Sfero and General Kland. "We need to stall them, until our FBBs are ready."

"What do you suggest we do, Timurud?" asked Glave o'Sfero.

I heard a gasp from General Kland at the revelation of my god name. By now it was OK for them to know who I really was.

"I suggest that I communicate with Orbyzykhan and drag on the conversation to buy some time."

"Thank you, Timurud," said Glave o'Sfero. "Go ahead."

A channel was opened to *Mauler*. "Thank you for your magnanimous offer, Orbyzykhan the Great. This is Timurud, the god, speaking." I wanted for as many of those listening to our conversation to know who was speaking: *Timurud the god*.

"What!" shouted Orbyzykhan in outrage. He then bellowed Maggotroll-flavored obscenities at me. A lot of those bad words had to do with my dog, which I didn't have. Or maybe he was referring to me as a dog. Or was it because "god" spelled backward is "dog"? Whatever.

I had infuriated him. Maybe this was the wrong strategy on my part. The mad Maggotroll could forgo all reason and attack Nisip at once. The channel to *Mauler* went quiet.

Oops!

"Timurud." A silky female voice came over the comm, sounding as if it were happy to recognize me. "This is Groznikhan the Stunning. It's been a long, long time since I last heard your voice."

"Groznikhan the Stunning, I am stunned to hear from you. I hope Orbyzykhan the Great did not have a nervous breakdown at hearing my godly name," I said in my smoothest, accommodating voice.

"You dog x@x!?zyw f—" shouted Orbyzykhan, but the sound was cut off, and there was silence again.

I imagined Groznikhan slapping Orbyzykhan to quiet him down. She had a reputation for being one tough broad, they say. I looked at the clock: minus-22 minutes.

"Timurud, are you there?" Groznikhan called.

"I certainly am, Groznikhan the Glamorous. What is going on at your end?" I asked with pretend concern.

"If I get my hands on you, you dog's a—" Orby howled, and the sound went off again.

I wished I could see what was going on over there in their command center.

"Timurud?" Groznikhan asked.

"Yes, my dear, I'm waiting here with bated breath. Is Orby doing well?'

"Well, my brother seems to have become—how should I say this?—energized, knowing that you're still alive." I heard in the background Orby asking, "What did he call me?"

I didn't have to make much effort to drag on the conversation. Orby was doing it for me.

"Timurud, are you there?"

"I'm alive and well. When did I die, oh, Spectacular Groznikhan?" I'd call her anything to buy time, and she appreciated my over-the-top flattery.

"He was told that you were killed in Tandalo."

"A god cannot be killed, oh, Splendid One. He was lied to. Your soldiers killed the Coshmars, not me. I'm sure at least you, the Superb One, are happy to hear the great news that I'm alive. And let me tell you…" I continued, going on a tangent to tell her about my fight with the Coshmars.

"Timurud, I'm heartened by your valiant fight with the Coshmars," her voice turned cold, "but we must talk about your surrender."

"Now when you say 'surrender,' do you mean me or the Sferogyls?" The time was now minus-15 minutes.

"Both of you, of course."

"Now when you say 'both of us,' do you mean together or separate, because there is only one of me and millions of Sferogyls, dear Grozny the Suave."

"What did you call me?"

"It is an endearment, Grozny, for Groznikhan the Stunning."

"How sweet of you! I want *you* first."

"And when you say you want *me* first, what do you mean by that?" Always answer with a question to stay in control, but also in this case to drag the conversation on.

"You alone, damn it!"

"Me alone, unescorted?"

"Yes."

"And where should I go?"

"What the hell? Are you dense or something? Get your unaccompanied ass up here before we destroy the whole planet with you on it."

"But you see, last time I did that, you wouldn't believe what happened to me..." And I began telling her how I was entrapped in a force field and fighting with Orby's dogs.

"Cut the shit," she ordered me. "If you're not on *Mauler* in five minutes, this benevolent offer of surrender is over. Over!" she repeated, as if through gritted teeth.

The time was minus eight minutes.

"Absolutely, I'll comply with your wishes, oh, Dazzling One, but I don't have a craft to get to *Mauler*."

"Is that so? Get on one of the Sferogyls' craft and get your ass up here. I'm running out of patience." I heard Orbyzykhan cursing about my dog again in the background. I still didn't get the meaning of those insults.

"Sorry, oh, Affectionate One, but the Sferogyls don't have that kind of spacecraft."

"What are those meatballs flying around?"

"Ohhh! The meatballs. Let me tell you what they are..." And I gave her my most dishonest version of what an FBB was and she let me finish, no doubt interested in the details I was giving them about the Sferogyl craft. "So as you can see, even if I could fly one, I couldn't get out of it without a special can opener, available only down here." The time was minus two minutes. The Sferogyls around me looked completely confused at what was going on. Glave o'Sfero, with his hands on his belly, seemed to be enjoying the charade.

"I'm going to send a fighter for you. Where are you?"

"I'm in Tandalo."

"You're in Tandalo? We're occupying the city."

"Yes, I'm in Tandalo. Come to the Assembly House."

"Orbyzykhan just told me the Assembly House was destroyed."

"I'll be on top of its ruins."

"Surrender to General Ambronkhan."

"I'll only surrender to you, oh, Exquisite One, as you know I am a god."

"You'll surrender to me on *Mauler*. A shuttle is two minutes away from your location. If you're not there, we'll kill everyone on Nisip."

I looked at the clock: minus one minute.

General Kland messaged me. A silent attack order has been given to the FBBs. They were storming toward *Mauler*.

I couldn't resist. "Dear Groznikhan, I want to remind you that I am a god, and it's time to rock-n-roll."

A new clock showed the time when the FBBs would arrive at *Mauler*: three minutes.

"What does 'rock-n-roll' mean, Timurud?"

I never answered her.

Chapter 45. *Mauler*

From all around Nisip, thirty squadrons of over 900 FBBs, each with a specific mission, headed at their maximum speed of 10 km/s toward *Mauler*'s bow and aft sections. One thousand fighters, ten frigates, and one hundred missiles launched from the frigates, gave pursuit to the FBBs. The enemy space-warp missiles were on target to impact the FBBs from behind at the thirty-second mark before the FBBs crashed into *Mauler*. If that were to happen, our FBBs would be thrown into disarray, and many would be destroyed. Our pilots knew better and reversed course, going backward before the impact. The missiles couldn't do that, so they made a wide U-turn loop to strike the FBBs. But our craft seemed to be caught between the missiles and the enemy fighters now. At the same time, *Mauler* launched several hundred missiles as well, joining the frigates' missiles. Our FBBs reversed course on a dime again and accelerated toward *Mauler*, taking evasive actions around the oncoming missiles.

Not all our FBBs were to impact Mauler at the same time, since the warship orbited Nisip with its bow pointing toward the planet. The impact on the aft appendages and DU tunnel would lag the impact on the bow targets by a second or less. Although a second might seem to be a short time, it was not for the *Mauler*'s computers, which figured out the FBBs' strategy. Even a partial destruction of any engine would cripple it.

Mauler identified the swarm of FBBs approaching its bow and moved more turrets at that end, which began firing continuously at the FBBs. Besides the wall of proton and laser fire coming from the turret guns, *Mauler* fired its three big proton guns at our FBBs.

We began taking casualties, as the firepower increased from deadly to hellish. Even the enemy fighters and missiles were hit by their own friendly fire. The frigates took evasive actions and encircled the FBBs, while firing proton and laser blasts at them. They didn't fire any more missiles, as the attack was getting closer to *Mauler*. We lost over fifty FBBs just in the first part of this frontal attack at the bow.

Getting into the DU tunnel was impossible with so much firepower coming out of the bow. The only good thing was that many of the missiles were wiped out by *Mauler*'s own fire. Whatever was left of the three squadrons of FBBs that were heading to the DU tunnel reversed course and began orbiting around the mouth of the DU tunnel. The enemy fighters harassed them, and their formation broke into cat-and-mouse chases. Both we and the enemy were taking losses, and soon the FBBs at the bow couldn't withstand the assault and retreated.

At the same time, twelve squadrons assigned to attack the arrowheads approached the energy shields. If the timing didn't work correctly, they would be bounced back, and *Mauler*'s guns would have an easy time destroying them. Just about all of them were deflected, except for five that broke through the first shield and then the second one. But to our surprise there was a third shield, and the FBBs were trapped. These FBBs disengaged their VALs and plunged against the hulls of the arrowheads. *Mauler* warped the space around itself and its many guns opened fire, destroying our five FBBs in the blink of an eye.

In the meanwhile, the other fifteen squadrons attacked the aft targets, and to my horror, they suffered the same fate. Nothing seemed to penetrate *Mauler*'s defenses or space warping, no matter how valiant and persistent our FBBs were. We were losing more FBBs than the enemy was losing fighters. The whole orchestrated attack against the bow and aft targets disintegrated into chaotic fighting. The enemy fighters and the frigates engaged our FBBs, while *Mauler* was shooting at them with all its firepower. The stats on the board showed that over 300 FBBs were destroyed. We were losing badly.

Mauler was indestructible.

Chapter 46. The Final Annihilation

I opened a comm with Logrn. "What's going on, Logrn e'Sfero?"

"Tim Andrus, it seems the bow and aft appendages are mission critical, and *Mauler* has extra shields and embedded guns to protect their engines."

"What now?"

"The final annihilation, Tim Andrus."

What was he talking about? "What does that mean, Logrn e'Sfero?"

An announcement blared over the broad comm: "Begin the final annihilation."

Logrn didn't answer my question, so I watched the unraveling of this "final annihilation" on the central hologram. Thousands of FBBs left Nisip's atmosphere and headed toward *Mauler*'s main hulls at maximum speed.

I thought that we had only about 600 FBBs left undestroyed. Where did those thousands of them come from? When did the Sferogyls build them? I opened an information channel, and indeed, there were 5,000 FBBs about to assault *Mauler*. But *Mauler* and the frigates didn't seem to notice them yet, as they were battling the remaining FBBs in space.

"Time to impact, sixty seconds," an announcement blared.

I looked in the direction of General Kland, and he seemed to be calm and detached from what was happening. With 5,000 more

FBBs on the attack, he and all the other generals and officers should have been feverish in coordinating the assault. But all of them watched as if they were spectators about to see fireworks. Something was not right.

It was even more unnerving to see Glave o'Sfero with his hands on his belly and eyes retracted, as if he didn't want to see what was about to happen. I waited to see the results of this latest wave of attacks.

"Time to impact 10, 9, 8..." A countdown was announced as the 5,000 FBBs were racing toward *Mauler*'s hull from all directions. *Mauler* initiated space warp. "... 4, 3, 2, 1. Impact."

Nobody cheered with joy when all these new FBBs penetrated the energy shields and crashed through *Mauler*'s hull.

Another display began a new countdown. This time it counted down from fifteen minutes.

"Logrn e'Sfero, what just happened?" I asked.

"My apologies, Tim Andrus, for not answering your earlier question, but I was busy at my station. Rather than tell you what's just happened, please inquire about KBBs on the information channel."

"What's a KBB?" I asked as I was retrieving the information.

"Killer Busting Balls," he replied.

I stopped asking questions as I reviewed the KBB specs. These Killer Busting Balls were kamikaze balls. My jaw dropped as I assimilated the information. A beetle piloted each KBB—not just any beetle, but a beetle controlled by a small section of a Sferogyl brain. I couldn't believe what I was learning. The part of a Sferogyl's brain associated with mechanical ability and orientation was no larger than a shelled walnut. This part of the brain was removed from a live Sferogyl, implanted in an *in vitro* cocoon, and its nerve connections were spliced into the beetle's nervous system to control the beetle's six legs in flying the KBB. The pilot in each KBB was part insect and part Sferogyl, flying on a suicidal mission.

The KBBs were much smaller, only about 10 cm in diameter, just about the size of a 4-inch-diameter cannon ball. The KBBs had VAL capabilities, which was disabled just before reaching the energy shields. Once past the energy shields, the balls re-energized their VAL, hit *Mauler*'s hull, and penetrated it. The holes were small enough that the hull self-sealed immediately, retaining the craft's internal atmosphere. But the real damage began after the KBBs were imbedded in the hull or passed through it.

Each ball released its weapon: high-energy positrons, also known as anti-electrons, positively charged particles equal to electrons. When a positron and an electron meet, they are attracted to each other, annihilate each other, and produce gamma rays. A deadly high-energy radiation ensues, and that continues traveling through other atoms' electrical fields, causing pair production of new electrons and positrons, which continue to annihilate each other until their energy decays.

The result was havoc on the craft's electromagnetic fields and the nuclear structures of the warship's material. Batteries of neutron and proton containment fields were destabilized, letting protons escape and neutrons begin a rapid decay. All systems were affected, ceasing operation. Computers were rendered useless, as everything using E-M forces was thrown out of balance, and software and data banks were corrupted. *Mauler*'s entire nervous system was annihilated.

The estimated time to obliterate the craft and all life aboard was about fifteen minutes, slightly longer than it took for the neutron batteries to decay when breached. During that time on board *Mauler*, it would be Armageddon. The craft's systems would begin breaking down or freeze altogether. The environmental and onboard grav systems would begin malfunctioning. The energy shields protecting the craft would halt, and all guns of any kind would be rendered useless. Vacuum, poisonous gases, high temperature gases, short circuits, electrical discharges, and deadly gamma rays would begin killing the crew. The gamma radiation would destroy the atoms in the crew's bodies. Weightless, with no controls or help of any kind, the crew would soon be dead. Even escaping by emergency pods was unfeasible, as the crew wouldn't be able to reach the pods, and many pods would eject empty because of the electrical mayhem raging on *Mauler*. Just about all hatches would fail open, spewing into space everything that was unattached, including the remaining breathable air.

I looked up from the info display, shocked at what I had learned. *Mauler* had no chance of recovery and was soon to be dead. What the heck? But was this outcome any different from how *Mangle* was destroyed? Almost all its crew died, and so it would be on *Mauler*.

Just as it was for the 5,000 Sferogyls whose brains were used.

"Logrn l'Sfero, where did the Sferogyl brains come from?" I asked.

"Volunteers."

"You killed 5,000 of your own kind?"

"No, they are not dead. They are in a vegetative state. They made the ultimate sacrifice to save us all," replied Logrn.

A broad announcement was made: "FBBs, retreat to bases."

The fight was over. Now it was just a matter of time, less then ten minutes, before *Mauler* and its crew were dead.

I looked up, thinking about and waiting for the inevitable, when my comm beeped.

"Timurud, it seems you are shocked at what you've learned," said Glave o'Sfero.

"Yes, you could say that, Glave o'Sfero."

"It was not until recently that we discovered the KBB technology in our ancestors' files. Again, just like the FBB, it was never implemented. And perhaps the use of a Sferogyl's brain for each unit was a big obstacle to our deploying them earlier."

"Why didn't you use a mini-bot with artificial intelligence to perform the task?"

"AI doesn't work in a busting ball with an active VAL, Timurud. We did not make the decision to sacrifice our people lightly. As a matter of fact, the part of the brain needed to fly the KBBs was not extracted from the volunteers until we realized that our FBBs were not going to win. We waited until the last minute."

"Sacrifice 5,000 to save hundreds of millions," I said thoughtfully.

"Yes. I hope you can forgive us, god Timurud."

"You had to do what you had to do to survive, Glave o'Sfero," I said, having to contend with the reality of war.

"Thank you for your understanding, Timurud."

Some of the enemy fighters chased the FBBs, but once in the atmosphere, the FBBs had the advantage and the enemy fighters retreated in orbit, awaiting further orders. None of the fighters and frigates returned to their warship base, although I was sure that they needed energy and more missiles. I think *Mauler*'s command realized the danger they were in and did not allow their craft to board the warship. The last two frigates that were still parked on *Mauler* and were never used in the fight blasted away from the warship.

A new announcement came on the general comm: "Preliminary communications from *Mauler* indicate that Orbyzykhan and Groznikhan have left on the two frigates."

Orbyzykhan and Groznikhan had run to save their hides, abandoning the doomed warship. Some leaders those Maggotrolls were! I looked at the countdown: T minus three minutes.

The remaining enemy fighters in the occupied pockets on Nisip took off into orbit to join the rest of the craft up there. It was a mystery why, considering that *Mauler* was obviously dead. They must have known that all was lost with the end of *Mauler* and that the situation on the ground was hopeless. Without *Mauler*, where would they go?

"T minus two minutes," the broad comm announced.

And then, all of a sudden, all but one of the enemy frigates departed from their orbits into vast space, following the previous two. Surprisingly, some of the fighters followed them as well.

"Enemy frigates have engaged their NLS engines and are heading out of our solar system," the broad comm announced.

The frigates with NLS capability fled, approaching the speed of light, without taking on board any of the fighter pilots. The fighters did not have NLS engines and were marooned in Nisip's solar system. They were left behind, and the only livable planet was Nisip. Soon, one after another, and then all of them, would have to come down and land in Tandalo.

"This is General Kland speaking. *Mauler* is dead and the enemy has been defeated. We've won."

Everyone in the command center broke into cheers and loud whistles. A few cried. Yes, the enemy was defeated, after losing millions of lives and destroying the enemy's two capital warships.

"Congratulations, General Kland," I said over the comm.

"Thank you, god Timurud. We couldn't have done it without you."

"Yes, I second that, god Timurud," said Glave o'Sfero.

"God helps those who help themselves," I said.

Epilogue

My assignment was complete on Nisip. The Sferogyls had won their right to live in freedom and peace. The Maggotrolls, led by Orbyzykhan, lost two warships, and four million of their people died or were taken prisoners in their misguided invasion. I doubted that the Maggotroll emperor would send additional warships to subjugate the Sferogyls. Nisip didn't seem to be a worthy prize in the first place.

It may have been Orbyzykhan and Groznikhan's scheme to expand their wealth and influence, but they lost badly as well, as losing two capital warships. I was sure they blamed me for their losses, just as they blamed me for the losses a hundred years before. They were fleeing at near light speed toward an unknown destination. Since their frigates did not posses DU travel capabilities, they would be spending a long time in space, unless they were rescued by DU ships and returned to Vestrallum.

The Sferogyls informed the Maggotroll Empire that they had taken millions of their citizens as prisoners. The Maggotroll Empire promised to reply in due time. Unless compensation was paid, the prisoners would work for the Sferogyls to repair the damage they caused. The wannabe colonists ended up working on Nisip, not as landlords but as prisoners. And the icing on the cake for the Sferogyls was the capture of a nearly intact capital warship with all the advanced technology it possessed. I hope they'll use it wisely.

I'd seen horrible things during this war, and I did horrible things by killing other sapient beings, but in the heat of battle I had to do what it took to survive and help innocent people stay free. I didn't stay long on Nisip after the victory, and I left for Gardenia.

My EBT took me back to Gardenia in the blink of an eye. It's a wonderful thing to be a god and have such technology.

At the spaceport, Freggor was waiting for me. "Welcome back. As expected, you were victorious," he said smiling.

"The Sferogyls were," I said as I walked from the opened-up dipyramid. "I cannot think of what I did for them other than what they did for themselves."

"Modest Timurud," he quipped.

"Is Anu around?" I asked.

"No. He's in the Andromeda Galaxy. What do you need?"

"You knew me from before, right, Freggor?"

"Of course, every god knows you," he said with a knowing look.

"Do you know why Anu didn't want me to divulge to the Sferogyls that I was Timurud?"

Freggor sighed. "I could speculate, but my guess is because of your reputation."

"What kind of reputation?"

"You still don't remember, do you?"

I shook my head.

"Maybe that's why you decided to die as a god and be reborn as a mortal." Freggor raised his eyebrows.

"What's my reputation?"

"First, you scared the shit out of most of the bad sapient

creatures in Milky Way Galaxy," he said in language unbecoming to a god. "No one, not even Anu, knows what you did in the last decades of your life as a god. But you put the fear of the devil in them. God forgives, Satan does not."

I looked at him, stunned, as if he had just told me that I was Satan's son. "Aren't there repercussions for what I've done?"

"No one has filed an official complaint," said Freggor matter-of-factly. "And since you have amnesia and don't remember, who's to tell what really happened?"

I stood there, wondering and churning over the possibilities of what had happened in the past.

"Don't worry too much about it. Maybe one day it will come back to you, or you'll find records or someone who has firsthand knowledge about what you did." Freggor smiled. "But in the meantime, you have one month for R&R until your next mission. And someone is waiting for you." He winked at me.

"Dalia's back?" I asked eagerly.

"No. Dalia is still busy on her mission. But Aphrodite is back and wants to see you as soon as you arrive."

I stared at him. "Aphrodite?"

"Get used to being a god, Timurud," Freggor snickered. "Aphrodite, the goddess of beauty and love, exists, and she knows you. *Intimately*."

I collected myself and asked, "All right, then. How do I go about seeing her?"

"Take that pod," Freggor pointed to a craft with a clear bubble. "The pod knows where to go." He paused. "Remind me to teach you how to teleport while on Gardenia. And other stuff as well."

Aphrodite, the goddess of beauty and love—I couldn't believe my ears. And she knows me intimately! I hopped into the craft and in no time I was brought to the white sand beaches of a Caribbean-blue sea. The perfect place for some R&R.

Nearby I heard someone playing a wind instrument, an oboe, and I went in that direction. In a cove surrounded by palm trees, I saw a Greco-Roman beach villa made of white marble, and on its front steps a beautiful woman sat cross-legged, playing the oboe. The tune reminded me of Italian Renaissance music, melodious and romantic.

I approached, transfixed by Aphrodite's beauty. She was blonde, with blue eyes and a voluptuous alabaster-like body, scantily covered by a light-blue silk gown. She stopped playing and looked at me with an inviting smile. I gasped, seeing her deep blue eyes looking at me with so much longing.

"Timurud, love. Finally, you're back." She spoke through moist red lips. She stood up, extending her hand to me.

I took it and felt love energy ignite in my body. "You know me?" I muttered, melting with desire.

"You've forgotten. Let me bring back some sweet memories." She took me by the hand and pulled me inside her love nest.

The best parts about being a god are the fringe benefits.

The End.

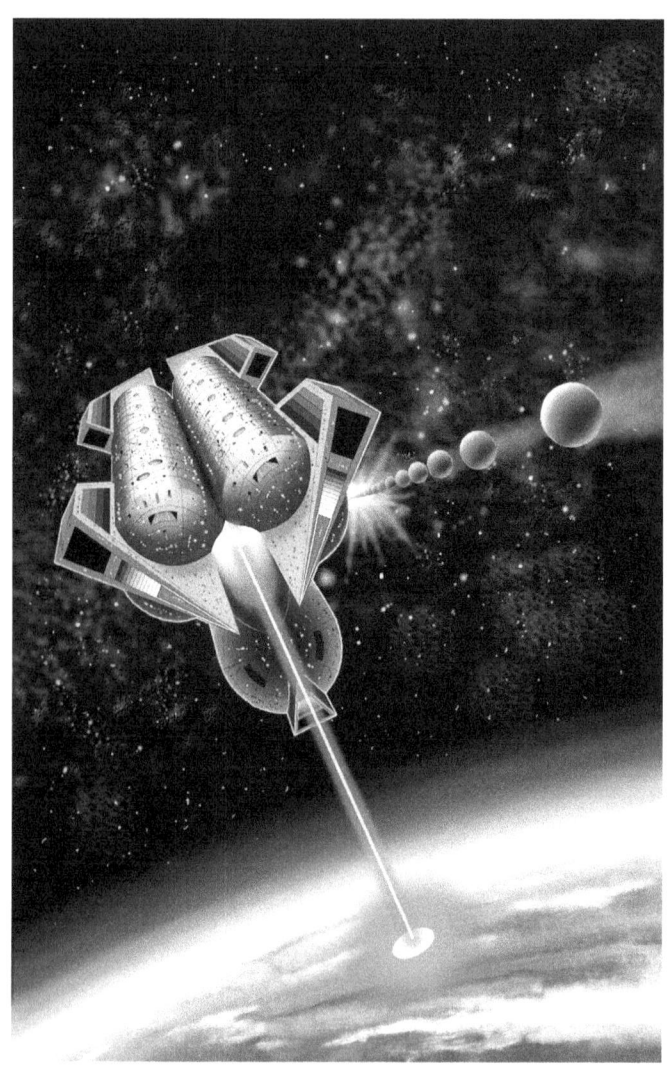

If you enjoyed this book and would like to help other readers with your comments please write a review on Amazon, which I appreciate very much.

For more information about my books and my art please visit my website: **sandru.com**

Other Books By Sandru:

Science Fiction

Gold Rush Mystery (Terraspantion Chronicles, Bk. 1) by Mit Sandru.

America is back on the Moon, and we intend to stay and establish a self-sustaining permanent base for tourism and mining. The work is challenging, the environment is deadly, but the astronauts Mia, Geo and Roby succeed in building the moon base, even if they landed in a mysterious crater.

Time Hole, (Terraspantion Chronicles, Bk. 2) by Mit Sandru.

Mining on the moon is a hazardous affair. Deedee and Arno, two lunar generalists, find perils beyond what they signed up for when they travel on the lunar surface at night . . . on the dark side of the Moon. Time will not be the same after they fall into the *Time Hole.*

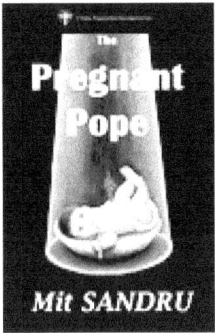

The Pregnant Pope (TIO Series), by Mit Sandru.

The 92-year-old Pope is pregnant. Although he hasn't undergone any medical procedures, he carries a human fetus in his abdomen. Is this a case of self-cloning, or a mutation? Is this an Immaculate Conception, or Satan's work? Find out how Clair, Travis, and Prescott, the members of the Capuchin Trinity Team, are solving this mystery.

Folding Reality, by Mit Sandru, a Paranormal, Time Travel Adventure.

Experiencing a new reality is just a paper-fold away for Mike the insurance salesman. But those realities are not by his choice and he ends up being crucified, or gassed at Auschwitz, or marooned in space in a Russian capsule.

Arboregal, the Lorn Tree, by D.G. Sandru.

Four youngsters, Melissa, Perry, Nathan and Michelle materialize in a desolate world where giant, mile-high trees, support all life. They find shelter in the Lorn Tree among the Lorns. Soon after they discover that an evil spirit, Hellferata, wants them dead. Fearful Lorns want to expel the youngsters from their tree, which would be a dead sentence since monsters roam the land at night.

Will their ingenuity, cunning, and courage help them escape, or will Hellferata mete out her wrath before they can escape?

Vampire Thriller & Romance

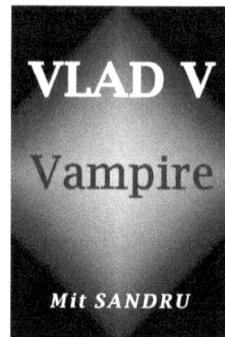

Vampire (Vlad V Series), by Mit Sandru, a Vampire Romance.

Vampire (Vlad V, Book 1) by Mit Sandru.

Meeting a vampire isn't something that happens every night, even on the New York City subways. Even in her wildest dreams Cat never expected to meet a vampire or survive an encounter with one. Instead, she becomes his confidant. Why is she so lucky?

R.I.P., The Death of a Vampire (Vlad V, Bk 2) by Mit Sandru.

Vlad V Draculesti is dying because of an incident that happened decades ago. Unfortunately for Vlad V, the US intelligence agencies investigate him to find out his true identity, and centuries old life. Will Cat Sanders and vampire friends be able to help him die in peace, or will Vlad be discovered for being a vampire and die in a US Federal research laboratory?

Vampire Slayers (Vlad V, Bk 3) by Mit Sandru.

Cat Sanders is a billionaire, but not all is well. Her nemesis, Veronica Seyler, allied with a vampire-slayer drug cult, demands extortion money or she will be killed.

Cat's vampire friend, Angelique, comes to her aid. But the cult is more cunning and dangerous than even her vampire friend could handle. Would Cat and Angelique be able to come out of this alive even if Cat pays the ransom?

Vampires of Transylvania (Vlad V, Bk 4) by Mit Sandru

Cat Sanders has a simple task: spread Vlad V's ashes in Transylvania at midnight, during full moon. But in Transylvania Vlad V has centuries old enemies who take her and her friend Tudor hostage, placing them in iron cages among zombies and proto-vampires. Will they be able to escape from the blood sucking proto-vampires and flesh-eating zombies, or become zombies themselves?

The Queen of Vampires: A New Queen Arises (Vlad V, Bk 5) by Mit Sandru

The Vampire Queen, Eleonore von Schwarzenberg, is bloodthirsty and vengeful on Cat Sanders and her friends. She plans the most painful death for them. Cat and her friends find themselves entrapped and helpless to avoid her wrath.

Will Cat and her friends be able to escape and survive the Queen of Vampires' fury?

Other Books:

Escape from Communism, by Dumitru Sandru, a True Story and Commentary.

Life under communism is cruel and inhumane. Communist countries have a "Berlin Wall" around them, and the whole country is a giant concentration camp. I risked my life to escape from hell and reach freedom.

T-Shirts and other stuff:

Sandru's Shop or Sandru's Products

Visit my e-Gallery at:

http://dumitru-sandru.artistwebsites.com/
http://www.artistrising.com/galleries/Sandru

  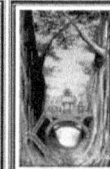  

About Dumitru "Mit" Sandru

Dumitru "D.G." "Mit" Sandru was born in the greater area of Transylvania in the last century. He is an artist, composer, and author. He paints in the classical, surreal, and modern styles, and most of the music Dumitru composes is of the New Age flavor. As an author, he prefers to write Science-Fiction, Paranormal, and Teen/Children Fantasy & Sci-Fi novels.

Dumitru resides in California with his wife. They have one daughter and two grandsons.

Visit him at sandru.com